A FEW LAST WORDS FOR THE LATE IMMORTALS

Other Fairwood Press /
Kudzu Planet Productions titles
by Michael Bishop

Brittle Innings

Ancient of Days

Who Made Stevie Crye?

Count Geiger's Blues

A Funeral for the Eyes of Fire

Philip K. Dick is Dead, Alas

Joel-Brock the Brave and the Valorous Smalls

Other Arms Reach Out to Me: Georgia Stories

Transfigurations

The Sacerdotal Owl and Three Other Long Tales

The City and the Cygnets

Unicorn Mountain

A FEW LAST WORDS FOR THE LATE IMMORTALS

50 Short Stories & Poems

edited by Michael H. Hutchins

MICHAEL BISHOP

KUDZU PLANET
· PRODUCTIONS ·
BONNEY LAKE WA

A FEW LAST WORDS FOR THE LATE IMMORTALS
50 Short Stories and Poems
A Fairwood Press/Kudzu Planet Productions Book
November 2021

First Edition

Fairwood Press
21528 104th Street Court East
Bonney Lake, WA   98391
www.fairwoodpress.com

Edited by Michael H. Hutchins

Cover image © Josef Bartoň
Cover and book design by Patrick Swenson

Kudzu Planet Productions, an imprint of Fairwood Press

ISBN13: 978-1-933846-12-5
Fairwood/Kudzu Planet Productions Trade Edition: November 2021
Printed in the United States of America

For Michael Hutchins,
my right-hand man through many years
of my writing career
and always an undaunted friend

CONTENTS

ACTS OF CHUTZPAH
An Introduction

Sarah Pinsker

M y own introduction to Michael Bishop's work occurred accidentally. I found *Unicorn Mountain* in the library at an age when I'd finished all the books in the childrens' section with horses or unicorns on their covers and had started on the adult section. This book, unlike some adult fare with *horse* or *unicorn* in the title, actually featured unicorns, but also darker themes. Adult themes. Some of it may have gone over my head, but I surely must have liked it because my reading list for that year also included *Philip K Dick is Dead, Alas* and *Ancient of Days*.

After that, I began noticing Bishop's stories in my father's magazines and anthologies, for once a name becomes familiar you see it everywhere. And the stories appeared everywhere—in *Year's Best* volumes, in *Omni*, in *Asimov's* and *Analog* and *The Magazine of Fantasy & Science Fiction*—and with their catchy hooks, layered meanings, and complex characters they challenged me to be a better reader.

All of which meant that when I received the invitation to write this introduction, I felt altogether intimidated. Who am I to introduce this lion of science fiction, fantasy, and horror? What can I say about his work that hasn't been said in reviews and a recent entire critical volume analyzing it?

Here's what I've settled on: I am writing an introduction to a specific new collection, which I've read and you haven't, though I hope that won't be true much longer, for I am possibly introducing some readers to Michael Bishop's work for the first time, in which case the really polite response would be to stop writing or to urge you to skip the rest of this introduction and head for the first story.

Go! Read! I'll wait until you get back . . .

If you're back, I'll tell you why I consider this collection such a delight: it is, frankly, an act of chutzpah. These aren't the novellas upon which Bishop made his reputation. This is not a "best of" consisting of his most lauded stories; I believe only one of his many award-nominated works actually appears herein. (Which is not to say that these stories aren't excellent, only that these are not pieces that caught the often fickle eyes of award voters). This is not a book of early stories, later stories, or stories on a single theme. It's not even all prose. That pretty well covers what it isn't.

What is it, then? A collection of prose, of poetry, of prose poems, and of stories playing with poetic forms, and even a short play. A collection spanning the fullness of Bishop's career. A collection of horror and dark fantasy and real-ist works, of futures near and far running the entire gamut of fantastika. Works that disturb and provoke thought. Works political or profane or both. Works darkly humorous, or just humorous, or just dark. Stories that defy concrete con-clusions. Stories that are human, except when not; humane, except when not. Together, a mosaic made of photos of human faces, which, when viewed from a certain angle, reveals itself as a larger image, although here that larger image may change each time you look at it anew.

The main commonality here resides in each item's brevity, but a freedom inheres in that restriction. These are short pieces, chosen for their precision, their surgical strike. A short piece is a dare that its writer can drop you like a paratrooper into a new situation, a brand-new head, an amnesiac head forced to gather all clues as you travel, a sentence at a time, with no compass but a title, yet make that character, that entire world, real enough to carry you for-ward to an ending that must feel inevitable but not predictable, so that when you reach the final sentence the whole experience feels both rich and complete. No big deal.

Or maybe that's the wrong metaphor. Maybe I should call it a magic trick. A sleight of hand whereby the magician convinces you that you are experiencing a moment in a life not your own. Ink on a page, words in an order as precise as any spell, miraculously conjuring, straight into your brain, characters who obviously had lives before you started reading about them, yet you don't seem to notice that you're watching alongside them out of their eyes.

Three thousand words later the magician must do it all again, with new eyeballs, new characters, a whole other world with entirely different rules. Most collections intersperse longer pieces among the short, but this one tilts the other way, with poems to punctuate the short stories. You'll experience entire lives in these whip-fast changes. Here we converse with the dead "In the Memory Room"; here we release our hopes for Balloon Day, only to have them return to haunt us in an ongoing war.

We often talk of how the genres of fantastic literature converse with one another, and here you can find those conversations at play in stories and poems that reconsider Borges and Philip K. Dick, but also in "The Contributors to *Plenum Four*," which turns alleged contributor notes in a future anthology into a story all their own. You see it in the handful of stories written in collaboration with his son Jamie's story files, and in pieces that reconsider and recontextualize Bishop's own earlier stories, for he is a writer unafraid to revise published work to a point where we must consider it a new thing entirely. That's yet another form of chutzpah, I believe, one that I'm familiar with from music but rarely see in fiction. Musicians know that there's a version of a song fixed in time—the album version—but every time we appear on stage, we have a chance to play it differently, nor is it unusual to record new versions that speak to new understandings. The original story here, "Yahweh's Hour," does exactly that.

Near the end of this collection appears a one-act drama, "The Grape Jelly and Mustard Method; or, How to Write Science Fiction, Maybe: A Short Play." This piece, written for a real museum in Eatonton, Georgia, features a conversation between a guru in a humanoid robot body, a chimpanzee-ostrich with augmented intelligence (COA), and assorted other animal amalgams. The COA approaches the guru on his mountaintop, or in this case, a planetarium on the dark side of the Moon, to ask how it can write science fiction. There commences a conversation wherein the guru gives all the good advice that a good teacher of science fiction gives, starting with the basics of "read more" and "learn the mechanics" and moving on to analyzing how the writers you admire set up their stories; to creating courageous, daring, and sometimes absurd hybrids of the elements of story; and to noting that "regardless of your genre, or medium, or audience, the real goal for all artists is Quality."

Here, then, is one more take on what this collection is, rather than what it is not. It is a shining example of everything a chimpanzee-ostrich amalgam with augmented intelligence would want to read: a collection that spans genres and mediums, striving for Quality in each, daring to mingle grape jelly and mustard and serve the mixture to guests as a fondue option, knowing they'll appreciate the taste whether or not they know what went into making it. It's all here: the sweet and the sour, the experimental and the familiar, the mundane and the fantastic. Grab a skewer and enjoy!

Sarah Pinsker is the author of about fifty short stories, the Nebula Award-winning novel *A Song for A New Day*, the Philip K Dick Award winning collection *Sooner or Later Everything Falls Into the Sea*, and, in 2021 the near-future novel, *We Are Satellites*.

A FEW LAST
WORDS FOR
THE LATE
IMMORTALS

PROEM

Astyages' Dream, Which He Relates to the Magi

i.

From out my daughter's private parts,
Budding slowly in its growth,
There grew a monstrous vine:
Darkly leafed it was
And of such verdure
That its prolific runners
Voluptuously did seem
To make of Mandane's naked limbs
A living trellis.
Then those green tendrils
Filled the chambers of my palace
With a thousand budding flowers,
Expansive in their bloom,
Weaving delicate nets of green
To enmesh my lush fantasia.

ii.

Through this I slept with heavy starts,
Never waking, like some sloth
Made lurching-drunk on wine.
As an infant rose,
Keening in manure,
Cries petals to the hunters
Of its insensate dream,
I awoke, full of stupid whims,
And strangely jealous.
To you wise scoundrels
Came I raging. You were callous,
And dispensed through occult powers
A prophecy of gloom—
For what in wild sleeping I had seen
Was another king in Asia.

Part One

✦

LOVE'S HERESY

LOVE'S HERESY

"The heresies we ought to fear are those that can be confused with orthodoxy." —Jorge Luis Borges

When John Pannell and his small son Bubba came into Swainsboro from their farm in the Valley View community, the green at the heart of town stirred with people. The cars around the square shone like mirrors, and an intense seersucker-clad young man harangued the crowd from the bandstand. After glancing at Osborne's Hardware and the little grocery beside it, Pannell led Bubba into the park.

"You're not the only you there is!" the fox-eyed speaker shouted, pausing to survey his audience. "By no means. In heaven you have a double, another you more real than you are. In fact, this double is the *real* you. Everyone here in Swainsboro is just a reflection of your real self in heaven."

Dabney Whitlow, a middle-aged druggist, scoffed, broke from the crowd, and met the Pannells halfway across the green. "Hey, Bubba." He tousled the boy's unruly hair. "Hey, John. You're not here to listen to that joker, are you?"

"Who is it?" John Pannell asked.

"He says he's a preacher without a church. A Baptist, same as you and me and nearly everybody else hereabouts. But—"

"But what?"

"He talks damned unbiblical craziness. Listen a spell if you want. It's interesting enough, and he ain't so stupid he's tried to take a collection." Whitlow pulled the neck of his undershirt away from his throat, nodded goodbye, and crossed over to his store.

Bubba twisted his daddy's forefinger. "C'mon, Papa, let's buy our stuff."

Pannell eased his finger from his son's hot grip and neared the bandstand wearing a grim, set expression the boy had seen only twice before: once when someone gave his two-hundred-dollar birddog a near-fatal dose of poison, and again in Savannah after Mama's surgery when the doctors offered a one-word verdict: *malignant.*

"*Daddy!*"

"Hang on, Bubba. I want to give this fella a listen."

"What we do here on earth," the fellow was arguing, nodding at the pair as they wedged their way forward, "influences what happens in heaven. That's how it is. We may be made of moist and heavy clay, we may be earthbound in our poor, sick lives, but for better or worse our actions are reflected in heaven, and they're reflected exactly backwards of things here on earth. In a mirror, your left hand appears to be your right.

"Well, in heaven the evil you do here is transmuted into good, the good into evil. If your false earthly self drinks and honky-tonks, your double in heaven, the real you, is chaste as snow. If your false self comforts the sick and gives of its time and money, your double above is cruel and tight-fisted to balance your false self off. When you die, your spirit wings to heaven and becomes your other self, your *real* self."

"How do you know all this?" asked a woman in a straw hat with a green plastic window in its brim. "Where'd you get these silly notions?"

"My name is Eugene Forbes, ma'am, and I get my silly notions from the Bible."

Several people laughed. "Well, Mr. Forbes," said the woman, a faint green shade on her brow, "it don't much sound like the Book I know."

"I'm sure it is, though. Matthew 11:12 proves that what we do here influences what happens in heaven—'*the kingdom of heaven suffereth violence,*' it says—and 1 Corinthians 13:12 tells us that everything on earth is seen '*through a glass, darkly*' and isn't truly real. I know my Book, ma'am. I wouldn't be up here explaining it to you if I didn't. My credentials may not be your everyday ones, but they sure as hell ain't a bit phony."

The man's casual "sure as hell" offended the woman, and Bubba hoped that his daddy, likewise disgusted, would lead him out of the park to Osborne's Hardware or the grocery store with its cooler of Nehi sodas. But Pannell, who only rarely cursed, raised his right forefinger like a man signaling an auctioneer's attention.

Forbes saw this gesture, "Sir?"

"If our actions are reflected backwards in heaven, what are we supposed to do here on earth? Should it be good or evil? I don't get what you're driving at."

"That's because I'm describing, not prescribing. I'm just pointing out the nature of the situation, that's all. The thing to keep in mind is that heaven is what counts, heaven's the reality. Everything here in Swainsboro"—Forbes pointed to the trees, the scalding-hot automobiles and pickups, the store fronts across the street—"everything here has meaning, but it ain't real. How you yourself wish to influence genuine reality, sir, is a measure of the kind of man you are. As for me, I'm going to grab a sandwich at the Mayflower Cafe so my real self in heaven can show his piety by fasting. I bid you all good-day."

Forbes came down from the bandstand without ever passing his hat, and in a few minutes the crowd had dispersed to park benches, motor cars or trucks, or nearby businesses. Bubba dogged his moody father across the street to the hardware store, where Max Osborne apologized three times for having to deny them credit.

Six months later, Mrs. Pannell died. When they buried her in the rocky cemetery behind Valley View Baptist Church, a white-washed building near rice and cotton fields belonging to the Pannells' neighbors, Eugene Forbes appeared among the mourners.

He wore a black rayon jacket, cordovan penny loafers, and a silver buckle as bright as a mirror. The understated funeral rites were presided over by Valley View's young pastor Brian Alverson, who, Bubba heard someone whisper, had once attended the same divinity school as Forbes. That meant that there was nothing deeply mysterious about Forbes' presence at the funeral; he'd just happened to drop in on his former classmate when Leah Pannell failed for the final time and died. His standing at graveside merely signified a courtesy to Brian Alverson and the Pannells.

A *double* courtesy, John Pannell supposed.

"Your wife has joined her real self," Forbes told Pannell after the burial. "For the first time in her immortal life, she's complete in the only reality that counts."

Wiping dirt from his hands, Brian Alverson approached the trio from the flower-heaped grave. His eyes glinted fiercely, and his usually placid face betrayed an un-Christian resentment. "Don't plague them with your heresies,

Gene. This isn't the time." Then he said, "John, Bubba, our prayers are with you. If there's the tiniest thing anyone at Valley View can do, let me know. I'll see it gets done."

His voice as dark as winter, Pannell asked, "What's Mr. Forbes' heresy, Brian? Is trying to give me a bit of comfort heretical?"

Embarrassed, the former classmates exchanged a glance.

"Of course not," Alverson said. "I just don't see much comfort in Gene's take on Leah's death: this business of her being complete for the first time in her life."

"It's what got me kicked out of divinity school," said Forbes, studying his penny loafers: "insisting on the falseness of our earthly selves."

"And the existence of doubles in heaven," Alverson added.

Then Bubba's sniffling drew the men's attention. Pannell knelt and wiped his son's eyes with a handkerchief. "It's all right, Bubba. We may be earth-bound, but heaven knows who we are. Never believe it doesn't."

"That's right," Rev. Alverson said, touching the boy's shoulder.

"That's exactly right," Eugene Forbes agreed.

Perplexed by this rare consensus, Bubba put his arms around his daddy's neck and turned his face to the cloudless sky. His daddy lifted him. The adults bid one another goodbye, and the son sensed the intensity of his father's love— warmth felt through pressure—as Pannell carried him across the churchyard to their dilapidated pickup. On the bumpy ride home, Bubba saw that his father's eyes glinted with moisture.

"It's hell, isn't it, Bubba? Earthbound's the same as hellbound now she's gone." A little later he said, "O, that this stinking truck could fly."

Bubba put his hand on the window. Crops flashed dimly by in the gathering dusk. When their truck crossed a wooden bridge over a ditch, its tires played the slats like hammers on a toy xylophone, and Bubba knew that the old Chevrolet was much too heavy a contraption to get off the ground. Why did his daddy want it to fly?

That evening after putting Bubba to bed, John Pannell visited the welding shop next to the shed housing his dry-docked tractor and picked-up pieces of scrap iron. Not since the doctors had diagnosed Leah's ailment as pancreatic cancer had he sought to make his living by farming. Instead, he'd advertised himself throughout the Valley as a mechanic, blacksmith, and machinist so that he could work at home, maybe forty yards from Leah's bedroom window. Business had never been good, maybe because he was a so-so mechanic.

Now, Leah dead, Bubba asleep, he wielded an acetylene torch in his musty shop to create a huge, vision-inspired sphere.

The "sphere" was neither solid nor truly round, but irregular in shape, open between its iron struts, and therefore hollow. It resembled a globe conceived and assembled by a student of avant-garde metal sculpture, but to Pannell it was less a work of art than a means whereby his double in heaven could play Daedalus to his son's unsuspecting Icarus. He worked for seven straight nights, sleeping only in the final hours before dawn and always hiding the project from Bubba, whom he finally sent to the Alversons saying that he needed time alone to recover from his loss. The Alversons understood.

The sphere itself hung from two iron girders so that its bottommost strut was only three feet from the floor. Once completed, its great size and crude intricacy its most conspicuous features, the sphere dominated the shop, and Pannell spent the hours after finishing it walking about the open-faced globe in order to come to grips with its weight. No one could possibly lift it. A calendar given him by a man who sold Atlas tires hung in the gloom over his workbench, mocking his assessment of what could or could not be lifted, but he'd never believed in any myth but the orthodox ones of Christianity and love, and one piece of calendar art had no power to affect his plans.

"I'm ready for Bubba to come home," he told Muriel Alverson on the telephone that afternoon. "May I come get him?"

"Come ahead, John. But Brian and I would be glad to keep him longer."

"Thanks, Muriel. I miss him. Besides, I've got a surprise for him."

"That's good. Boys like surprises."

On the trip home from the rectory, Bubba said, "Mrs. Alverson said you have a surprise for me."

"Yeah. I do. Just you wait."

The pickup swung between the unkempt hedges of the Pannells' gravel driveway and slammed to a stop in front of the tractor shed. Man and boy sauntered toward the welding shop. In its doorway, Bubba halted and gaped at the massive metal globe gleaming blue in the dark. Then he scurried inside, closed his hand on one of the grease-blackened struts (a bent crowbar welded into place), and tried to turn the globe by extending his forearm against the bar.

When it failed to yield, Bubba glanced shyly at his father.

"That's all right. It's not supposed to move. If it weren't for those two chains holding it in place, it would, but those chains are brakes." Pannell pointed at the girders and the oily chains hanging from them in taut opposition.

"What is it, Daddy? What's it for?"

"Come here. Duck under the globe and let me help you get into this harness." Pannell attached a pair of leather saddle straps to the underside of the sphere, and, obeying his wishes, Bubba crept under it and donned the harness his father had made. Now the globe rode his back like a meteor caught a scant three feet off the ground, all its crushing weight negated. "I know that isn't too comfortable," Pannell said, "but I'm clueless about how else to rig it."

"It's okay." Bubba felt powerful and frightened, grateful and uncertain. But even in the gloom-ridden welding shop, his daddy's face radiated such pride in accomplishment, such love, that his fears and uncertainty lifted.

"Abraham didn't know what I know," Pannell said. "If he had, he'd never have gone up that mountain with so heavy a heart." He knelt before his stooping son, kissed him on the lips, and withdrew. With a self-made device, he released from the shop's girders the chains holding the globe. They fell like two crumpling iron snakes, and Pannell's lovingly crafted sphere drove Bubba into the shop floor's oil-caked dust.

Ten minutes later, Pannell telephoned the Alversons. "Muriel," he said, when she at last picked up, "Bubba's dead."

The sheriff in Swainsboro asked Pannell if he'd let the Rev. Mr. Alverson into his cell for an interview. Pannell told the sheriff, "No. Get me Eugene Forbes."

Forbes was in Savannah, and Alverson had to hunt throughout that city to find his friend, who roamed about preaching his heresies to longshoremen and whores, poor whites and poorer coloreds. But Alverson found Forbes and returned with him to Swainsboro and the tumbledown county jail.

"You murdered your son, Brian tells me." Forbes sat next to Pannell on a bench in his cell. "You dropped a big metal sphere on his back, crushing him to death."

"So his double could fly. I wanted Bubba's real self to fly."

"Then you did exactly right."

"I know I did. I just wanted to tell you."

"Bubba's real self is whole for the first time. He's flying around heaven like a bird. So, rest easy."

"I do," Pannell said. "That's how I rest."

For four days after this interview, Eugene Forbes remained in Swainsboro preaching from its bandstand and explaining why John Pannell had done what he'd done. Forbes did not stay in the Valley View rectory with the Alversons, with whom his relations were irreparably strained, but in an end unit of a motel outside of town run by Dabney Whitlow's brother-in-law, Clinton Rule.

On the night of Forbes' fourth day in Swainsboro, a car carrying an unknown number of passengers sped past this motel. A firebomb was hurled into the unit where the mad heretic was thought to be sleeping. Although the fire department arrived in time to save ten of Rule's twelve units, Forbes' body was later found in the ruins of the bombed-out end unit, and the county had a second murder case on its hands.

Some time later, Pannell was transferred to a state hospital. For reasons stemming from his initial sanity hearings, the sphere he'd crafted was brought into town. The following year, Swainsboro's mayor charged a young councilman with disposing of the cumbersome but oddly beautiful sphere, and the councilman, enamored of it, suggested that it be put on display in the bandstand park. This was done. Today the sphere is an enigmatic monument. Walking across the town's well-trimmed greensward, one should not be surprised to encounter children clambering all over it, ignorant of its history.

HONEYMOON WALK
July 20, 1969

When Armstrong, that stalwart pioneer, put his boot
Into the lunar snow, we had been married a month
And were watching from banks of linen, our bodies
Aerodynamically naked and as cool as liquid oxygen.

Outside, it was a magnesium-white July in Colorado.

DARKTREE, DARKTIDE

Although he didn't want to go, they took him to visit the old woman lying ill and gasping in Darktree Sanatorium. She wasn't actually his grandmother, his father had explained, but a step-relative with a tenuous familial ligature binding her to one of his parents. He didn't know which and didn't care. All that mattered was that he'd ride in the musty backseat of his father's limousine to the ornately landscaped building with antique cupolas and straw-colored shingles and stand, as if teleported there, in the unsettling sickroom that always signaled a submersion of his own personality.

Chloe was the old woman's name, and he liked it no better than he liked her. It didn't suit her. But she had appeared in his family—from where?—less than two years ago, ill with the disease that had confined her to the institution, and he struggled for his parents' sake to accept her, even though without warning they'd grown indifferent to many things once important to them. He came to see that, since Chloe's arrival, he had lost status in their eyes. Their activities and talk now revolved about the old woman almost solely. Still, he'd even tried, unsuccessfully, to love her. But in these past two unreal years, how many times had he felt emptied of the very qualities that made him Jon Dahlquist and not someone else?

Many times, he perceived. Dozens . . .

On the evening she'd first stepped from his family's new car into their yard, she'd been a tall patrician woman with a face cruelly wrinkled. Jon Dahlquist pumped away in a swing that fell like two knotted hangman's ropes from a twisted oak near the driveway. Legs cleaving the air in the tree's cascading shade, Jon watched her unravel from the backseat and stand without help. She looked six feet tall, not at all sick, but sadly worn, the dust inside a mummy's grave-clothes. Briefly, she swayed beside the contrastingly stolid car.

The car was older than the one they'd owned before moving to the Hilltide area, but it looked newer. That was a paradox. Jon's father said that owning an automobile with tradition behind it was better than owning the new. This ma-chine, he said, had an ingrained mechanical knowledge that the annual outflow of vehicles from Detroit could not duplicate. Background. Tradition. Ingrained knowledge. Only lately had his father thought on such matters.

His father saw him. "Jon, this is Chloe. Say hello."

Chloe came to his swing and looked down on him with rheumy eyes, like teaspoonfuls of mud. How could she even see him? He must look blurred to her. Seeing someone through a dirty jalousie window, Jon felt sure, would ap-proximate her image of him.

"Ah," Chloe told his father, "a fine young man. I hope to get to know him."

"You will," his father promised, his smile weirdly crooked. He took Chloe to the house with the deference of an old familiar, but never once touched her.

Jon looked at the dark earth a few inches beyond his swinging feet and won-dered at its existence. How wonderful, that such firmness could exist.

That night and several following, Chloe slept in his room. The Dahlquist house was huge, one of the largest and oldest in the Hilltide neighborhood, but painters and decorators had been at work preparing Chloe's suite. His family had moved into the house from a smaller and newer one just before Chloe joined them, and because of the ongoing work, Jon had to share his room with her. It held two well-fitted brass beds, and he was only eight. What necessity for privacy could either the very young or the very old summon in such circumstances? None on the old woman's part: she welcomed the chance to share his room, and Jon yielded because his mother had smoothed his hair and kissed him.

"Just a few nights. Chloe needs to be close to someone now. You can help her and she in turn can instruct you."

The urgency in his mother's voice persuaded him, even though its gentle-ness held an unidentifiable nervous quality. He wondered what Chloe could teach him but nodded assent for his parents' sake.

After lights out, Chloe turned her head on her embroidered pillowcase and spoke long past the time he was usually asleep, mesmerizing him with stories about lovers, forests, and preternatural animals. Sometimes, she turned a small gold figurine in her hands. In the nighttime shadows he could hardly see it, but he knew it depicted a naked man and woman pressing against each other in a long-held kiss. Once, she'd let him cup this little sculpture in his hands, and he'd been troubled, but not because it offended his boyish morality. Something glistening and sinister haloed the object. It became an even more unsettling totem in Chloe's hands. Purpled with age and incapacity, her hands contradicted the indwelling life force of the kissing statuettes. Even Jon felt the incongruity . . . and shied from it.

But the stories—

He never remembered them. Always in the morning he realized that the moonlit image of Chloe's filmed-over eyes and mobile crablike hands was all he possessed of their night together. He had no memory of living, of *being*, with Chloe at the same moment in time. The six nights he shared his room were an upsetting absence, a wholly inexplicable sensation, but he knew that the incursion of sleep did not account for the time lost, and he grew older without clearly processing his diminished life or his unsettling nocturnal aging.

One story he did remember.

But only because Chloe told it on the last night they shared his room and because he took steps requiring all his will and stamina. He *had* to know what was going on. Childish intuition told him he could not go on being drugged away from life, suffering the nightly theft that Chloe carried out. Only a concerted effort to recall what spells she wove could return to him the dark moments she stole, so he focused heart and mind on remembering.

The story was about an immortal blackbird. Chloe told it in a hypnotically droning way, her collapsing equine face studying him in the dark. All during the story, Jon pinched the inside of his thigh and kept pinching until her voice stopped and he heard only the soft inward whisper of the lace curtains.

"This regal blackbird," Chloe intoned, "lived to bear ten thousand generations of young. She lives even yet. For whenever she repaired to her nest with a morsel, she broke it in her beak, sweetened it with her saliva, and doled it out among her fledglings, begging with outstretched throats. But even when she had no more to offer, she plunged her beak repeatedly into the throats of her babies, drawing off their hot life's blood. Thus, she increased her years but ruined the tiny creatures she appeared to foster. It was her way. But the blackbird never required help," Chloe said, almost as an afterthought, a chronic echo in Jon's mind.

Whereupon he excused himself, hopped from bed, and hurried to the bathroom down the upstairs hall. There he splashed water on his eyes and reviewed the story's words until he had them memorized. His face in the lavatory mirror looked sallow and skull-like. But the look of consternation on Chloe's wrinkled face when he went back was even more disturbing: he had never seen it before. The blackbird story, he mysteriously felt, held the key to his ambiguous predicament, but he could not sort its implications. Chloe breathed heavily all night, giving no clues, and other noises in the house disclosed that his parents were puttering about.

Consequently, he could not drift back off to sleep.

The next evening, after speaking with his father, Chloe moved into the suite so long in preparation for her, even as Jon's mother protested that the decorators had not finished hanging the drapes. But now they were in place, and the fresh paint on the suite's walls had long since dried. Jon had sneaked in to check.

In succeeding months, Chloe's health worsened.

At length, his parents took her away to Darktree. Nothing could be done to help her, at home or in the hospital, they said. All they could do was let her *pass* in surroundings replete with nature's consolations, amid trellises and birdsong, in the deep green mercies of the wood. Did Jon have no idea of how Chloe would react to the antiseptic white of a hospital, where gurneys and syringes aggravated a dying person's horror of *letting go*?

He did. He actually did. But that made the prospect of visiting her in the sanitorium no more appealing. Darktree's building resembled a leaf-grown gingerbread house, quaintly evil, and he wanted nothing to do with it.

Nor with Chloe.

The old woman had materialized out of his childhood nightmares to haunt the childhood he still had left.

But they always drove Jon with them to visit her. And each time Chloe, who could no longer speak, gestured at him to approach her sickbed and let her kiss him. Not on the cheek or forehead, but on the lips. Always she held him too long to her mouth, her oddly strong gnarled hands clenched on his shoulders. Her breath on these exchanges was stale, like the smells in the rugs and the upholstery of furniture in funeral homes, two of which Jon had visited when his biological grandmothers had died. It scared him. And as Chloe held him, *his* breath funneled away, threatening to empty him, a vastly alarming prospect.

But he never protested.

Because when Chloe finally released him, he found approving smiles on his parents' faces. Only that salvaged Jon's pride. The regard his father and mother had for his mannerly compassion, even if both were forced, somehow made up for the indignity of kissing Chloe's lips as she compelled him to do.

Now, again in her sickroom, he was two years older than when she'd first come to their house. Chloe lay propped in a mechanical bed, looking even more embalmed and mummy-like than on that first occasion. The orchard on the Darktree lawns was visible through the window by her bed, and Jon kept looking at the trees' colliding leaves rather than on her sunken face. But even without gazing upon her, he knew that as soon as his family had entered, she had seen him through rheumy eyes. He stood at the door, transfixed or terrified, as she stretched her pale claws toward him, wordlessly moaning.

"Jon!" his father said. "Come to Chloe. It's been weeks since she's seen you."

"Hello," he said from the door.

"Jon!" His mother grasped his sleeve and led him to the bedside. "Forgive him, Chloe. He's at that stage where he believes any kind of affectionate display unmanly. We're trying to purge him of that spurious notion."

The old woman reached for him as if he were a piece of driftwood, a means by which she could save herself from drowning. The look in her clouded eyes implored, scolded, intimidated. How could they expect him to submit this time? He wanted to bolt, never to return to Darktree, but her hands seized his arms, and her face grew more insistent as she pulled him to her withered lips. Jon scented the orchard air.

"We'll leave you with Chloe a few minutes," his father said. "Your mother and I have financial matters to attend to downstairs, and Chloe told us in a letter that being alone with you, even briefly, would make her feel years younger."

As soon as his lips touched Chloe's, he knew his parents had left. The door to the room closed, and she forced him to her breast. Frantic, he looked over her head into the orchard. Huge shadows drifted there, like tidewater. Her teeth touched his. Devouring shadows under the trees, dark shapes sucking light from his optic nerves. Her tongue enwrapped his. The orchard became a black square of black columns. All his breath rushed from his lungs. He fell into a spiraling pit. His consciousness swept away on a dark tide.

Jon let go of the other's shoulders and opened his eyes.

Although he hadn't heard the door reopen, three people neared his bed and stood by its foot, blurred as if by a jalousie window.

Weird. Still, he recognized the adults as his parents. But what about the boy leaning over him? Unable to speak, he extended his crablike hands imploringly and tried to induce Mother and Father closer. They did not approach. When the boy, who resembled him, reached down and slapped him across the face, he had no clue what had just happened . . . until the boy gave him a gratified look drained of long-borne frustration, and his parents smiled at their new son as if they'd adopted a more-than-worthy stand-in.

"Being alone with Chloe was good," the boy told his parents as they left Jon's bedside together. "Very, very good."

I, CARTOGRAPHER

As we scrape our upstairs bedrooms, blue paint flakes and old plaster dust sifts from the walls. Built in 1890, my wife's mother's childhood house undergoes, under scraped hands, a tedious renovation. A new family, we and our children, have moved in. Its five rooms have swallowed us like a rainforest, a desert, the rock gardens of a moraine. The bedrooms teem with secret fauna, invisible denizens whose languages thwart our understanding. The stairway drops into a foyer that emits from its scarred hardwood a backboil of memory, a mist roaring with voices that my wife may hope to recognize; but I, never. She scrapes the master bedroom, I the one our son will occupy, and as marshes and lake countries take shape on these walls, our infant daughter awaits a passport to her designated domain.

Maps. In the fifth grade, Mrs. Carter made us draw them: France, Bulgaria, string-bean Chile. All the protean nations of Africa, their cellular borders bulging in and bulging out, collapsing and reforming even as the Crayola tips we guided over the tracing paper lifted and fell for our latest squint-eyed realignments. Like Age of Discovery explorers, we were cartographers. In my classroom, our desks bolted to interlocking grey and white tiles, we sailed with Columbus, Cabot, Verrazzano, and Magellan. Like Hakluyt, we also compiled maps, for from our waxy hands nations, emperies, and the hungry terra incognita of our ignorance fell like sheafs for a coffee-table history of the "Post-War World." That long ago, we never heard the machine-gun fire in the rattling of our traceries and did not realize that cartographers draw lines that divide and may even vivisect.

I use a Red Devil scraper. My clumsy technique has worn both edges of the blade, humping it in between. I invariably tilt the scraper's blade to pull off time-bonded paint. I fail to exert the pressure evenly when I pull. Hence the callus on my right palm: two chafed knuckles, one on each hand. On the walls, at shoulder level: an expanse of gouged plaster. Below it, extending to the baseboard, an undercoat as glossy brown as hardened bee's wax. Everywhere else, oceans of powder-blue—probably the favorite color of the house's former tenant, my wife's bachelor uncle, who lived here after his father, Dr. Ellis, died. The uncle scraped these walls, too, right down to the porous masonry that we've struggled toward for two months. Once, Ted also put up new paint, which finally blistered like a hand, split into seams, and spalled into patterns like those caused by the tectonic movements of continents, the topographic shaping of wind, water, vulcanism, and even the minor dickerings and divvyings of man. Through the wall I scrape (the wall itself a map of an unknown foreign territory), my wife chips out harbors and fjords from the powder-blue wastes on the largest accidental mural. Like me, she surely stoops ankle-deep in snow.

As I pause in my mapmaking (in an Asian inlet or a tropical estuary fingering through the main landmass of another planet), I find a pearl lodged precariously between the nail and pad of my right forefinger. It is indigenous to these parts. It must have accreted its round nacreous self about an irritating bit of plaster or paint inside the scallop of my nostril. Now the pearl has emerged to shine arrows of rippling light over the seascape that, powder-blue silt at my feet, I am enmired in. Is it likely that men would kill for a necklace of these? In the master bedroom, silence. I flick my prize discovery away—there are more where it came from—and resume charting the wall's alien shorelines with a singlemindedness built on riches recklessly lost and loved ones forsaken.

From the interior, someone charts my progress. Yes, it's true. Through the steel of my worn blade, I register replies to its stridulous scraping, which emerge from deep within the masonry, from beyond the spidery inlet whose banks I crumble with each downward tug. For eight years, Uncle Ted dutifully paid his pest-control bills, so it cannot be rats scrabbling through the uninsulated canyons between our walls. Nor do the replies to my scraping echo only my wife's work in the master bedroom. For months I haven't heard her. I've mapped a private trade route into the heart of a region still unfound. When I return, I will arrive with strange spices, creamy porcelains, the scrimshawed teeth of leviathans and manticores, having taken them in trade for my mucoid pearls. Meanwhile, first contact nears. The restless machete of my double inside the wall slashes down the foliage and rattles the lath-supporting studs rampant within his interior country. His breath, even at a distance, shreds my olfactory sense as would a flamethrower's exhalation, the corona of its odor like the halo over Hiroshima. In our February chill, the wall plaster sweats and I sweat too.

Across from *Chica con flora*, a lithograph by Alvar, hangs George F. Cram's Panoramic Map of the World. As I toil, I recall the wall in my study, the first room we assaulted with scrapers, primed with sealer, and repainted. In there, the colors of *la chica* are two muted shades of blue, a dull burgundy, and some subtly interwoven browns. The colors on Cram's map, by contrast, are a watery blue (for oceans, seas, lakes) and orange, green, yellow, pink, and purple (for all the various countries). Does one artifact qualify more as *a work of art* than the other? Surely. But Cram's gaudy cartography belongs to my wine-colored walls in a way that Alvar's Grecian girl cannot. The blue flower in her hand is like a lollipop or a plastic pinwheel—too fragile to last. And though the outlines of countries are also fragile, I find in my dream reverie that they have more substance than the flesh of Alvar's human subject. Maybe, now, my dark-haired wife walks barefoot over the migrating ruins of Mauritania. Maybe sands have engulfed her, and *mano contra mano* Cram has defeated Alvar . . .

"Hello, Red Devil," I say. As I knew would happen, a Japanese man rises toward me out of the plaster, his flesh neither red nor yellow, but a soft brown like that of the *chica con flora* on the study wall. Glancing back, I see into our son's empty room and understand that the masonry I've scraped for so long has just closed behind me, blocking any escape. After an odyssey more strenuous than Magellan's, I am at last to meet a representative of one of those countries I knew I would one day map. We almost bump noses inside the walls. I scrape my counterpart's arms, he scrapes mine. For a time, this happy reciprocity obtains. Then an exhalation of his breath informs me that this ostensible poet-cum-warrior is a samurai who has lain with dragons, and we duel with our blades in the boundless space between this world and that. Although we are boxed, if not boxing, in the house of my wife's grandfather (once a doctor to our new hamlet), it might as well not exist. But it does, this house, and I learn the agony of hand-to-hand combat in such cramped vastness. Then the samurai, his face that of a rabid mythological beast, morphs into a Sumo who smothers me under his wide nude buttocks in the powder of our scraping and, laughing volcanically, suffocates me.

Eventually, wallpaper goes up. On my belly, I peer through it into the room beyond and easily distinguish the pattern on the paper: raccoons, rabbits, mice, foxes, robins, and assorted grasses that repeat endlessly atop the continents and waterways that my wife and I once effaced beneath a coat of white sizing. She, back from Mauritania, makes a bed. Our three-year-old, astride his red plastic locomotive, pulls a stuffed rabbit along the floor in an empty Kleenex box. From her crib in another room, oceans or continents away, our daughter burbles, *"Damn you,"* and I tell the mutating samurai-Sumo-beast whose buttocks still pinion me while he inscribes maddening archipelagoes down the ridge of my spine, *"Let me up! Can't you see there are people living out there?"* But Cram's Panoramic Map of the World has overcome the Iberian gal with the lollipop flower, and the walls keep calling my name . . .

TEARS

When True Stanford—Mister True to everyone who knew him—left his house and crossed Orchard Street into my yard on his way uptown, I almost went inside to keep from talking to him. I was picking up pecans and dropping them into a paper sack, and his route would have brought him right past me. Still, I called out, "Hey, Mister True, howya doing?" Guilt? From hoping to avoid him?

Two years back, the bank made him retire. To keep busy, he puttered about his and Miss Carolyn's yard. In the fall he raked oak and pecan leaves. In the spring he set out tomato plants in topsoil surrounded by old tractor tires. All year, he drove his beat-up Impala to and from town with his fedora jammed on his head and an at-loose-ends look on his face. Miss Carolyn said he haunted their house like a specter, drifting from room to room and fading off into the yard when he had visited them all.

Hearing me, Mister True turned on a grand smile, but for his crooked teeth. He stood two inches over six feet but looked taller because he was skinny and wore his trousers up under his ribcage. He wore his famous felt hat, his famous button-up sweater hanging off his shoulders like an ashen cape. His *walk* was what got me, though. His legs looked to move only below the knees, and his hands clasped his hips with his thumbs pointing toward his belt buckle in a way reminiscent of a girl modeling a bathing suit.

Anyway, he arrived an arm length's off, a crust of egg yolk stuck to his bottom lip and a night's growth of beard stubbling his jaw. He looked down as if he had something vital in his shirt pocket, but only to keep from meeting my eye. "It's not on. It's off," he said. "They have 'em up there. It'll do, if I get it again." He held his thumb and forefinger apart to show me the size of the mystery item and nodded toward town. "It's a problem. We need one. I've got to get it. It's off, that's why."

Mister True talked that way now: fuzzy pronouns, verbs that didn't go any-where. To follow him, you had to make loopy mental jumps. For which reason the bank no longer called him in for part-time teller work. In a grown man, it was irksome. You wanted to grab him and demand that he put real names and places to his formless mutter.

"Look," I said. "Is there something I can do?"

He swung his chest around toward his house. "—out and won't stay on." I couldn't hear the rest of what he said.

"Is it your car?"

Mister True's head rose, his smile got sunshine bright.

Thinking I'd hit the jackpot, I told him that although I wasn't a mechanic, I could check under the hood and maybe give him a notion of what was wrong. Then he could tell Errol Cruz or one of the other guys at the Amoco station. That idea was hunky-dory with Mister True. He waved at the blue Impala in his driveway, inviting me to go there with him. I put my pecan sack on a lawn chair, and we crossed the street.

I went to the Impala's hood, but Mister True climbed to the porch and walked into the house, maybe for a flashlight or a screwdriver. But when he didn't return, I stepped through a flowerbed onto the porch and knocked on the screen door. Miss Carolyn let me in. Saying she was grateful I'd come, she led me into a dark parlor with painted wainscoting halfway up the walls. In this parlor, Mister True stood before the space heater staring down at it as if it had hurt his feelings.

"Its handle came undone," Miss Carolyn said. "True's fretted it all morning."

I used a screwdriver on a lampstand by the heater to tighten the handle. It took thirty seconds. The Stanfords beamed as if I'd just run a pack of mad dogs out of their yard. In the parlor's chilly gloom, Mister True's eyelashes had a gluey look. He put one long hand atop the heater and rolled his knuckles over the ugly amber metal.

In the hall I said, "I thought it was the car. That's what he made me think."

"True gets confused these days." Miss Carolyn was nearlybout crying.

"Don't we all," I remarked.

*

The next time I saw him, he sat on a folding chair in the voting-machine room of our new City Hall. Miss Carolyn was an election official checking the name of each person who came in against a list of registered voters. She had Mister True at the end of the table, not far from her, because she didn't like to leave him alone: he'd wander or go outside for a walk. His driving had also deteriorated. Miss Carolyn had begun to hide the car keys to protect him and everybody else in town. A short line wound about her table. My wife Pam and I made it longer, but voters kept throwing levers in their booths and opening curtains for the next person, so the line kept moving. The people going past Mister True asked him how he was doing, told him how good he looked, patted the shoulder of his musty cardigan. "True just went to the post office," Miss Carolyn told everyone. "Says we've won the lottery."

I looked at Mister True. When my sister and I were kids in the pew across from his and Miss Carolyn's, she noticed that although he crossed his legs at the knee, the foot of the upper leg still rested on the floor, right next to the foot of the uncrossed leg. He was sitting that way now, and his smile seemed to have as much to do with this impossible posture as it did with any lottery victory.

"This is what we'll get," Mister True told everyone. "This here. Hundreds of thousands of dollars. Millions maybe." He held an aluminum-siding-company brochure. With one spidery finger, he tapped a toll-free telephone number on the brochure. To him, this number was the prize money he and Mrs. Stanford had won. Miss Carolyn looked at each person going past with a message in her eyes: *Please don't make him think anything else.*

"Congratulations, Mister True."

"That's wonderful."

"Going to Hawaii soon?"

Pam and I stood next in line. Leaning her forehead into my back, she whispered: "I swear to God, Al, it makes me want to cry."

A few days later I came home to an empty house. At the kitchen window I looked out over our dead lawn at Orchard Street and the Stanfords' tall tar-papered roof. Pam pushed open their house's screen door, spoke to someone inside, and came down the steps. Soon, she joined me in our kitchen with cups of coffee at the breakfast bar.

"What's going on?"

"Miss Carolyn and I put Mister True to bed. It took some doing."

"It's not even six. Is he ill?"

"Wrung out. Miss Carolyn, too. The both of them."

"Yeah, it's tough puttering about the house all day."

Pam grimaced. "They attended a funeral in Sylvester. A double funeral for the teenage grandchildren of an old family friend who were killed in a crash. The Stanfords were away two days and just got home. Didn't you know they were gone?"

"I was at work. Same as yesterday."

Pam tapped her spoon on the Formica, harder and harder, until I seized her wrist. Like Mister True, she averted her gaze then declared, "Miss Carolyn's nearlybout the bravest woman I've ever known. No, the *absolute* bravest."

"Is that something to get angry about?"

"Listen, will you? The funeral flummoxed Mister True. He saw two coffins. Two coffins for two young people. He thought their own grown-up sons had died. Their whole two days in Sylvester he thought that. He cried like a baby in church and at graveside when they lowered the caskets—the caskets were closed because of that damn car wreck—and he thought his own kids were being buried."

"Nobody set him straight?"

"Al, Miss Carolyn didn't realize he didn't know whose funeral they were at. It seemed a tad out of proportion, how he carried on, but Mister True's always been a softie, and folks there knew he's been declining. It touched them, Al."

In a modest sort of way, this was a fantastic story. I sipped my coffee and waited for Pam to go on: "Driving home, Miss Carolyn figured out what had happened. True started mumbling the boys' names—'Cliff, Cliff,' 'Martin, Martin'—and about how it wasn't fair, him and Miss Carolyn living longer than the boys when they still had their own families to raise, so it hit Miss Carolyn like walking through a big pane of glass, invisible one minute but the next you're all cut up with too many hurt places to count. She had to stop the car to tell him it just wasn't the way he supposed."

"Didn't that do it?"

"Stopping the car confused him. He got out and peed at roadside, then told Carolyn they had to get home and check their insurance policies. He figured there was money owing Cliff's and Martin's families, which was pretty sharp for a mixed-up old man. She tried to say again that the closed caskets hadn't held their sons, but he'd seen what he'd seen, and all she could do was get him back in the car and drive home."

"You mean he *still* believes their boys are dead?"

"Miss Carolyn called me as soon as they arrived. I went over to help her set Mister True straight. We showed him school pictures of the kids who'd died, explained about the car crash, told him Cliff and Martin were fine. What finally did it, though, was calling Cliff in Birmingham and letting him and True talk. Cliff talked to his daddy just as sweet and reassuring as you could ask. He wasn't a bit annoyed, just truly concerned."

"And Martin?"

"He's up in Atlanta. We couldn't reach him. Which was okay: talking to Cliff did it for Mister True."

Pam carried her cup to the sink. After a while, looking out the window, she said, "You should've seen him, Al. He clapped his hands like a kid. He yanked his hat off and flipped it at Miss Carolyn. He blubbered into her shoulder. Sobbing, sobbing to beat the band. She got started too, tears of joy because their boys were still alive. And I was right there with 'em, just laughing and crying all at once."

"You're doing half of it again."

Pam turned on the cold water and rinsed her hands. "I don't know how Miss Carolyn stands it." Then she leaned down to rinse her face. Taking a dish towel with her, she went past me and upstairs to bed.

I made my own supper.

Mister True got worse. He found the car keys and wrecked the Impala . . . without killing anyone or damaging anything besides the car but a garbage can. He wandered off at odd hours, and a patrolman brought him home a few times.

By spring Miss Carolyn was spoon-feeding him and doing the kinds of chores that people with babies do.

In June, Mister True fell off a stool trying to unscrew a light bulb that hadn't burnt out and broke his hip. His time in the medical center seventeen miles up the road grew longer, and Miss Carolyn was hardly ever home. Evenings, a porch light burned until midnight or later. Pam kept up with her and reported her doings whenever we sat down to eat.

One evening, a TV program we like had come to a place where the detective stalks a heavyset baddie in a fatigue jacket. The telephone rang. Pam got up to catch it: folks always call when you're just shy of a big shootout. The program ended, another started, and Pam returned and sat down on the sofa with wrecked-looking eyes.

"Mister True's dying."

I turned off the TV. "He's been dying for weeks."

"He's dying *tonight*. Won't last till morning. She thought we should know."

"I'm sorry."

"I asked if she wanted me to drive up. She said no, she just wants to sit with him alone, holding his hand, kissing him goodbye until he can't feel it anymore. She'd be self-conscious doing that stuff with others around. She'd feel obliged to talk because they'd come such a ways to keep her company."

And it hit me. Never again was Mister True going to saunter out his door with his hands on his hips like a Miss America contestant. His famous felt hat and ratty sweater would go into a box. So would Mister True.

"A blessing. He hasn't been himself since the bank let him go."

Pam didn't register this. "I started crying. That got Miss Carolyn going. I apologized, but she said not to fret. Over the phone, crying's something better than talking that two gals can do together." Pam took a breath. She wasn't crying now, but her eyes were even redder. "Damn. So many stupid goddamn tears."

I had no idea what to say to that. Pam didn't either. TV was a lost option. I walked to the front door, let myself out, and stood on the porch with my hands in my back pockets looking at the clouds ghosting the dark sky and listening to semis growling through town toward Columbus and other points south.

THE CONTRIBUTORS
TO PLENUM FOUR

P LENUM is a *continuing anthology of the best original holovistic universes now being conceived. PLENUM FOUR represents the latest entry in this series. Editor Ethelstan Bem, has culled these compelling universes from literally millions of submissions. In the three years its selections have been eligible, universes from PLENUM have won five of the Apotheo Awards given by HVMW (Holo Visionaries of the Milky Way), not to mention two of the Yahweh Awards bestowed by HV fandom at its annual Galactic Cons.*

THE CONTRIBUTORS

Daphne Deirdre Dubose ("Quasars and Cumquats") has gained an enviable reputation over the last eight years for her inimitable "mood" programs in this and other HV-venues. "My intent," Daphne lasers from her home in the Australian Outback, "is to develop a schema of interlocking universes that overwhelm the male imbiber by their cumulative evocativeness and make the chauvinist son of a bitch cough up his delusions about how reality operates." With her life-person, Bruce, and their two whelps, Daphne lives in a large crater, one of many topological changes in Earth's terrain precipitated by the lamentable Cobalt Galas. In this secluded Eden, four thousand kilometers from the nearest citsite, she brings her HV universes to fruition and teaches a special course, "John Milton and Introductory Worldshaping," via satellite, to dozens of students around the globe. Many of Daphne's full-length cosmoses have appeared in free HV editions from AC/DC Dispensers. Since the stunning success of her Yahweh-copping *Rib of Chaos,* her newer cosmoses have been reissued in minicoins @ 10,018 inflated georges per unit (as Daphne wishes me to remind you).

S. K. Sullnan ("Black Hole Blues") surfs with a tidal influx of sardonic young holo-visionaries who hope to extend the range and techniques of holo-vistic programming. Sullnan's universes are darkly engrossing. He neither gives nor asks for quarter. The maelstromic fragmentation of his method, initially confusing, ultimately holds a glass up to the sensualist in which one recognizes one's self and feels a cathartic revulsion. With such cosmos coins as "Up Yours, Life" and "The Incredible Shrinking Élan," Sullnan has enraged long-time HV addicts and traditional worldshapers alike by attacking many of the field's sacred cows. In "Black Hole Blues," for instance, he forthrightly questions the *necessity* of existence.

"Faster Than the Speed of Love!" marks the fourth appearance of **Benjamin Bacaruda**'s work in *PLENUM*. Bacaruda is one of the very few active HVers whose career spans the entire specialized history of our field. His first cosmoses arrived during the Golden Age of *HYPNOTIC*, back in the glorious but vaguely reprehensible days when we downloaded our HVs from pedwalk Vend-O Dispensers and slunk home to enjoy them in the privacy of our delta-coves. (Who in those days had the georges to buy a fully equipped plenarium?) Even then, though, Bacaruda was lifting our field's standards. His universette "More Than Megacosmic" is still often anthologized because its use of sensual and deific motifs was an ether-breaking step in the development of modem HV. Recently, Ben has been exploring the manifold dramatic possibilities of relativistic meiosis. (As a past secretary-treasurer of HVMW, he wants to inform members that ballots for last decade's 2143 Apotheo Awards will soon traverse the ether toward you to be voted upon and retroactively submitted.)

Harmony Shadrach ("Hallucinogengineers") is, along with Benjamin Bacaruda, the only worldshaper whose work has appeared in each number of the *PLENUM* series. She is our only contributor to slip more than one universe into a single coin (i.e., "Time's Last Gasp" and "The Philosopher's Stone Regarded as a Hemorrhoid," both in *PLENUM THREE.)* Seen by HV creators as a member of the new generation, Shadrach has startled her fans by creating cosmoses that are painfully absorbing on many levels. Her cosmos here presages the start of a series about the epistemological effects of universe-expanding stimulants. Her coming full-scale cosmos, *The Eye-Scream Clone,* is set for universal dispersal. In standard time, Harmony is the life-person of editor Ethelstan Bem.

Pfara "A'ra"pf's "The Otherworldly, the Otherwise" marks the first appearance in our *PLENUM* series of work by an alien. Pifi, as they are known by their close admirers and friends, has mastered thirty-three different sensory complexes. Further, entity "A'ra"pf ' has translated the lovely and moving "The Otherworldly, the Otherwise" from the Vegan sensory complex into our own auditory-gustatory-olfactory-tactile-visual system. Astute imbibers of this tastily strange creation will no doubt find it unique among their hours of HV-ing. We anticipate more good work from Pifi and wish them a successful alternate-cycle estivation this summer on Vega II.

R. Ron Golightly ("Fifth Moon in the Corner Pocketa") is the unpigeonholable loony in the pantheon of HV developers. He has created universes from back to front and from the middle to both sides out, breaking rules less brilliant talents don't even know exist. "Microminiaturizing Andromache" in *PLENUM ONE* restructures the Welsh *Mabinogion* as a cowboy love song about unrequited entropy, hilariously. A recent wrinkle in his work has been the introduction of robot solar systems that wind up, down, and all around, using the rules of three-dimensional mechanistic snooker. Golightly tells us that, for a lark, he has recently retranslated Pifi's "The Otherworldly, the Otherwise" back into Vegan. "Where it always belonged to begin with," he adds facetiously.

Asa C. Mach, whose universella "Doomdrop" is the feature cosmos in *PLENUM FOUR,* has long been known for his work's impeccable scientific grounding. Like Bacaruda, Dr. Mach had his start in Vend-O Dispensers like *HYPNOTIC* and *HEADFUL*. "I got 1½ semi-inflated georges per amp back then and sometimes pumped up the voltage to no real purpose but to keep body and soul together. My inspirations were the Big Bang and wind erosion— I know, that last smacks of faddishness—and I tried my damnedest to create programs combining the dynamism of the one with the delicate aestheticism of the other. Still, many of my early universes were the products of a technology-struck hacker, short on style but long on spectacular effects. Hopefully, I've learned a few things over the years." Dr. Mach's cosmos "Doomdrop" attests that he has. Its sensitive delving of the synched occurrence of binary supernovas is a *tour de force* of last-days HV programming, one that few inveterate imbibers will ever forget. "Actually," the estimable Asa C. Mach lasers us, "I got in over my head with this one. Its breathtaking realism stems from the fact that I induced an ultra-delayed neutron chain-reaction in the atoms at Sol's core, did some under-crust holography by means of three ESPer-eye plasma-glide waldos, extracted them along with a spectrum of sensory-complex images, re-combined the lot with a biscopic mixer, and—*voila*! Sadly, the core explosions will surface within the next two years as an annoying pseudo-nova. However, its effects will not be *pseudo,* the term refers only to the manner of its initia-tion. But surely, Stan, you know how this business is: a real HVer will sacrifice almost anything for a synapse-boggling holovision." Regular imbibers of the *PLENUM* series will doubtlessly agree that "Doomdrop" is totally worth it.

For reasons stemming from Asa C. Mach's creation of "Doomdrop," PLENUM FIVE, to appear late next year, will most likely be the final number in this distin-guished series. We hope it gives you as much pleasure as PLENUM FOUR is sure to.

TO A CHIMP HELD CAPTIVE FOR PURPOSES OF RESEARCH

Argument: An idealistic young researcher at a facility making extensive use of primates, particularly chimpanzees, addresses a male animal under her supervision.

I

Your heart aches. I can see it in your face.
    Do you dream of the day when you were orphaned?
Or is it the sterile stench of this place
    That makes you gnaw the heel of your own hand?
Either, I think, would be reason enough
    To etch that pitiable expression
        On your wretched, rubbery, manlike mask.
        It must also be tough
Having to contend with our compassion,
    The feckless ways we take ourselves to task.

II

Eleven years ago, they shot your mother
    From a treetop, and down she came with you
Astride her shaggy back, just another
    Silent Zeno for our surgical zoo.
They tore you wide-eyed from her warm body,
    A terrific wench only lead could tame,
        Loveliest coin of your lost pongid wealth.
    Yes, it does seem odd, we
Sanctify such ruthlessness in the name
    Of our superior species' right to health.

III

And then, of course, the funk of the cages,
   The deadening wages of quarantine,
The drug-fogged hours—virtual ages—
   While we test what our tinkerings must mean.
Little wonder, then, that you wear your gloom
   Like the hairshirt of a saint, a threadbare
      Mantilla of regret, a monkish frock.
     Still, I'd like to assume
That we could cure your melancholy stare
   Merely by jimmying a fast-jammed lock.

IV

Not likely, prominent ethnologists
   Warn, for after long confinement a chimp
Uncaged solely to stalk our research lists
   Becomes, in social terms, a hapless gimp.
What simian Guinevere could grapple
   Gracefully with your uncouth gibberings,
     Your taste for crap, your ignorance of sex?
    Even Eve with her apple
Would have thought you the saddest of beings
   Upon whom to bestow a mortal hex.

V

The Interagency Primate Steering
   Committee (of the National Institutes
Of Health) fears your species may be nearing
   The bourn of countless other bygone brutes.
No one comes back from that dolorous state,
   Not dinosaurs, or quaggas, or dodoes!
     Though sometimes we grant you sabbatical sun,
   Expecting you to mate,
You coolly disdain to breed in the throes
   Of our own lively race to extinction.

VI

The vaccine you gave us for hepatitis B
    Might hearten you a little, or the hope
Of harvesting from your hemoglobin, see,
    A melanoma-neutralizing dope,
But no, you deeply disturbed prisoner
    Of our devotion to our research roles,
        You'd rather we determine why you grieve,
    Put our heads together,
And ask if apes have apprehensive souls.
    That, however, we simply don't believe.

VII

Or perhaps I do. I've heard your high screech
    Carry through the antiseptic cell block
Like the cry of one called upon to preach
    Rebellion to his shy, phlegmatic flock;
And I've trembled to think, not that you would
    Really pull down these godforsaken tiers,
        But that you do possess an upward-yearning
    Spirit that might have stood
In the same nearness to mine as Shakespeare's . . .
    Given but love and hypnosis-led learning.

VIII

Idiocy! You were born for torment,
    Not the presiding role at Sunday mass,
The lifting of a bleeding heart's lament,
    Or your potential mastery of chess.
The sufferings you abide ennoble
    All of us, giving a grave, selfless laugh
        To those who vow our vanity's too large.
    If the dearest foible
Of our kind is to err on our own behalf,
    Why, then, to forgive is a chimp's clearest charge!

IX

Ah, but do you forgive? Can you forgive?
    Racked, stuck, implanted, cut upon, and dosed
With caustic rays and chemicals, you live
    A galvanic dream, half junkie, half ghost.
All right. I'll renounce the outward human
      To reassert my rogue humanity:
        I'll don a gaudy gorilla costume
      That may yet illumine
My mad return to moral sanity:
    I your heinous bride, you my hirsute groom!

X

No marriage made in heaven, I grant you,
    But the late Charlie Darwin and the Leakeys
Of Kenya will sit in a spectral pew
    As we exchange rings, and a few rueful fleas.
O let my more unfeeling colleagues scoff
    To catch me cavorting in apish drag,
      Funny-farm foe of their humbug refrain!
    Brute spouse, I'll not take off
This suit until the butchers cease to brag
    They're putting an end to reasonless pain!

A FATHER'S SECRET

Y ou're not thinking about Dad again, are you?" Tina asked.

Gordon, on his knees, leaned up and away from her in the early summer dark like an oarsman slick from the exertion of a moonlight race, and she was the scull he'd been rowing. His eyes closed with the fatigue of a disappointing finish.

"Gordy, lie down next to me. I'm not comfortable like this."

Gordon's eyes opened. They studied Tina as if she'd emerged on a silent mechanical lift from the heart of the mattress. Sighing defeatedly, he stretched out beside her, and she eased the sheet over her body.

"That was good," she said hopefully. "For a man processing his grief, that wasn't bad." She tried to put a smile into her words so he wouldn't mistake them for bitchiness disguised as sympathy. Gordon's hurt was hers even when he tried to hide it with an outdated Gary Cooper stoicism.

"It's so quiet tonight." He sounded amazed. "So quiet you can hear the crickets singing."

"Then it isn't *that* quiet, is it?" Tina meant this as banter, but it sounded like naked contradiction. Given Gordon's simmering touchiness, that was dangerous. What was she doing?

"I mean inside, Tina. It's so quiet inside I can hear the world outside. That's rare. We're usually trying to figure out how in hell to take care of—"

"Shhhh. Be grateful he's resting easy."

To Tina's relief, Gordon let himself be shushed.

"I *am* grateful," he whispered. "I just can't believe the crickets, the whole Georgia Cricket Philharmonic in our backyard."

Tina cuddled him. "Did you even hear me say it was good, Gordy?"

"Really, it was like letting go of a rubber band before I had it aimed good.

Same sort of feeling. Thinking just of myself, of course."

"Three weeks is a long time, Gordy. Three weeks is—"

"I also heard you say something semi-annoyed about my dad."

"Not about Dad. Just about your preoccupation with him during . . . you-know. Thinking just of myself." Sarcasm could dent his fenders, too.

Gordon propped on an elbow and looked into her eyes. His face hung gargoyleish above her, shadow-etched into unfamiliarity. "I'll tell you something, ma'am. Even before Dad died, I thought of him—I think I always thought of him—during our bouts of . . . you-know. I couldn't help it."

This confession, if it *was* a confession, had no handles for Tina. She couldn't pick it up. "You mean you think of your father while we make love? That you *always* think of him when we're doing it?"

"That's a pretty good paraphrase."

Beneath the surface ridicule, Gordon's "teasing," she sensed the body of the indistinct monster making these disturbing waves. So far, though, the monster's body had no shape: it was a blip on her emotional sonar. "Why would you think of Dad, Gordy? I don't understand. Is this some sort of parable?"

"A terrible parable." He eased to his back again, his hands like cast-iron gnarls on his thighs. "If you believe the world, anyway. If you believe the pious hoi polloi."

"Gordy, talk in an alphabet I understand!"

"Shhh. Keep it down. The kid needs his—"

"Okay, okay." Now Tina was staring down into his face, the tips of her hair brushing his shoulders. "I'm supposed to believe that every time we—"

"—you-know."

"—make love, damn it! That every time we do it, apparently back to our very first time in Daytona, some part of you is mulling memories of your dad? Is that it?" Incredulity coated her words like a glaze. He was putting a riddle to her, a bedtime tightening of the brain screws. Only it was something more than a riddle or a game.

"It's true, Tina. I swear it."

"But why? That doesn't make sense."

"Let's just forget it, okay?"

"I won't forget it. You brought this up. Halfway up, anyhow. Haul it all the way into the light, please."

Gordon's lips met in a semi-scowl. His eyes blinked as if he were clearing them of sleep sand. "It's a secret, Tina. I promised him I'd never tell anyone."

"He's been dead almost three weeks. I'm your wife. Use me as a sounding board."

Surprisingly, he smiled.

"Among other things," Tina said. "Besides, if your promise held only while he was alive, what harm in telling it now? You've kept your part of the bargain."

"Maybe." He seemed to consider the matter. "But it can't go any farther than this room. No one else ever hears it."

"Gotcha."

"Pinch your earlobe and swear."

With an exasperated snort, Tina pinched her earlobe. "I swear. Now talk."

"My father was an unusual man—"

"Gordy, I'm no stranger to that fact. Please skip the memorial preliminaries. We ought to be sleeping."

Gordon rose to an elbow so that Tina and he were nose to nose, and she drew back. "Between the ages of eleven and fourteen," Gordon said, pursuing her with his shadow-distorted features, "I was my dad's little live-in boyfriend. Is that clear enough? Does that acquit me of shilly-shallying around?"

Tina, to hold her own, stopped retreating. Outside, the crickets' unearthly thrumming sounded like a deranged gloss on Gordon's confession.

"Dad sexually abused you? Your own father?"

"I imagine a psychologist or a social worker would call it that: sexual abuse. Yeah, I'm sure they would."

Now Tina stroked the silvering hair above his ear. "Gordy, I never suspected. Never. He was always a gentleman around me."

"It's still true, Tina."

"But you took him into our home. When the others jumped ship, you paid for nursing services. Your cousin from Knoxville—Hazel?—was the only one of that sorry bunch to attend his funeral. You stuck by him in spite of what he'd done to you." Tina's lips touched Gordon's brow. "That's amazing. If it had been me, I could *not* have forgiven him, but you never let on. It's a wonder, Gordy. It really is."

Gordon lay back again. "Maybe. If you want to know the truth, it just never occurred to me I had anything to forgive him for."

"He took advantage of you."

"Well, you'd never catch me calling it sexual abuse. I don't know about other such cases, but Dad never hurt me. He taught me stuff. We had secret times when he instructed me in stuff other kids my age just weren't getting." He barked a laugh of reminiscence. "It was all learning by doing, that's all."

"You're joking!"

"I'm not, Sometimes I look back on that three, almost four-year episode with nostalgia, not with guilt or revulsion. In fact, every sexual encounter reminds me of Dad, if only fleetingly, at some crucial point in the process."

A sensation like that spurred by ice cubes popping in a tea glass struck Tina, and she shuddered. "*Process*? Jesus, Gordy!"

"Come on. It's over. Dad's in the cold, cold ground, and I'm here at your beck and call. Maybe I wasn't so hot tonight, but I'll lay my daddy's ghost the next time I lay you. You can count on it."

"Wait. If you liked your grab-ass sessions with Daddy so much, what made you stop? Why didn't you all keep on horsing around forever?"

"Girls, Tina."

"Girls?"

"I got interested in girls. I had more than an inkling of what to do with them too. It gave me a leg up, forgive the expression, on my teenage rivals. It gave me confidence."

"So, you sent your father a Dear Dad letter or something?"

"I just didn't meet with him anymore. I avoided him. He understood. It made him sad, but I was getting to be a big boy and he knew I had undiscovered countries to explore. Besides, he knew I still loved him. For the head start he'd given me."

"Wonderful."

"Anyway, I think he'd already found a replacement: Hazel's boy, a kid three or four years younger than I. Everything worked out."

Tina stared at Gordon, who lay staring at the inverted stucco dunes stippled across the ceiling. The deranged choiring of the crickets had begun to subside, and a dog barked, far away, its voice both lugubrious and frail.

Closer, just down the hall, another sound: a sobbing intake of breath followed by a series of desperate gasps.

She and Gordon bolted upright, but he hurried to step into the bikini briefs he'd recently taken to wearing and yanked on his jeans.

"Poor tyke," he said, struggling with the zipper. "God, Tina, I thought he was going to outgrow these attacks. I figured by now he'd be roughhousing his bike through every flowerbed on the block and playing shortstop for a little-league team."

"*I'll* see about him."

"Tina, it's my turn and, look, I'm dressed." He snapped the button on his jeans. "For once, thank God, we weren't asleep when the hacking began." He quick-timed down the hall to where Derek lay. Tina imagined their son blinking in the glare of the tensor lamp at his bedside and groping for his inhaler. His gasps drowned the insipid music of the crickets.

"Hey, boy-o," she heard Gordon say. "Daddy's here. Everything's gonna be okay."

Tina lay back, turned her head, and bit her bottom lip, hard.

WISHED-FOR BELONGINGS

My mother didn't want me. Like a Victorian foundling, for reasons never clear to me, I was dumped on the doubtful charity of the world in a battered Igloo cooler lined with strips of paper torn from the sports section of the *Atlanta Journal-Constitution*.

It was February when, as if by hobgoblin messenger service, this cooler materialized on the backseat of a Ford Fairlane parked by a rural Georgia farmhouse. The owner of the Ford and the farmhouse rescued me from the automobile, carried me inside, and, despite the reputed pleas of his wife to keep me, telephoned the police in Hogansville.

I became a ward of the state. Over the next seventeen years I lived in a dozen different foster homes, usually in the care of kind-hearted people whose affection for me depended in part on the stipends they received for sheltering me. Some families let me go because their primary breadwinners lost jobs, because I couldn't reach lasting truces with my new siblings, or because they found fostering other folks' children less profitable, emotionally and financially, than they had expected.

So, over time I became a wary expert on lower-middle-class housing in western Georgia: tin-roofed shotgun houses, double-wide mobile homes, tall-ceilinged drafty boxes with screened-in sleep porches. My opinion of and trust in people suffered in direct proportion to the accidental increase in my architectural savvy, but I never gave up on either myself or others.

Instead, I became a reader, thinker, and onlooker, always hoping to join any group that welcomed me. Passed over in grade school for such semi-honorary positions as Fire Marshal, Hall Monitor, and Lunchroom Attendant (I actually *heard* the capitals fronting these prestigious titles), I got into the Library Club because all you had to do was state your interest, sign up, and report on a book every other week or so. I read Walter Farley and Anna Sewell, A. A. Milne and Ross Macdonald. I ran for office every nine-week period for two years (the longest I ever stayed in any foster home), but never won a single election. Then the Library Club's advisor appointed me its historian, a post in which I worked hard, both at that job and at being liked.

To some extent, I *was* liked. My accomplishments threatened no one. When my peers vied for recognition, I faded obligingly into the background, even as an ostensible competitor. And, come the sure end of each foster relationship, I faded away entirely, exiled by exasperation to other paid parents and to other schools where the glacial cast in my eye and the lovelorn way I piloted my desk always identified me as a professional transient. It was okay to like me because, hey, I'd soon be gone again.

Throughout high school, I made above-average grades, but after failing an Air Force physical, for a year I bummed around the Gulf Coast doing odd jobs and haunting the history sections of local public libraries. Back in Georgia again, I wound up at the state university in Athens. Because the scholarships I applied for went to others, I paid for my tuition, board, and books by working at an off-campus fast-food franchise.

Well known for its greasy chili dogs and equally oleaginous teenage hires, this place set me among poor but likable gray-aproned kids with aspiring hearts and fast-food jargon as their presiding vocabularies. One skinny counter guy rarely said anything but *"Walk her through the garden!"* This cry alerted me to confetti with coleslaw the next hot dog on our frantic assembly line, but he also used it as a retort to any suggestion that he speed the processing of orders. None of the other countermen was as old as I, and during our rare breaks and downtime I found myself excluded from every inept practical joke or adolescent two-minute bull session. I knew nothing of Otis Redding, Camaros, or the fabled goings-on at Effie's place, and my acne-scarred peers didn't care beans about the Sepoy Mutiny in India or British colonialism in Southeast Asia. Why should they? They were high school boys with more immediate ambitions.

By this time, I had long since recognized the insidious pattern unifying my life and knew better than to register for fraternity rush. I thus escaped rejection by packs of besotted blazer-clad SAEs or Sigma Pis. I had no family, no connections, and no money, and no fraternity on campus had any incentive to sign me. To give the Greeks their due (though I never put them, or they me, to the ultimate test), I also conspicuously lacked a hail-fellow-well-met personality.

But consider my background.

In graduate school, which I reached by dint of hard work and kindly rec-
ommendations from a few senior faculty members, I fell in love with Melissa
Ahmadjian. I loved her exotic name, her short fair hair, her strapping golden
body, and her capriciously lively mind. Melissa reciprocated my interest, if not
my love. She drove a yellow Mustang (another product of the Ford Motor Company with a crucial role in my personal history), and on its cramped back seat,
not far from an undergraduate trysting place called Slippery Shoals, she indoc-
trinated me into the fibrillating rituals of sex.

By this time, I'd ceased walking dogs through greasy-spoon gardens and
earned a fairly decent salary as a research assistant in the history department.
The world looked bright. In spring quarter of that year, potentially solvent for
the near-term future, I asked Melissa Ahmadjian to marry me. She did not
say no.

She said, "I'll think about it, Jonathan."

Over the summer she meant.

To keep Melissa stage-center, I could protract this part of my story, although
you may have already concluded that she returned in the fall to decline my offer.
But you may not have foreseen her coming back with a full-fledged fiancé behind
her Mustang's wheel, yet that is what she did. The interloper hailed from her
Tennessee hometown, where they had resumed a romance that they'd mutually
broken off after Melissa's senior year.

My rival stood five inches taller and weighed a hundred pounds more than
I. He owned stock in a company up north that did certain mysteriously mer-
chandisable things with tritium, a radioactive isotope of hydrogen. Knowing
that I'd proposed to Melissa, he loathed me. Worse, he stayed in town living off
tritium dividends and behaving like a middle linebacker drafted into essaying
the title role in a local production of *Hamlet*. I had no chance against him.

A year or so after Melissa married this hulk, I found the happy pair ap-
proaching me on an interior concourse of the Georgia Coliseum during a basket-
ball game versus Kentucky. Melissa's hubby spotted me and the jostling halftime
crowd gave me no room to retreat. "Open your coat," he ordered Melissa. To her
credit, she did not obey. Besides, she didn't have to part the wings of her navy

London Fog trench coat for me to see that—as round, firm, and fully packed as a Lucky Strike—she was pregnant.

Buckling down, I took two advanced degrees in history, but started to job-hunt when college-level teaching posts in the humanities were as rare as snow leopards. How could you bag a creature that was nearly extinct? Although I interviewed for positions in four different states, no one hired me.

Totally demoralized, I gave up the search, moved to the small mid-west Georgia city of Tocqueville, and went to work for Piedmont United Mills as an apprentice loom operator on the night shift. I was lucky to get this job, but it wasn't what I wanted to do, and sometimes I swore that my machine was chanting, *"Walk-her-through the-garden, walk-her-through-the-garden."* I had no friends at the mill and spent my afternoons, when I should have been sleeping, knocking on doors of Tocqueville Junior College with transcripts of my grades from Athens.

I worked at Piedmont United Mills three and a half years before someone in the history department at the junior college had the ill luck and consummate kindness to die. This was a young woman killed when, after a severe winter storm, the ice-weighted branches of a pecan tree cracked and dropped on her ten-speed bicycle at the instant of her passage, burying her and the Gitane beneath a glittering demi-structure very like a fallen chandelier. Thanks to this grotesque accident, I was hired on a contingency basis. If I didn't work out, a hotshot Harvard grad would swoop down from Massachusetts to send me packing.

This threatened event never occurred, and I began to feel gingerly at ease in both the department and the classroom. True, the papers I wrote failed to earn favor at any of the requisite journals, and my awkward approaches to undergraduate women whose eyes, during my lectures, seemed to engage mine in colloquies of ill-disguised desire finally led me to conclude that I was an eye-language illiterate. These women were not flirting, but striving to appear intelligent and attentive. Maybe they *were* both, but when I invited them to films or pizza parlors, they lifted doe-like eyes to note they already had boyfriends. *That didn't stop Melissa Ahmadjian,* I wanted to say. At least not at first. But this unspoken rejoinder simply served to accent the dismaying possibility that Melissa had never had very good taste in men.

One goal kept me going, as prof and aspiring campus swain: I'd earn tenure if I stayed on the faculty five straight years and won departmental approval. With tenure in my grasp, I would now surely exude the ravishing pheromones of Eligible Bachelorhood.

Sadly, my failure to publish arose to haunt me.

To slay this specter, in the year before the formal review of my credentials I cranked out eight papers on different crucial episodes of imperial British history, which all limped home with rejection slips . . . until I placed a psycho-historical profile of the flamboyant explorer Richard Burton with *The East Alabama Review of Nineteenth-Century Approaches to Cartography*, a little magazine in the most exacting sense. (Each issue contained one medium-length article, a reproduction of a nineteenth-century map, and a page of subscription coupons.) Unfortunately, my piece would not appear until the quarterly's fall issue, months after my tenure hearing, and I must hope that word of this pending publication, along with my legitimate skills as a lecturer, would carry the day.

It didn't, and like a carny who has goaded a backwoods Nolan Ryan into flinging a ball at the metal bull's-eye triggering the carny's plunge into a tub of icy water, I fell—*kerplunk!*—from my precarious perch. Denial of tenure meant dismissal. Despite the many daunting lessons of my past, the shock of my dismissal overwhelmed me. Drowning, I thrashed, sputtered, and cried for mercy, but to no avail.

I passed three days naked and unshaven in my apartment staring at a jade plant whose small cushiony leaves, like emeralds with pleurisy, took turns falling to the floor with sorrowful clicks. (Maybe out of a Freudian desire to offset others' niggardliness toward me, I overwatered my house plants). Now we had both drowned, my jade plant and I.

"Poor baby," I murmured. "Poor baby."

Then, to my idiot amaze I found that I'd stashed almost two grand in the local Farmers, Merchants & Mill Workers Bank, and my doldrums ebbed. I'd withdraw the money, pull up stakes, and light out for Alaska. Losers, loners, bankrupts, outcasts, drug addicts, and drunks made one glorious Walt Whitmanish fraternity there, and I would join it by landing in Juneau and buying a round for the house in the city's most companionable bar. Yes, sir. That was the ticket. I'd relocate to the land of the timber wolf, the lucky strike, the pipeline, and the effusive tritium-glow of the aurora borealis.

I walked straight into a bank robbery. Three determined persons in ski masks, parkas, baggy pants, and jogging shoes were pointing stubby weapons—illegal submachine guns assembled from mail-order parts?—at patrons lined up two or three persons deep at the tellers' windows. Grabbed by the elbow, I was spun into a line near the door and told in oddly dulcet tones to behave myself.

As two of the thieves fanned out across the lobby, the one who'd just spoken to me drew a set of gray draperies across the bank's plate-glass entrance. A fluorescent twilight enveloped every actor in our surreal little drama.

The robbers were women. Two began working the customer lines collecting wallets, coin purses, jewelry. The eyelike bore of the machine gun trained on my gut by the third woman held me immobile. Soon her pals were moving from teller cage to teller cage passing zippered money pouches from hand to hand. No one spoke, time passed, and at last the wailing of distant police sirens sounded like the cries of peacocks on a muggy summer's night. The robbers, conferring heatedly now, decided they needed a hostage but wasted precious time puzzling the matter out among themselves.

"Me!" I shouted. "I'd make a wonderful hostage!" They took me. Out of all the people fixed in the quivering aspic of apprehension in that hijacked lobby of that bank, they chose me, Jonathan Smith, to see them to safety.

Resolute at last, the leader jabbed me with the barrel of her weapon, and the four of us performed a mincing retreat to the rotunda housing the drive-in window. Here, while the leader held patrons and bank officials at bay, the other women shed their outer garments, revealing rumpled Sears Catalog floral-print dresses and the frowzy, flattened mops of their hair. With loot-packed purses they burst through the rotunda's outer door shouting, *"Don't shoot! Don't shoot!"*, a pair of terrified hostages who'd just escaped their captors. I, the real hostage, looked on in wondering admiration.

The other young woman and I got out about five minutes later. Lady Pat (for so I call the wily maiden who masterminded both the holdup and the getaway) put her head and shoulders up under the cape of my windbreaker and the barrel of her submachine gun right into the hollow at the base of my skull. In the parking lot, we must have borne an alarming resemblance to a pair of vaudeville performers in the ill-fitting halves of a horse costume.

The police barricading the lot, brandishing their shotguns and bullhorns, froze and fell silent. They were stymied by my many loud proclamations that the holdup man was a Vietnam veteran in dire need of psychiatric help, a spiel I rattled off at Lady Pat's promptings. When her two accomplices squealed up in a commandeered police car to take us aboard and spirit us away, right under the noses of the deputies and patrolmen, the rescue operation—our Great Escape, if you will—was a breathtaking *fait accompli.*

"Why aren't they following us?" I marveled as we shot through alleyways, down side-streets, over bumpy tractor trails, and then along a stretch of county-maintained asphalt west of Tocqueville.

"Dee Dee and I took the keys out of their ignitions," said Dee Dee's sister, Mary Faye, and all of us laughed.

Ten or twelve miles farther on, in a stand of loblolly pines, we transferred to a civilian vehicle left there for just that purpose—a cute little Escort, another product of the Ford Motor Company—and headed into a heart-stopping Alabama sunset. Three poor-white former bank tellers with a grudge against the system, and their graying, far-from-reluctant hostage.

Oh, what a sunset!

I have stayed with Lady Pat and the girls. They all took a shine to me. Such is their trust, I have helped them with a half-dozen additional heists. Between forays, we hole up in Lady Pat's deceased parents' lakeside cottage in rural Alabama, a place you'll never find because I am lying about the lakeside. The house has a garden, unfortunately fallow nowadays, and every evening at sunset I walk my gun moll through it thinking on my fruitless bygone years.

Then we kiss, and I stop thinking altogether.

Poverty drives some to crime, avarice others, and a wish for vengeance or a craving for the perils of mortal gamesmanship yet others.

My motive, though, was something else entirely. I plan to marry Lady Pat, and one day it's conceivable that she and I, with or without our cheerful henchwomen, will relocate to Alaska to escape the heat. Meantime, the number of folks who want me—really, *really* want me—grows larger by the minute.

VERNALFEST MORNING

Priesman calls the place us kids live Little Camp Fuji. Fuji is short for refugee, and Priesman is—was—a lieutenant with the guerrillas on the rampart side of City. Since most of our mothers and daddies are, or were, sympathizers, one of his jobs is seeing after us. Already he's shown us how to keep the juvies from Deeland, Viperhole, Poohburgh, and other nearby kiddie camps out of our gardens and barracks, and twice this month he's visited Fuji with a side of wild greyhound.

I like the way Priesman takes care of us and the way he looks. He always wears camo, combat boots, an Uzi over his shoulder, and bristly 'rilla burns that sweep down from his ears and over his cheeks like wings. My dad, shot dead through his temple, had burns like Priesman's. I have a photo.

About a week ago, four days before Vernalfest, Priesman came into Little Camp Fuji's central barracks and lay a skinned bloody side of an animal down. I was sitting on Li'l Mick's winter thermals playing bodycount with Lajosipha Joiner, our twelve-year-old self-appointed witchwoman. Lajosipha had made bodycount markers out of spent machine-gun shells and old rampart-side safe-passage tokens. A bunch of us got up to see the meat Priesman had dropped, but he turned to me.

"You're the oldest here, aren't you, Neddie?"

"I'm fifteen."

Hands on hips, Priesman twisted to stare all the other kids in the eye. "Anyone older than that? No? Okay." The looey swaggered toward me, hooked a finger inside my shirt, and led me onto the porch. While his big hands squeezed my shoulders, all I could see was the broken button below the X of his cartridge belts.

"Fifteen, huh? If you weren't so damn puny, Neddie, you'd've probably been promoted out of Fuji by now."

I just waited. Priesman already knew that in the last six months his unit had run me back half a dozen times. Then, his stocky colonel, Simpson, had said, *"Stay away until you're asked, boy, or I'll have your scrotum for a dice bag."* Honest.

"Listen, Neddie," Priesman said. "You ever heard of Maud Turska?"

"She's in your unit. She's the Poohburgher proctor."

"Yeah. Simpson thinks she's passing holdfast locations and potential bomb targets to the airport-siders and using her kids as runners."

I looked up, wrinkling my forehead.

"Listen. We can't give you any metal, Neddie, but on Vernalfest morning we want you to hit Poohburgh. Do it right and, swear to dog, you'll be promo'd out of Fuji."

I went back in to tell the others, but most of the kids had rumbled down the rear steps to spit Priesman's gift and roast it. But Lajosipha was still there, hunched over shells and tokens, and when I told her about striking Poohburgh she leapt up and paced all over the barracks like a stork on stilts. Her head seemed to sit right atop her legs.

"It don't matter, getting no metal. Other ways will do, lovely ways. We need cardboard, Neddie. And lumber. And rags. Eight or ten old tires. I think Lt. Priesman's done asked the right folks to get this done, Neddie."

The next day, three before Vernalfest, I led Li'l Mick, Awkward Alice Gomez, and two other Fujiniles from barracks 4 through the rampart-side ruins to the trucking warehouses under the expressway. Li'l Mick had a noisy wagon with wheels that we'd wrapped with torn bedding, and it bumped along *whump-bam-whump* slowing us up.

Over the drooping bridges, drifting up from City's burnt-out heart, oily smoke plumes wriggled. I imagined Lajosipha conjuring with them, voodooing the airport-siders but kissing us rampart 'rillas with magic gobbledygook. She wasn't worth a poot on a scavenger hunt, though, and I was glad we hadn't brought her.

As it was, Li'l Mick nearly did us in as we flattened pasteboard crates near the warehouse incinerator and lay them in our wagon. He got punchy with success and started jigging around every time we stomped and stacked a box. Just as a gigantic green copter with rocket launchers tilted over the expressway toward the mountain's ack-ack emplacements, Alice tripped Li'l Mick and hauled him up to the dumpster. That may have saved our bums. Priesman says airport-siders like to go tadpole-gigging.

But we got back to Little Camp Fuji okay, and the next day while two other dog-parties hunted paint and lumber, Brian Rabbek took the wagon and a pair of thirteens over by the Pits to dig inner tubes and tires out of the sand. They ended up being gone past dark. Lajosipha started muttering about death and weaving her arms in front of her like two black geese trying to knot a double hitch with their necks. The littler kids got spooked, so I told her to do her witch-womaning in a closet somewhere. She kept it up. Brian and the others returned okay though, and that mostly undid the worst of her spooky mumbling and jerking. Damned good thing.

The day before Vernalfest broke clear. Awkward Alice said the smoke over the airport across town and among the trees on the mountainside looked laundered, it gleamed so white and fluffy. Everyone in Little Camp Fuji busted butt that day. Cross-legged in the yard between barracks, we cut tires and inner tubes into long pieces to make helmets, breastplates, and shields from cardboard. We painted designs on the shields and cuirasses. The plans for all this getup and for the coats-of-arms and mottoes we painted on it were all Lajosipha Joiner's. She told us what everything was supposedly called, showed us how to use strips of rubber as flexes on our shin- and arm-guards, and insisted that every flimsy lance have a banner tied to it. A few of us made broadswords from scrap lumber, and Li'l Mick found some odd-sized tins that he cobbled to a board for marching drums. Lajosipha supervised. Her arms were streaked with three different colors of paint up to her elbows.

Priesman came by that afternoon with gray circles under his eyes. "What in hell, Neddie? You think you're going on a goddamn *crusade?*"

"No metal, you said. We made our own stuff."

"The first Children's Crusade was a fiasco. If I know diddly about first-strike advantage, Neddie, this one won't go a bit better. They'll hear you. They'll *see* you. It'll all turn out a botch, and Simpson'll have my neck."

"You mean your scrotum for a dice bag," I corrected Priesman.

"That's okay," Lajosipha answered the lieutenant, not me. "We *don't* sneak." She sported a cardboard breastplate with a drippy red eagle outlined off-center against it. A white handprint, like Indian war paint, prettied one of her cheeks.

Priesman turned to me. "Neddie—"

"It'll be okay," I assured him. "We don't have to sneak to hit 'em right."

Not looking at anybody, he said, "Shit!" Then unslung his Uzi, fired three pinging bursts at the weather vane on barracks 4, stalked to the entrance of Little Camp Fuji, and turned to say to me, *only* me: "*Our* scrotums, Neddie. Yours and mine. Simpson wants Turska taken out, but her dad was a field commander with the first rampart force, fifteen years ago, so we've got to do it obliquely." His eyes roved over our gear. "That don't mean backasswardly. I swear, boy, you don't get it." He wiped his face with his sleeve, spat, and disappeared up the hillside between an ashy-gray truck and some dented oil drums.

On Vernalfest morning Lajosipha was first up off the floor. And the first to get down on it again to pray. Keening, moaning, coughing from the spring chill, she woke the rest of us. The barracks were dark, and when some kids in barracks 3 began slamming doors, I thought first of gunshots.

With Li'l Mick's thermals under me for mattress, I lay staring at the ribbed ceiling and remembering how until I was four, I'd lived in the lobby of the International Hotel. Then the airport-siders had dropped the building with mortars, and it was almost two years—I got good at looting and grubbing even as a tyke—before the first kiddie camps were "bilaterally organized." Priesman says there's a six-year-old treaty outlawing military activity in or around the camps, but Fuji's been strafed before and so have Viperhole and Mouse Town. Maybe the kids at airport side have caught it, too, I don't know, but if you glance up, you can see colander holes above the rafters.

"Let's go, Neddie," Brian Rabbek interrupted my reverie: "It'll be light soon."

Everyone dressed. Everyone pulled on cuirasses, casques, and greaves, old Lajosipha right there to say which was which and to lace you in if you couldn't do it. Outside, as the ridge aspens began to twinkle, we grabbed lances and formed two columns. Li'l Mick started bongoing his peppermint and tobacco tins, but somebody knocked him on his ass and the stillness turned nerve-tweaking again.

Pretty soon, we shuffled out of Little Camp Fuji like pallbearers at a propaganda funeral. It was eerie, marching in front of them at first light. I wasn't really in front though. Lajosipha marched ahead of even me, in a long white dress that had been her mother's, without an ounce of cardboard armoring. Her gooseneck arms wove weirdly as she walked, as if she was spelling the sun to rise. I didn't mind her going ahead because I kept waiting for a 'rilla unit, ours or theirs, to break from the rubble and mow everybody down with words or rifle fire. That morning, gunfire didn't seem much worse than words. Also, it was okay by me if Lajosipha wanted to lead us to Poohburgh. It sits about two miles off the perimeter expressway in a place called Sand Spire and I felt like she knew the way better than I did. She had a sense for that kind of thing, so all I had to do was wonder why, not counting our flapping banners, it was so still and quiet.

"Vernalfest truce today," Rabbek said. "We're breaking it, kid."

I guess we were, going against a rampart-side camp on the first Sunday after spring's first full moon, but what mattered to me was doing what Priesman asked and getting promoted into a big-guy unit bivouacked on the mountain overlooking City. I was too old for Fuji. Only a couple of kids had seemed like family to me, which was how Priesman told me I should think of *all* of us. Anyway, I'd heard Simpson say, *Truces are made to be broken.*

"Play, Li'l Mick!" Lajosipha ordered as we straggled into Sand Spire toward the quonsets of Poohburgh. "A tat-and-a-tum to march to!"

So Li'l Mick bongo-banged and all us Fujiniles fluttered along, lances high, peering into the pale light seeping over the eastern plains and the ruins of City to the rock garden surrounding Poohburgh. A sentry heard or saw us. He raised a piping shout to rouse his barracksmates. They got up in a hurry too, a lot faster than we had so that whatever first-strike surprise Priesman had wished for was lost. That didn't seem to matter though. Our visors, shields, and other stiff-paper whatnots put even the older Poohburghers in a panic, and Lajosipha led us up their main avenue before any of them thought to fling a rock at our boxy-looking heads.

By this time, we'd spread out across their camp like iodine tinting a bucket of water, pricking at whoever not from Fuji got in our way. I don't remember a whole lot that happened, except that it didn't seem cool after we'd tramped into the Sand Spire area. Many small kids on the other side came out of their quonsets half-dressed or less, and two little men were stiff from dawn shock. When we chased them up against a porch or a boulder of sandstone, their bellies gave way just like wet sponges. Mostly I remember scuffling, screaming, and me feeling sick because everything took so long. It all just went on and on, and in the midst of it all Lajosipha wove arm spells to charm us undefeatable.

Finally, someone threw a rock. It struck Lajosipha in the eye, and she crumpled into her tattered white dress like a wilting flower. Then more rocks, and as I tried to pull her out of camp, rocks bouncing off shields and breastplates made sickening *thwumps.* On one side, Brian Rabbek retrieved stones to chunk back at the juvie throwers. Awkward Alice did the same thing on the other side. Pulling Lajosipha along, I saw that the dust was clotted and sticky, but stayed focused on getting her home. Throwing rocks and lance-jabbing, we hurried out of Poohburgh, tore our armor off, and tossed our weapons aside. Beyond the Sand Spire overpass, we regrouped to help one another other back to Fuji.

Lajosipha died. We buried her in her mother's dress in a trough where we used to roast the greyhounds Priesman brought us. Li'l Mick and some kids from barracks 2 never returned. Not counting one kid's banged head and some others' scrapes and bruises, those were our only scary losses. Rabbek says we were gone just an hour and twenty minutes, most of it to get down to Sand Spire and come home. Three days later, in spite of my bad memory about some of what we did, I felt we'd spent the whole day in Poohburgh. The rest of Vernalfest is a shadow thrown by the morning, even Lajosipha's burial. We dug her down and covered her up. No one thought of toting her in a prop-march here on rampart side, but we probably should have. And so I say the rest of that Vernalfest was a shadow thrown by the morning.

Only yesterday did Priesman drop by to see us again. I got so worked up waiting that two or three times I nearly went looking for his bivouac, to ask how us Fujiniles had done. When he at last strolled in though, he wore *two* assault rifles and a badger's smile.

"Turska broke, tough old Maud. Her daughter by an airport-sider was in Poohburgh on Vernalfest morning, and that wiped her out. She fessed the whole schmeer under sedation, and Simpson's higher than a Canadian goose."

Priesman tossed a rifle. "Here's your payoff, Theodore. Let's get the hell out of Fuji."

"I've been promoted?"

"Sure." He bent his fatigue collar down so I could see the new insignia on it. "And I have too, Theodore, I have too."

THE EGRET

As usual, the telephone rang at dinnertime. McGruder winced, and from around the table Polly and the kids gave him pleading looks that meant *don't answer it, for once let the damned thing ring*. As always, McGruder ignored their silent pleas, rose, and spoke a weary hello into the mouthpiece of the instrument of torture on the kitchen wall.

"Did I catch you at dinner?" Harry Profitt's reedy voice asked. "Too bad. But at least you got somebody to make it, don't you, Stork? Me, I fry up taters or eat from tin cans. A one-eyed fella, a guy more than half blind, never had a pauper's chance to find a helpmeet to do him sweet domestic stuff. You know whose lousy goddamn fault that is, don't you, Stork-O?"

"You'll never let me forget, Harry."

"Damned straight. Why should I? You ruined my life, you bastard. You've got a wife and young-uns. You're a big-shot ranger at the state preserve. You wear a uniform and strut around. Me, I got nobody. No position. The birds I like to watch fly over, sometimes I can't half tell 'em from tatters of smoke or cloud. And it all goes back to you, don't it, Mason? Oh, forgive me, I meant *Stork the Dork.*"

McGruder took it, as he did every time One-Eyed Harry Profitt called. Still guilt-ridden after thirty years, he could not shrug off the specter of his culpability.

As a tall skinny thirteen-year-old, Mason "Stork" McGruder had shot the fateful BB. It had been a bitter-cold December day, and the boys had all worn thermal parkas or heavy coats. The idea had been to score war-game points by making their BBs go *ker-thunk!* in the folds of their enemies' winter clothes. That evening, hearing this news, McGruder's father had taken off his belt and repeatedly walloped his son before everyone in Harry's family. But Harry had lost his eye anyway, and an infection had settled in the other, heaping even more guilt on the young McGruder.

So, thirty years later, he answered the phone every time it rang and resignedly took Harry's abuse. Tonight, after enduring a good five minutes of it, he said, "Still sorry about what happened, Harry, but it's time you shut up about all that and did something with the days you've got left."

"Like what?" Harry railed. "A job? I can't see worth a mole's butt. I get dizzy spells. They grab when I least expect them. If it wasn't for my empty-bottle returns, I couldn't keep body and soul together." Yeah, maybe. Harry had other income, from somewhere, and spent some of it on birdseed—watching birds was his only healthy recreation—but a helluva lot more on cheap bitter beer in lanky amber bottles. Those weren't the bottles he returned for piddling amounts of cash, though.

At last, Harry was tiring. "Damn you to hell, Stork!" he ended, as usual, and slammed his handset down with such force that the bones in McGruder's inner ear vibrated. Polly squinted at him across the table with dismayed, dismaying reproach.

One morning, slurping a mug of lukewarm instant on the top step of his tumbledown backstairs, Harry Profitt thought he saw something moving in the weeds at the far edge of his yard. He had to squint, one-eyed, to bring this living object into focus, but the focus he got made it difficult to espy much but a cushion-sized white torso floating above two spidery gray legs. A serpentine neck, also white, coiled up from the torso, and atop the neck sat a narrow head with a feathery crest pointing one way and a dagger-like beak the other.

"A snowy egret?" Harry muttered. "In my backyard?"

Usually, like herons and ibises, the egrets just flew over: long-legged tatters of soiled silk on the china-blue sky winging inland to their rookeries. Never, in Harry's experience, did any of these birds drop down to scout the weedy terrain of his two-bit barony. Now, though, realizing that a graceful egret had *landed* on it truly fretted him. About fifty yards away, after all, lived a pair of tigerish yellow toms who, when it came to birding, took no prisoners. They were too thin and impatient to toy with their victims. Already this summer, Profitt had seen them butcher a mockingbird, three brown thrashers, four robins, a gray catbird, and a couple of bluejays. Pecan trees full of squawking relatives couldn't hold those toms at bay, and Profitt was too achily slow to scare the bloodthirsty felines off.

"Egret, they'll get you." He blinked at the small, long-legged bird mincing through the weeds. "If you're hurt, you're damned well doomed." He set down his mug and went to see what he could do. Shuffling to keep from pitching headlong into the ratty bushes marking his yard's far boundary, Profitt stalked the egret. (Yes, *definitely* an egret.) The bird, high-stepping, eluded him, but never panicked or tried to fly. It couldn't fly, Profitt decided; something had happened to one of its wings. So, their pointless do-si-do continued, the egret moving to escape him as he, lurching, half-blind, reached to gather only egret-less air.

"To hell with this!" Profitt straightened, turned his back, and limped back to the house. Once inside, he thought, Only a real sonuvabitch would leave an egret out there to fend for itself with those damn cats around.

Finally, it occurred to him to telephone Stork McGruder and ask how best to handle a downed bird of this sort. Even if it meant calling the joker for some other reason than to remind him of how McGruder'd ruined his life, he'd do it to save the egret. Profitt dialed the number of the ranger station at the preserve and asked for McGruder. A woman on the other end told him that the ranger hadn't reported today, that he'd come down with a virus and was at home. Well, *great!* Profitt could inconvenience buddy-boy Stork and do something for the downed egret all at the same time. He dialed again.

Mrs. McGruder answered, recognized the voice of their tormentor, and told him angrily that today Mason just couldn't listen to his abuse.

"Damn sorry to hear it," Profitt said. "But this is urgent. Get your dear Mason up off his sickbed. Tell him who's calling."

"Good day!" Polly said, and Profitt knew she was about to hang up with one of his own notorious handset slams when McGruder intervened.

"What is it this morning?" the ranger asked, and he did sound weak.

Profitt, clearly to the ranger's surprise, told Stork about the snowy egret in his yard. He asked McGruder's advice. He wondered if maybe someone couldn't come out to his house and get the poor bird before the area's damned marauding cats did.

"*You've* got to do it," McGruder said, warming to a problem that for once had nothing to do with a thirty-year grudge. "Harry, *you've* got to go out and fetch in that egret."

"Damn it, I've tried. I'm more than half-blind, as you damn well know, and that sucker, hurt like he is, dances away every time I try to grab him."

"You got any meat in the house?"

"No steak, Stork. No bites of tender beef."

"Some hamburger? A can of sardines, maybe?"

"Some raw bacon that's about gone bad. Would that work?"

"It'll do, Harry. Take a strip and duck-walk out there holding it in your fingertips. Your egret's probably hungry. Somebody's shot it or something, and it's been tiptoeing around your backyard looking for vittles. If you go out to feed it, you can grab it as it's lifting its beak to take your peace offering."

"And when I've got it in hand?"

"Take it inside, Harry. You've got to get it out of the yard. Snowy egrets are valuable birds. They're legally protected, but those cats over there don't know that and wouldn't care if they did. I'll call the preserve and send someone your way to take custody of it."

Profitt set the handset down with mocking gentleness, found a strip of near-rancid bacon in his icebox, and limped down the backstairs, squinting into his lot for a sign of the egret.

Ah, there!

With the slimy bacon extended, Profitt began duck-walking toward his prey. The bird scented the bait and high-stepped toward the one-eyed man shuffling its way . . .

McGruder slumped to the couch beside the telephone stand. He was grimacing, but in his grimace, Polly thought, resided something weirdly akin to a smile.

"What is it?" she asked him. "You feeling sick again?"

"Much better. Might as well be hung for a hitman as a horse thief."

"I don't understand."

"He'll never stop calling."

"He would if you wouldn't listen to him, Mason." "

I *have* to listen to him. I put out the crackpot's eye. I *deserve* to hear what he tells me. Some of it, anyway."

"That's foolishness, Mason."

"Well, from now on, it'll be easier to take. A whole helluva lot easier."

"What are you talking about?"

"It's instinct, Polly, biologically dictated egret instinct from ages and ages past."

"Do you still have a fever? You're not making sense."

"They go for the eyes, that's all I'm saying. They take their daggerlike beaks and go straight for the glistening eye."

It took about an hour for the phone to begin ringing again, but when it did, McGruder insisted on answering it himself.

IN RUBBLE, PLEADING

Sibyl, Kansas: 1954

Justice Weir sat in the shoeshine chair in the narrow shop's rear and stared past two scuffed red-leather barber chairs at the rain.

For months it had rained, and the storms had spawned whirlwinds, which, roaring like waterfalls, had flattened several grain-belt towns. Tornadoes kept roaring in ever-widening circles from a point dead-center in the state, even destroying communities on the northern and southern borders of Kansas.

Justice sat waiting in Ral Wagner's barbershop abutting the Pixie Theatre. The stucco overhang capping the theatre also shielded the thin front of Wagner's shop, so that the boy, seated on a raised shoeshine chair, stared out the rainy front window, a wide eye under a saluting stucco hand. He watched Wagner cutting the hair of a dour-faced fiftyish man in the chair nearest this window. His scissors went *sclip-sclip*, and the men's talk droned on beneath the spattering rain as if they spoke not words but the words' blurred aural shadows.

"They've hit all around Wichita, Lawrence, Kansas City," Col. Aspenshade said more clearly. "It's uncanny." He was retired Army. A year ago, he'd returned from the Far East to retire in Sibyl, where he'd been raised. "The twisters haven't hit a city bigger than six thousand inhabitants yet, Ral."

"Sibyl has eight thousand, Colonel."

"Yes, but they're hitting larger communities every day. I think it's a purposeful thing, like they're working their way up from villages to towns, from towns to small cities, and so on to Wichita, where we've got a big military base and lots of aircraft factories. A kind of pattern."

"I don't know, Colonel," Wagner said. "It's Tornado Time."

Outside the window, a truck with boarded sides jounced into view, weighted with fallen branches, lopped by last night's high winds, and with other debris.

Before the truck clattered away over red cobblestones, a man leapt from its running board and almost fell when he hit the bricks. Staggering, he plunged into the shop ushered by wind and the *ting* of the bell over the shop door. He wore a slicker with a removable hood out of which his damp face peered exhaustedly.

"Look." Wagner nodded at the newcomer. "Mulc'sta's drenched in sweat."

"Rainwater," the colonel said jovially. "Schoolteachers don't sweat."

Mulcusta's cowled features betrayed a coy glee. He tore off his hood, tossed it on a chair, stalked through to Justice and halted. His angular face looked huge, wet, alien: an oiled mask behind which two weary red eyes burnt. When Mulcusta pointed a finger, his khaki sleeve fell back to his elbow to disclose an arthritic hand. "He wasn't any older than this kid, but I couldn't do a damned thing to help him."

"Mulc'sta," Wagner cautioned, "you'll scare the boy."

"I ain't scared," Justice declared, eyeing the teacher, who turned agitatedly to Wagner. Even though he'd worn a hood, Mulcusta's hair was so wet its strands had knit together into a shiny plastered helmet.

"Scare the boy!" he cried. "*I'm* the terrified one. I've been in Arles all day, where I saw enough scary shit in its ruins to last me forever. Heartbreaking shit." He lurched to the chair where he'd flung his rain hood and dropped into it.

Col. Aspenshade undid the apron from his neck, shook hair to the floor, lay the apron over the shop's radiator, and reclaimed his barber chair, his old soldier's hands on his thighs. "Go on, Mulc'sta. We won't spoil your show. Give us specifics."

When Mulcusta began to talk, Wagner took the chair facing him. Mulcusta grabbed and wrung his rain hood. "The tornado battered Arles about three, damned early. It tore hell out of everything. Phone lines down, poles and boards strewn everywhere. Cars and pickups crushed, like in a train wreck. And Arles is just nine miles from here. Here in Sibyl, we missed it all but some rain and the twister's outside spinning edges. It could've been us, the funnel veering our way and following the river. It's only nine miles . . ."

"We was lucky," Wagner said.

The colonel grunted. "It wasn't our turn yet. Arles isn't as big as Sibyl, not so many folks there."

"O the folks pleading in blown-in houses," Mulcusta continued as if no one had spoken. "Arms and legs amid the flinders, battered beds, and chifforobes. Iceboxes and shattered toilets in the same rooms, except there aren't any rooms now. Shingles. Shards. Tree roots lying like gigantic weedy footstools. It's a long shit-scattered mess, Arles' front street—even if the Red Cross, Sheriff Cluny, and a few dozen other volunteers and I met to clean up the place and dig out the pleading dead."

"Good on you all," the colonel said, "but cleaning up and calling a disaster aren't enough. Nobody's coming to grips yet with *the pattern*."

"What should we do?" Wagner asked. "Put soldiers in every Kansas town and let them lob mortars at anything that looks twister-ish?" Then he looked guiltily at the boy, lowered his gaze, and tapped a comb against his thigh.

"No, Ral," Col. Aspenshade said, "but you're right: there aren't any battle-lines in this conflict. It needs analysis, is all I'm saying."

"The water tower toppled too," Mulcusta said, undeterred. "The rain was still spattering and never stopped. The Red Crossers stuck beds and blankets in the school gym, which was fine but for some windows knocked out that they quick-fixed with plywood. Not beds, though: *cots* with stiff green blankets. Up and down the walls lay gray-faced survivors scrunched under army blankets, sixty or seventy at least.

"Cluny asked why so many were hurt, and Dr. Wright, the principal, said there'd been no warning, it wasn't raining when the tornado waltzed through." Mulcusta dropped his voice to a stagy whisper: "So far as Dr. Wright knew, no one had seen it funnel in, but outside working I hit upon someone who had *watched it form*."

"Who?" Wagner asked. "The boy you mentioned?"

"Let me set it up, Ral. Let me tell it my way."

"Then get on with it," the colonel said. "It's fifteen till six."

"Hold on." Mulcusta, staring at Wagner's knees, resumed: "After we set up more cots, we got back into the rain. We dug at the ruins of houses, tossed bricks into truck-beds, cleared branches away. Broken foliage. You name it. Power trucks came to fix the downed lines, drivers telling onlookers to stand clear. I've no clue how many're still working there."

"The radio said two hundred volunteers," Wagner said, "not counting the paid pros. Now get on with it."

Mulcusta scowled but obeyed: "Later, I walked down the broadest stretch the tornado'd plowed. When I reached the boy, I was soaked. He stood in a ditch brimful of black water and colliding branches, the water just level with—"

"*In a ditch?*" Wagner said, scandalized.

"—level with his knees, his peejays a second skin. But he stood there because he couldn't lean or stoop. He wore this leather jacket, much too big, with wool round its collar. But it wasn't zipped, and—here's the scary part—a board pierced his belly, going in past his navel and exiting in back to one side of his spine. It looked carefully slipped in, like an envelope into a mail slot. The jacket hadn't been tattered, just slit. Anyway, the boy was stepping through greasy water, so I followed him at the top of the ditch."

"A *board?*" Wagner said. "How'd he *walk* with a board stuck through him?"

"Good questions." The colonel regarded Mulcusta warily. "Sounds like a tornado yarn from Dorothy's fabled trip to Oz."

"You don't believe me?" His eyes bleak cinders, Mulcusta glanced at Wagner.

"A board through his gut?"

"You're saying you don't believe me?"

A quarreling of thunder sounded over Wagner's reply: "I never said that, Mulc'sta." The shop's lone window rattled.

Defiantly, Mulcusta said, "The kid's nose was clogged. Snot coated his lips and chin. At first, I doubted he could see anything. He just walked through the roil, like a rooster tiptoeing in sawdust, raindrops pocking the ditchwater like bullets: *Tlac! tlac! tlac!* Making these sounds, he bared his meat-colored throat. Then he spread his arms. *Hey!* I yelled. *Get out of that goddamn ditch!*"

The teacher got up and paced, swinging his rain hood, his jaundiced face glaring orange along his cheek and jawbone.

"*Get out of there!* I hollered again.

"The boy looked at me, like he saw me and wasn't just staring at the spot he'd heard me yell from. He was Justice's age—twelve?—but in shock, a total daze. He said, *This water's cool. It feels good.* Blood peeped through his PJ shirt, a dark pink stain at the edges of the board. He'd stopped bleeding earlier and now he resumed ditch-hiking, ignoring his pain."

"How *long* did he ditch-hike, *ignoring* his pain?"

Col. Aspenshade swiveled toward the barber and then the schoolteacher. "Ease off, Ral." Then: "Go on, Mulc'sta."

Mulcusta nudged a fallen curl of hair with his boot toe and inexplicably faced the wall: "The boy broke down," he continued, releasing the words as if they'd lined up single-file in his throat, under pressure. "Maybe he was crying at me, or crying because for the first time he'd begun to feel the board *in him*. I don't know how long he'd been in that ditch looking for help, and now he didn't understand that *I* was his help.

"*Take the board out, sir.* His hands hung straight at his sides. *Take the board out, mister.* I just looked. I couldn't do anything. He shouldn't have asked me that because I was helpless. He kept pleading, and at last I cried, *Goddamn it, that would kill you!* And he said, *I've got money. Please take it. Please*, blubbering, crying through his nose. A siren started wailing. *Goddamn it!* I yelled over it. *I don't want your money. Don't ask that.* But he screamed, *You're afraid you'll get splinters in your shitty hands! Or blood on your clothes!*

"And I was like *Kid, stop it! What the hell's wrong with you!*"

Mulcusta let his hood slide from his hand as if it were a scarf, then slowly turned and faced Wagner and the colonel again.

"Still sobbing, the kid said, *I've got a board in me*, just like he'd *wanted* me to ask my stupid question so he could say, *I've got a board in me.* Then he reached up to grasp me by my raincoat's hem. *I've got gloves in the pockets of this coat. It's my daddy's coat. Put his gloves on and you won't get splinters. Please.*"

"What about him seeing the tornado take shape?" the colonel interrupted.

"Hold on. I got in the ditch with him and lifted him to the bank, rain ricocheting round us, the siren screaming. *Please*, he kept saying. I got him to stop that on the way back to the gym. Did he finally realize I couldn't pull the board without causing him to bleed out? No clue. He walked beside me, taking half steps and gazing straight on, not at the masses of sodden rubble all around us.

"And he started talking again. Said he'd gone out really early in his daddy's coat. *Lights inside my head said to go out and look at the sky*, he told me. *They said to fetch other people to go outside, too.* He feared to obey though. He wasn't supposed to go out at that hour."

"What in hell did he *see*?" Col. Aspenshade demanded.

"Pale green lightning. Not arrows or razor zigzags, but pale green sheets. Sheet lightning usually occurs off near the horizons, but this was different. The sheets glowed under the cloud bellies, reminding him of the lights that spoke to him before he went out. He understood some of what the sheets were saying.

"*They wanted me to get us all outside*, he said, *but I didn't want to. I wanted to shout,* Go down to your basements! *But I couldn't move, it was holding me.*

He said he could tell something hated him and paralyzed him for not obeying. He had to stand in his backyard and watch a funnel shape form under the ghastly cloud belly. It plunged like a big arm over rooftops to the west, by the highway we rode into Arles on. Everything exploded, the boy said: fences, roofs, barns, silos, everything."

"Holy smokes," Col. Aspenshade said. "That's it!"

Opening and closing his scissors blades, Wagner stayed mute.

"*The board came right at me*, the kid said. *On purpose, out of swirls of other trash. It drilled me.* He sobbed harder. *And now I have a shitty board in my stomach and I still want you to pull it out.*

"I got him to the gym. He kept telling the Red Cross people to put on his daddy's gloves and remove the board. Everyone had too much sense to do that, and he died lying sideways on one of their shaky cots." Mulcusta shut up and sat down, the rain hood on the floor testimony to his devastation.

"Did this boy have a name?" Wagner asked.

"I don't recall. The principal told me that he was two grades behind, but he seemed bright enough, especially for a kid in that condition."

"Report that pale-green business in your story to the commander at McConnell Air Force Base." The colonel looked at once entranced and unsettled.

"What you gonna do now?" Wagner asked Mulcusta.

"Go to bed." He arose shakily, adrift between uprightness and collapse, picked up his rain hood, and snapped it on. "Good night, gentlemen. Good night, Justice."

He left. The bell tinged. Wind gusted in. The apron on the radiator streamed off toward the shoeshine stand and plummeted at Justice's dangling feet.

Oblivious, Col. Aspenshade paid Wagner. "I'm off, straight to Wichita."

In the shop then, only the barber and the boy in the shoeshine chair.

Justice waited, smelling shoe polish, hair wax, shaving lather, greenish tonics, and the *peculiar* odor of the rain, an aroma that crept as if by osmosis through the beaded window into his nostrils. He was happy it was still daylight, happy that—for now—he did not have to harry anybody in Sibyl into the streets. Already, though, many townspeople dashed to their cars to get home for dinner.

Sheets of green lightning played in Justice's head.

The experiment with Arles and other small towns had concluded, and huge black funnels were forming over Wichita, Tulsa, and the two Kansas Cities. He wondered how long it would take the colonel to find out.

"Son," Wagner said, "I hope hearing about that kid in Arles didn't upset you."

Justice peered out the window, waiting. He figured that the kid in Arles had got exactly what he had coming.

GIVE A LITTLE WHISTLE

George Caspary, the owner of a dealership specializing in foreign cars, returned home early from a business trip to find his wife Lena having coffee by their pool with one of his better-looking salesmen. After an exchange that Lena did not interrupt or even seem to listen to, the salesman, stunned by the sudden loss of both his job and his dignity, turned on his heel and departed. After watching him go, Caspary strode into the house and climbed the stairs to his bedroom. The next evening, he returned home with a lanky gray puppy that looked as if it had jumped from a mud-caked pickup.

"That's a hideous dog," Lena said. "Why have you brought it inside?"

"For company," said George from a wingchair with a muted floral print, the puppy in his lap. "You entertain human curs. I prefer honest-to-God dogs." He held up a tiny choke chain and a set of jingling tags.

"It's shedding all over your suit."

"Dog hairs suggest a fairly innocent infidelity, don't you think?"

"You sound jealous." Lena poured wine into a water-spotted goblet.

"You give me cause. And do so on purpose."

"It's one of my chief pleasures, George. You're either jealous or boring, nothing in between. I prefer jealous."

George stroked the trembling dog, his pudgy fingers sending strands of pale fur drifting through the parlor.

"That puppy is a tactic," Lena said.

"A tactic?" George smiled at her over the animal's head.

"Yes. But that's all right. I can counter it."

"I'm sure you can," George said.

*

George found that he couldn't take the dog to work. Either it distracted customers in the showroom or soiled the ecru carpet in his business office. During the day, he kenneled it with a breeder and trainer with whom he'd gone to college. In the evenings, he brought the dog home and played with it, shoving its head about or pinning its forepaws to his knees so that it must lick his fingers placatingly.

"That *canine* doesn't like you," Lena said.

With a monogrammed silk handkerchief, George wiped slobber from his hands. "On the contrary: we're great buddies."

"And *you* don't like *him*. It's cruel to cage him every day. Let him stay with me."

"To alienate its affections?"

"*Affections?* He hates you. He only acts that way"—the dog was licking George's hands again—"because you terrify him."

"Terrify it? I never even raise my voice."

"He's waiting for you to. He senses your unpredictability."

"Me, unpredictable? I thought I was boring."

"When you're not jealous, George, you are."

"You think I'm jealous now?"

"Maybe he senses he's only a tactic to you, not a living creature."

"It's a companion."

"*It.* You call the darling 'it,' George. You've had him two months and you haven't given him a name."

"I call it—I call *him*—Paladin."

"Since when? A second ago? And that's the appellation of one of your overpriced automobiles, not a dog's name."

"It is now."

"Leave him here with me. Stop kenneling him."

At the end of six months, George surrendered and gave Lena the dog. She renamed him Squeedunk because she'd once owned a pet turtle by that name and because the name irritated George. She groomed, fed, and played with her wolfhound with a single-mindedness that added to George's annoyance. Squeedunk was soon the only name to which the dog would answer, and Lena exulted.

She also found that her interest in novice salesmen, wealthy customers, George's out-of-town colleagues, and the footloose Casanovas who flirted with her downtown had dwindled to a mere itch. She had eyes only for Squeedunk and the dog for her, and George was jealous without her having engineered either a real or an imaginary *human* affair.

"I got that quisling mutt for me!" George raged whenever he saw the wolf-hound nuzzling her hand or lying beside her chaise longue. Squeedunk always slunk away, with risen nape hair, and George would purposely kick over another garden statuette.

"You've become an absolute delight to live with," Lena told him, and she meant it: nowadays, George was a *much* more interesting man.

One night, Lena awoke and realized that Squeedunk no longer lay at the foot of her bed. Hearing a muffled skitter of claws on the gallery's marble floor, she bolted upright. Out of bed, she pulled on her nightgown, opened her door, stepped into the sheen of the electric sconces, and saw George leading the dog on a choke chain to the circular staircase.

"Stop! I've caught you!"

"Just taking the wretched brute for a walk."

Lena glanced at her watch. "At two in the morning? You can't expect me to believe that." Squeedunk, she saw, stood spraddle-legged on the slippery floor, tail down, eyes averted. "I'm not an *utter* nincompoop."

George yanked the choke chain. "I never thought you were."

"Don't flash that insulting quasi-charming grin at me: I'm not buying it."

"Sorry."

"And if you harm a single hair on Squeedunk's head, I'll make life miserable for you."

"More miserable, you mean."

"What are you talking about? I've been a good girl."

"You toy with me, Lena. I'm almost old enough to be your father, and you treat me like a brain-damaged seven-year-old."

"Let him go."

George unhooked the leash, Squeedunk slipped the choke collar, and Lena knelt beside the dog to whisper praise and comfort.

"Good God," George said, stalking off.

"Another round to me," Lena told Squeedunk.

Squeedunk lifted his eyebrows: darling, cream-colored eyebrows.

"But who'd've thought a man needing seven hours' sleep would sneak into my room so early to wreak vengeance on *mi piqueño pobrecito*?"

Squeedunk applied a ribbon of saliva to her throat.

"He gets better every day, Squee: Georgie-Porgie gets better every day."

Two months later, at George's insistence, the Casparys held a gala to celebrate another good year at the dealership. Chinese lanterns dangled in the garden from Day-Glo orange nylon cords, a dance band played on the lakeside lawn, and most of the salesmen with whom Lena had slept, the ones George hadn't felt honor-bound to fire, had come with their wives. All of them danced with Lena at least once (to suggest there was no reason not to) and partied to the limits of their instincts for self-preservation. Canapés were gulped, wines and cocktails sloshed, and lewd jokes and gossip swapped like commodities.

Near midnight, when only a few of the Casparys' favorite acquaintances still lingered, Lena called Squeedunk from the house to perform a series of familiar tricks. The dog fetched a stick, begged, rolled over, shook hands, "spoke," and jumped through a plastic hula hoop. Lena beamed. The guests applauded, politely.

To one side, George talked with Jim Slawson, his assistant manager.

"That's quite a dog Lena's got there," Slawson said, sipping a third martini.

"I bought it," George said.

"But it's plain to see who he belongs to now."

Lena, who had once scolded George for getting dog hair on his clothes, was squatting before Squeedunk in a Dior gown, an orchid on her bodice, silver-lamé slippers on her feet. Squeedunk, nearly in her lap, struggled to land a barrage of doggy kisses on her throat, cheeks, nose, and forehead. Caspary turned away.

"What's wrong?" Slawson asked. "Worried about her gown? It's only—"

At that moment, Squeedunk pushed Lena onto her back, sank his teeth into Lena's throat, and tore away a collop of flesh, exposing and piercing the jugular. When Caspary turned around again, women were screaming and men shouting abuse or impossible instructions at one another. Squeedunk, in this confusion, retreated from the body and ran at speed toward the apple orchard beside the lake.

"God have mercy," said Slawson.

"We never really know who loves us, do we?" Caspary sighed, audibly, then said, "Jim, go inside and call the police."

"And an ambulance?"

"By all means. An ambulance, too. The more the merrier."

As Slawson rushed to obey, Caspary pocketed a small metal device. The high-pitched sound that it had made—a sound *in*audible to human beings—echoed in his mind like the siren of an emergency vehicle. He suppressed his smile.

I've always been more interesting than Lena supposed.

Always.

FOR THE LADY OF A PHYSICIST

Although Bekenstein's hypothesis that black holes have a finite entropy requires for its consistency that black holes should radiate thermally, at first it seems a complete miracle that the detailed quantum-mechanical calculations of particle creation should give rise to emission with a thermal spectrum. The explanation is that the emitted particles tunnel out of the black hole from a region of which an external observer has no knowledge other than its mass, angular momentum, and electric charge. This means that all combinations or configurations of transmitted particles that have the same energy, angular momentum, and electric charge are equally probable. Indeed, it is possible that the black hole could emit a television set or the works of Proust in ten leather-bound volumes.

—Stephen Hawking
"The Quantum Mechanics of Black Holes"
Scientific American (Jan 1977), 40.

If I with her could only join
In rapturous dance, loin to loin,
Deep space itself would soon discern
Galactic rhythm in our burn.
Our bodies stars, our debts all void,
Then would we waltz and, thus employed,
Inflate with megacosmic thrust
Through night and death and sifting dust.
Godlike lovers, we would hang
Beyond the cosmos whose Big Bang,

All the mad millennia past,
Was but a popgun to our slow blast.
And as we reeled with raw élan,
Pulsing plasma in vast pavane,
We would shame the Pleiades,
Relume the Magellanic Seas,
Deliver all our Milky Way,
Ionic flux too fierce to stay,
In supernova, and so rehearse
Our own expanding universe.

But my small body is no star,
Albeit something similar:
A blind pool vacuuming into it
All the lambency it's not fit
To redirect and render rife.
The woman I would take to wife
Sees only blackness in my eyes,
Rapacious ebon, hungry skies,
An O-gape gravid with desire
To aggrandize itself in fire;
And so her light sweeps down the hole
That is the maelstrom of my soul.

Therefore, I have become for her
A dark entropic murderer,
Whose chiefest virtue is his pull.
Then, while my strength is at its full,
Let me draw her to my embrace,
Collapse her will and show my face.
With her my Beatrician guide,
We'd tunnel with the thermal tide
Into the arms of Betelgeuse,
With Quasar sets and Marcel Proust
Emergent with us, glory-bound,
Detritus of God's Lost & Found.
Thus, though we cannot create light
From love, yet we will vanquish night.

DEAR BILL

The man paces, worrying about Bill, who's been acting strange of late, filing a divorce action against the sweet young woman from South Dakota—Kathryn, Kate, Kitty, whatever name she now used—whom he'd brought home to Dougherty County five years ago. Further, Bill acts as if his and Kathryn's son Zach hasn't even happened. The unfeeling son of a bitch. How can he do this to Zach, an innocent tyke who needs his daddy?

Kathryn—or Kate—or Kitty—Bill's wife—she's got to be in a mixed-up mental state, too. She can't even settle on her own first name. Has her hubby Bill's erratic behavior launched her on a frantic search for herself, or has that harum-scarum search for her "true identity" kicked jealous Bill's pins out from under him? The chicken or the egg? Bill may now believe that he spurred the change in Kathryn, not vice versa.

An objective look at the suffering of Bill, Kathryn, and Zach suggests that Bill is the prime cause. If the guy doesn't get help soon, from folks who care for him and have the cojones to call him to accounts for his selfishness and kamikaze bouts of carousing, well, dear old Bill may end up taking a header into the flinty Flint River or sticking the barrel of a pawn-shop .38 into his mouth.

Splash!

Bang!

Bye-bye, crazy Bill.

The worried man has no idea what to do. Nowadays, Bill trusts nobody. Whenever Kate calls, he hangs up on her. He avoids his friends, and the man in the apartment fretting about him is sure that Bill avoids them because he's embarrassed to talk to them. He knows that they know that he's broken his marriage and left Zach fatherless. What can Bill possibly say to his former pals when everyone knows he's acting like a horse's butt?

The situation has Bill's would-be Samaritan stumped. He can't telephone Bill because he can never get through. Even making the guy's number ring is a chore, and if by some miracle he could make connection, the man fretting about Bill doubts his ability to say the right words. He's never been able to talk to folks about Really Important Stuff, and, besides, he *hates* the goddamn telephone.

A face-to-face meeting? He'd have to corner Bill, and lately Bill's been in no mood to let that happen. Anyway, you'd still have to mount a firm argument, to prove with each tongue-tied word that Bill's welfare, and only Bill's welfare, rests uppermost in your mind. Talk—heartfelt, off-the-cuff talk—presents a serious obstacle to a one-on-one powwow, and clearly Bill doesn't trust himself to get past the trickiness of an in-person confrontation.

Impossible, the worried man decides. You're an idiot to even consider it.

What, then? What can you do?

It hits him as he paces the apartment: *A letter!* He can write the son of a bitch a letter.

This thought excites him, and he scrounges for paper and pen. Because he hardly ever writes letters, the search takes a while. At last, he finds a ballpoint in a kitchen drawer and a wrinkled sheet of notebook paper in the back of a directory left in this place by a former tenant. He sits down at the kitchen table and thinks. And thinks.

Finally, he writes:

> Dear Bill,
> Your wife loves you. Your boy needs you. It's not their fault you're losing a little hair on the top of your head. They don't care how you look. They just want you around. Do you think boozing and chasing women younger than Kate and LOTS younger than you is going to make YOU younger? It won't. People grow older every day. It happens. There's only one way to stop getting older.
> Don't do that. It wouldn't make sense. You're not just worried about getting older, you're worried about lost opportunities. Because you married young and had a kid right off, maybe you missed some things. But if you just STOP, what opportunities will you have then? Answer me that?
> Snap out of it, Bill. For Kate's sake. For Zach's. And your

own. You're killing yourself slow and we're afraid you'll get to a place where you'll decide to do it fast. PLEASE don't do that, Bill. Think of everyone who's worried about you. Think about me. Would I write you like this if I didn't mean it?

Someone Who Cares

The man makes an envelope out of a brown paper sack and some strips of Scotch tape. He finds an uncanceled stamp on a letter from his attorney—the machine at the P.O. failed to cancel the stamp. He tears it off, trims around it with scissors, and puts it on his own envelope with another tiny piece of tape.

Looking out the window, he notes that twilight has gathered.

So what? He won't be able to sleep until he mails the damn letter. If he mails it tonight, it should reach Bill the day after tomorrow, soon enough to save him and do the poor joker some good. If nothing else, it'll let Bill see his screwed-up situation from the point of view of someone who's weighed all the factors that Bill has self-destructively ignored.

It can't hurt, can it?

The man grabs his coat, jams the letter into an inside pocket, and walks seven blocks against the December wind to the mailbox at the corner of Oglethorpe and Hart. To his dismay, Charlie Griffin stands at this box feeding a stack of Christmas cards into it, the drop he'd meant to use. Worse, Charlie has seen him.

"Hey, Bill!" Charlie shouts. "How's it going?"

"None of your goddamn business!" Bill takes out the letter he's just written, tears it into pieces, tosses them up like confetti, and turns on his heel to walk the seven cold blocks back to his empty apartment.

"Merry Christmas to you too!" Charlie shouts after him.

INDEPENDENCE DAY FOREVER

Here on the Moon, the annihilation of our primary
Afforded most of us a pyrotechnic display
Of great color and no little poignancy. I especially
Enjoyed the airbursts, the interthreading mushroom caps,
The way the turquoise marblings of cloud and water
Fell suddenly (or slowly, depending on the jet streams)
Behind a dozen drifting veils of brown and coral.
Flowers opening in timelapse photography look a bit
Like that, even if it would be a heartless irony
To emphasize the correspondence in the present context,
And, like most fireworks I've witnessed, they didn't last
That long. The aftermath plunged us all into something
Akin to lethargy if not to downright gloom, what with
Communications going out and the chances for resupply
Not even a hopeful fraction of what they once were.
Evans tells everyone we're lucky, declares humanity
May owe its ultimate preservation to our presence
High above the fray, but Schweninger keeps pointing out
Certain unignorable consequences of Earth's removal
From our contingency plans, matter-of-fact assessments
That dispirit me deeply even when I try to recall
The loveliest, most kaleidoscopic moments of what was,
Indisputably, an altogether magnificent show.

A FEW LAST WORDS
FOR THE LATE IMMORTALS

In her assumed aura, an alien strolled through a vast equipment mausoleum on Titan. Of an eerie tallness here, she resembled in her inner self the neon-blue skeleton of a long-armed bird. Occasionally, she paused to peer at banks upon banks of antique machinery and electronic units. A chronometric device, faintly aglow, gave oft-refreshed digital declarations of the time and date:

0104 5 Nov 3952 anno Domini

Lwevshed—an approximation of her name—explored the mausoleum's haunted recesses in quest of connections. Aloft, Saturn hummed like a clock.

0107 5 Nov 3952 anno Domini

To orient herself within a chronological matrix no longer anywhere in use, Lwevshed read the time-keeping unit's runes and strove to believe in them. It was hard. Still, she made the complex adjustments in a way allowing her emotions to shift again out of Loshaibron modes of perception into human ones. By will and practice, she was a human female in a place where no such entity had set foot in a thousand Earth years, and the profound weirdness of this fact made her assumed aura tingle with the suppressed inner music of her quasi-avian bones.

0112 5 Nov 3952 anno Domini

As she strolled, a message, keyed to a language with the cultural ground to which she'd surrendered, pierced her aura to note that she had a specific task to perform on this inhospitable moon.

—Tell me, Lwevshed tweeted.

—What's the facility's condition?

—Lifeless. Utterly uninhabited.

—Glean what you can from the structure and report back.

After a time, she found an electronic unit that, by a sly insinuation of her skills, she reanimated and brought online.

—They were immortal for a time, she told her Loshaibron overseer.

—*For a time?* Explain.

Lwevshed's unit pulled up fact after fact about the species' historical evolution, image after image. Each audio/visual was stylized and spare, in keeping with the unit's tiny console, and she repressed her newfound empathetic "humanity" enough to nudge its symbols into a mental code suitable for retransmission to her overseer. Still, she stayed human on a disturbing emotional level, and the unit's synopsis of the species' evolution enthralled her:

Australopithecine africanus. Homo habilis. Homo erectus. Homo sapiens. Homo sapiens sapiens. Homo sapiens immortalis . . .

—You said they were *briefly* immortal, Lwevshed. Skip ahead and explain how such a situation arose.

She skipped. Because scrolling images rippled past from an infinity of planes, she applied a virtual brake and held a random segment of *Homo sapiens immortalis'* history on her screen.

—Broadcast, her overseer tweeted.

Lwevshed obeyed.

[Moscow, 2096. The Murmansk Times-Mirror.*]*

Kremlin official Viktor Stavrin, 81, and his 28-year-old grandson Yevgeny have just celebrated the fifth anniversary of their parabiotic marriage. Joined back-to-back in an 18-hour surgical procedure allowing them to share a circulatory system, Viktor and Yevgeny remain not merely loving relatives but sterling friends.

"How can I not love this boy?" asked Viktor, replying to a reporter. "Parabiosis has reduced the levels of death hormone in my bloodstream and significantly lowered my cholesterol level. Also, after nearly seventy years of rotten sleep habits, I've learned how to lie at ease on my side. This boy taught me."

Observed Yevgeny, "My grandfather had aged prohibitively before the advent of the Hayflick treatments and couldn't safely undergo them."

"The parabiotic method was used instead?" asked our reporter.

"Yes," Yevgeny said. "I allowed it because I wanted to extend the life of my beloved grandfather, a high Kremlin official."

"Couldn't this parabiotic arrangement shorten your genetically allotted span?"

"Oh, no," Yevgeny said, "Everyone says I'll live to the full limit of my years."

Then, like convivial Siamese twins, the two men danced back to their hospital room in perfect light-footed synchrony.

Lwevshed lifted her head. More than a thousand E-years later, in an equipment mausoleum on a moon of ice and methane, she could almost hear the echoes of the men's celebratory footfalls.

—Parabiosis is a dead-end technique, her superior said.   —Even then, they'd successfully tested biochemical prolongation methods. Leap ahead.

Lwevshed again obeyed.

[London, 2241. Comfax advertisement.]

WorldWide Life Insurance Ltd announced early this year that it is dismissing the last of its human representatives. Henceforth, all straight-life policies [those excluding accidental termination] are available via our London hub, said WorldWide PR persons. Cost: twenty nuppence [new pence] a year. Rates decrease by a fourth every fifty years, ending at an annual premium of one tax-exempt Hayflick Penny, if holders' treatments go on unabated. Accidental-termination policies are a much wiser investment for most citizens with up-to-date biomedical clearances. These are available for 1,000 nuppunds (new pounds) per annum, if often higher in satellite colonies.

To date, insurability has been denied only to astronauts, recidivist hunter-gatherers, leisure-hour mercenaries, professional death-ballers, certifiable masochists, immuno-system deficients, and certain others. We further guarantee that "term insurance" is NOT synonymous with "accidental-termination" coverage. Please access our London hub for details . . .

—Uninterpretable, said the overseer irritably.   —Except insofar as it suggests the societal impact of their prolongation methods.

—How far should I skip ahead?

—Two more E-centuries, at least.

—Two?

—Find a readout with private emotional thrust. Your previous readouts feel somehow peripheral.

And so Lwevshed displaced item after item until accessing this:

*

[California, 2573. Testimony of David Rhys Bradbrook, Immortal. An excerpt from his autobiography.]

Yesterday, I visited Gloria Bradbrook-Wisdom, my aunt, for the first time in seventy-five years. She lives on an estate restored to our family after the Los Angeles Yuke [i.e., Eucomenopolis] was peaceably disassembled by its inhabitants. Aunt Gloria has never married, preferring feline to human companions. Her cats resemble those sleek haughty beasts depicted in ancient Egyptian statuary. I can't say I grok her devotion to the creatures.

Aunt Gloria's quarters were a-crawl with cats. They slept on sofas or ottomans, sat like china figurines near doorways, slunk along marble baseboards, and fouled the air with perfumes (applied) and catty poots (natural). Aunt Gloria was not herself.

"Another has died," she said. "The droids just buried the dear."

We strolled about her garden and stopped among holly trees on the edge of Bradbrook-Wisdom Memorial Park: a cat cemetery. Their shrines rise in the foreground, recede into the distance, and pass from sight beyond a hill delimiting my aunt's estate: obelisks, headstones, statues of feline angels, marble litter boxes, and a maze of catnip-lined paths.

"They're here so brief a time, and I get so attached."

My heart not really in it, I comforted Aunt Gloria the best I could . . .

—Cats? queried the overseer. —What are cats?

Lwevshed relayed a *Felis catus* image via standard Loshaibron psychic methods to her overseer. She understood something of Aunt Gloria's grief, more than had David Rhys. Even with Saturn fatly afloat in the mausoleum's observation ports, she inwardly simulated Aunt Gloria's bereavement and the fierceness of its ache.

—This isn't to the point, Lwevshed.

Rebuked, she leapt ahead to griefs occasioned by graver bereavements. Cats, as her overseer saw the matter, were an irrelevancy: they were denied treatments and had no stake in their masters' potentially eternal lives.

Lwevshed summoned a document readout more rigorously addressed to matters of *human* life and death:

[Oslo, Stockholm, 2855. A review by Bengt Matsson from the Oslo-Stockholm Omnichron-Star.*]*

Life and Death *by Claude Hojier is a compendium of one hundred E-vols totaling nearly 30 million words. The author created this profound entertainment— certainly his masterwork—between 2604 and 2789 during residencies in most of the interdependent political sectors of Earth, eight planetary metro-habitats, and all the major satellite cities of our system's colonized moons.*

Purporting to be the biography of an early member of Homo sapiens immortalis, *this far-ranging work takes the reader from Adam Olamsson's mundane test-tube birth in 2021 to his sudden death at the turn of the 26th century. When his magnetoglider drops into the entrained plasma of Jupiter's atmosphere and plunges into an immense cyclonic methacane, the reader relives that heart-stopping ride. Hojier drapes this death in ambiguity. Accident or suicide? The answer, subtly embedded in Hojier's text, invites exhilarating speculation.*

Life and Death *is now available in a neomech trans from the Franco-Jovian. (Hojier is a naturalized citizen of Ganymede, where he lives in a 14-room rad bunker of his own design.) All one hundred E-vols of his magnum opus, pent in a mini-Gutenberg facsimile, may be bought for a span of enslavement to Pansolar Publishing based on one's social-financial status. In return,* Life and Death *will repay many Saturnian hours of soporifically exquisite reading . . .*

Relaying this item to her overseer on Titan, Lwevshed felt her aura melding with Adam Olamsson's fictive self and Jupiter's storms enwrapping her in swirling methane gas. Instead, it was *Saturn* outside the computer mausoleum's port, and she was a living Loshaibron wraith, not a dead human adventurer.

—We're still at a literary remove from your species' lethal anxieties.

—I'm selecting at random. It's hard to—

—Jump ahead, Lwevshed, to a period when its extinction is imminent.

She obeyed, ultimately halting the information flow to show this:

[Ptolemy Base, Luna, 3116. Excerpt from an essay on thanatology by Sharon-Davida Weng.]

The four most prominent causes of death among the pansolar populations of

Homo sapiens immortalis *are 1) accident, 2) murder, 3) suicide, and 4) psychological surrender to a syndrome popularly called "immortalist grief."*

Number 4 may soon surpass all others as prime dispatcher, for with the assassination sixteen E-weeks ago of Titan's beloved Lunarch, Selena Panmanterra, we have seen the extent to which immortalist grief may work its fatal havoc.

Panmanterra's assassin was a man who learned in an atavistic deviant fashion that his private genetic code doomed him to early death. He was programmed at the molecular level for a pre-immortalist life span. For doctors to correct the scrambled genetic messages at this basic level, he learned, would be to sabotage his life and kill him sooner. Even immortalist wisdom is not proof against chance, human error, or the anomalies of technological malfunction. To err is human. Given that fact and the vastness of time, death is inevitable.

Thus, this young man fixated on the Lunarch as the symbol of his immortalist community and resolved to kill her. He did so in a heinous way that spared neither of them. Except to report that the act was vile past imagining, I will not divulge his methods. (Would it horrify or gratify the assassin to know that in his bitter self-pity, he took many more lives than one?)

The knowledge that Selena Panmanterra will never again give the blessings of her beauty and intelligence to her constituency has proved a heavy psychological burden for many Titanites. If grief intensifies in proportion to one's perception of one's loss, these persons perceived their loss as terrible indeed. The ghastliness of Panmanterra's murder also shaped this perception, undoing the communal wisdom, providing her peers a glimpse of the primeval chaos that they supposed they had fled. The death's-head behind the flesh smirked at them, and they recoiled to find it still extant. Panmanterra's loving consort of two centuries yielded to immortalist grief and suicided. Afterward, his grief spread like a lethal virus, one to which we are susceptible precisely because our genetic codes predispose us to long life. In any case, the intensity of these mourners' grief has risen exponentially, urging more and more members of our species to follow the dead Lunarch and her consort down the bleak highway to personal extinction.

A third of Titan's inhabitants have fallen into comas or paroxysms of self-directed violence. The means of restraint and treatment have failed to prevent death in all but a few cases. Art and commerce stand frozen, and the virus waltzes outward from Titan in pavanes too fluid for corseting. Could it be that only there were conditions right for its incubation, and that only in the inward reaches of the Sol system will it finally slow and cease? I know only that as the grievers die, they create more grievers.

These in turn fail and pull others into the expanding sickness, which has spiraled to other satellites, with an explosion of cases as near to us as Mars.

And I, after all these years, I now mourn again the death of my infant daughter during the merciless Himalayan winter of 2412 . . .

Before her overseer could interrupt, Lwevshed strode in an eddy of shifting blue light to the structure's airlock. In turn, she channeled Viktor and Yevgeny Stavrin; Gloria Bradbrook-Wisdom and her heartless nephew; Claude Hojier and Adam Olamsson; Selena Panmanterra and her consort; and Sharon-Davida Weng. It hurt to share such intimacy with them and the millions of others that their lives implied.

She exited the airlock and floated over ice and frozen ammonia beneath an atmospheric pressure four times as great as that of Mars. Her skeleton re-set on a denser, less avian model, and her aura flattened to receive the change. Under Saturn's immense bulk, she seemed a faint blue mist in a miasma of sunlight-absorbing methane polymers. Night and cold enveloped her like inorganic rinds. She was nothing. And, conscious of her smallness, everything.

The inhabitants of this system's third planet had discovered physical immortality and then trivialized it. Until near the end when their heightened empathy had helped to obliterate them. Ah, the melancholy paradox of having been *briefly* immortal.

Lwevshed convoluted and beheld the golden enigma of Saturn and its rings. Inwardly, she also convoluted, knowing that even *her* species' quest would end in no better than a finite triumph. Like the dead immortals of this far-flung solar system, she, too, was doomed. That old creature anxiety clasped her like chains, but many stars would flare and die before annihilation came upon her kind and her, and so a sympathy for her failed human counterparts erupted in her, and, in comparison to it, *immortalist grief* was but a paltry sting.

After a spell in the night and cold, Lwevshed strode inside and reassumed her aura to face her overseer's exasperated curiosity.

Part Two

☄

IN THE MEMORY ROOM

IN THE MEMORY ROOM

This isn't my mother!" Kenny stares at the dead woman in the Memory Room. He has a lumberjack's beard, glasses that magnify his eyes to snowball size, and a belly so large he cannot button his maroon leather carcoat. He tells other members of Gina Callan's clan grouped behind him, "This *mannikin* isn't my mother!"

"Who in hell you think it is?" his uncle, white-haired Sarge Lobrano asks. "Madonna?"

Aunt Dot, Gina's sister, says curtly: *"Sergio!"*

"It's not my mother! This woman looks like she's still in pain!"

"Your mama's kidneys failed," Aunt Dot notes. "That's why she's so puffy."

The hostess who ushered Gina's family into the Memory Room says, "Please. I worked so hard to make her lifelike."

"My mother wore glasses. What did you guys do with 'em?"

"Personal items are taken at the desk, Mr. Petruzzi," the hostess says. "Nobody passed them on to me."

Kenny frees his wallet from a pocket of his tent-sized pants and extracts a photograph. "Here's how my mother *ought* to look: beautiful." He thrusts the photo at the hostess, a chic fortyish woman in slacks and a fishnet sweater and, gesturing hugely, says again, "That's *not* my mother."

Vince—Sarge and Dorothy's son, a high-school football coach in Colorado Springs—takes his cousin's elbow. "Of course, it isn't your mama, Kenny, it's only her body. Her soul has ascended."

"I *know* where she is. But she doesn't look like *that.*" Kenny elevates the photo. "This is how I'll always remember her."

"That's five years old," Uncle Lyle says. "You can't expect your mother to look like she did while in near-to-perfect health."

"I expect these bums to put on the glasses we gave 'em!"

The hostess turns to Uncle Lyle, Gina's brother. "Mr. Sekas, I never received a photo of Mrs. Callan or her glasses."

"What you've done here's a disgrace," says Kenny, sneering.

The hostess reddens and purses her lips.

Aunt Dot puts her hand on the casket. "It's not just glasses. Gina's not wearing earrings. Sis would never dress up smartly and forget her earrings."

Claudia, Vince's teenage sister, pipes, "Gina isn't Gina without her earrings."

"Gina isn't Gina because these goofballs lost her picture. And her glasses."

"Mr. Petruzzi," the hostess says, the Memory Room seeming to contract about her, "if you gave us those items, we'll find them. But no one passed them to me, and I made do as well as I could without."

"Which was actually pretty shitty."

"Take this lunkhead outside," Sarge directs Vince and Frank. Frank is Uncle Lyle and Aunt Martha's son, a realtor in the Callans' hometown, Gunnison. Sarge turns to the hostess. "Kenny's upset, we're all upset, you gotta excuse him, ma'am. He depended like crazy on his mama. Even after he was this big grown man, he couldn't stop yanking her apron strings."

Like tugs flanking the *Queen Mary,* Vince and Frank take Kenny's arms. Their goggle-eyed cousin, unresisting, blubbers, "She did everything for me. Loaned me money. Bought my clothes. If I came home at two a.m., even then she'd fix me something to eat. Not just baloney sammiches. Gourmet stuff. Omelets. Polenta and gravy."

Vince and Frank ease Kenny, the adopted son of Gina and the late Ernesto Petruzzi, out of the Memory Room toward the parlor, and he cries, "She was my intercessor when nobody else gave a damn!"

Alone with the dead woman, the hostess perches by the casket doing repair work on the masklike face of Gina Sekas Petruzzi Callan. In the hermetic off-white room, she inhabits the remembered life of the deceased.

Frank Sekas' wife, Melinda, has gone into the February cold with Dorothy and Claudia Lobrano to buy earrings.

The other mourners—Sergio, Cousin Vincent, Uncle Lyle, Aunt Martha, Cousin Frank, and Kenny—have retired to the parlor to sit on lumpy divans or pace the worn carpet. An odor of lilies and embalming fluid permeates the

Memory Room. It seems to the hostess that her subject is eavesdropping on her family's one-room-away conversation.

Sergio—Sarge—says, "It doesn't have to be open-casket, Kenny."

"Aunt Dot wants it open."

"Kenny, Dorothy's not bossing this business, so don't say afterwards it was open casket only because that's what *she* wanted. Got that?"

"Uncle Sergio, I'm not—"

"That'd be a cheap trick, Kenny, unfair to Aunt Dot *and* to you."

"Hey!" Uncle Lyle objects, and Aunt Martha chimes, "Sarge, you haven't given Kenny a chance to—"

"He can't blame my Dot for making a mockery of Gina at her own funeral!"

Kenny's high-pitched voice startles the hostess: "I love Aunt Dot, Uncle Sergio! I'd never do that, so what in hell are you talking here?"

"Well, I—" Sergio begins, audibly abashed.

"I'm only saying, Whatever Aunt Dot wants, I want. So how could I ever trash her for something I've also okayed?"

"Yeah," Sarge concedes. "That's different."

"You didn't let me finish."

"Kenny, I'm sorry."

"It's okay, but don't tell me I'd ever do anything to hurt Aunt Dot."

"I won't. Okay, I won't."

Conversation lapses, and the hostess, studying Kenny's photo of his mother, adjusts the lines bracketing the deceased's mouth. An old claustrophobia menaces her.

Then Vince says, "Who'd want a total stranger trying to get her body presentable?"

"Shush," Aunt Martha tells him. *"Shush."*

"I want to be cremated. Scatter my ashes over the Great Sand Dunes. It's in my will."

"Can you do that?" Kenny asks Vince. "Have your ashes thrown on federal land?"

"Who'd stop you?" Vince says. "You just get somebody to help and you go do it."

"It won't be me or your mother," Sarge says. "Why's a punk like you got a will?"

"Be proud," Martha says. "At least Vince thinks of stuff beside new cars and ski trips."

"Yeah, like polluting a goddamn protected federal showcase for sand."

"So what?" Frank asks. "I want to be cremated too. Dead's dead, and it's cheaper than a fancy-pants show like this."

In the ever-contracting Memory Room, the hostess imagines Frank rolling his eyes at the parlor's cut-glass chandelier.

"Gina wanted a Catholic funeral," Lyle says. "So we're doing our best to give her one. Her marrying Wesley Callan"—who, they all know, was twice-divorced—"didn't make it easy to arrange. I talked to a gazillion priests before Father McFahey agreed."

"And that fart Callan isn't even coming," Sarge grouses.

"You sure?" Martha asks him. "I told Wesley by phone he'll regret that."

Kenny says, "He told me he wouldn't listen to a lot of R.C. mumbo-jumbo. He and his Gunnison cronies are having their own holy-moly memorial."

"Mumbo-jumbo?" Martha says indignantly.

"Yeah, so I told him: *You got your own mumbo-jumbo, don't you, Wes?*"

Sarge laughs. "What'd *he* say, Kenny?"

"He was pissed. But if you treat people lousy, you get treated lousy back."

"Those goddamn Jehovah's Witnesses drive me bats," Frank says. "'Live Forever on Paradise Earth.' 'Jesus Is the Archangel Michael in Disguise.' *Jesus!* Aunt Gina was a saint to put up with three years of that malarky."

"And beautiful," Kenny murmurs.

"Wes may be a Witness," Martha declares, "but when he dies, they'll cremate him—hear that, Vince?—and stick his jar into a vault across from Gina's Tower of Memories."

Kenny asks, "Where will *I* go? They didn't save a spot for me, Aunt Martha."

His complaint evokes no expressions of sympathy.

In the Memory Room, the hostess makes an incision in Gina's neck, swabs the rubbery flesh around it, seals it with a mortician's adhesive. Now she and her subject are straining hard and hearing snow whirl out of the overcast. It clings to the 1907 building like Colorado cotton, shingles of white flannel. Then a teenage girl enters with a manila folder and a leather glasses case.

"I found these upstairs, Mrs. Dennis." She presents them to the woman on the stool.

"I could've really used these *yesterday*." Mrs. Dennis takes a glossy photo from the envelope and tilts it to compare its likeness to the body's face.

"I wasn't here yesterday. I couldn't—"

"Hush, Heather. Go back upstairs."

The girl collects herself and leaves, going through the smoky parlor past Kenny, the Sekases, and the Lobranos. Mrs. Dennis gets only a glimpse before the door drifts shut and she must return her gaze to Gina Callan.

Forgive my Kenny, the client says. Ernesto and I spoiled him when he was little.

He's no longer little, Mrs. Dennis rejoins.

His thoughtless behavior isn't his fault. He never learned responsibility.

And why not?

I couldn't have kids so we adopted. We were so glad to get Kenny, we went overboard. Ernesto gave him a diamond ring when he was six. A day later he lost it.

Mrs. Dennis stares blankly at the unmoving face.

Kenny was the only thing Wes and I argued about, except for his new religion.

Aloud, Mrs. Dennis says, "Yeah. A kid always dislikes a parent's stand-in spouse."

It wasn't that. Kenny was thirty when Wes and I wed. Ernesto died when Kenny was nine and Kenny *loved* Wes. Or did before them Witnesses got him.

Then I had it backwards, Mrs. Dennis thinks, working on the throat: It was Wes who didn't like Kenny.

Wes couldn't stand Kenny's flightiness. When we wed, Kenny was back from Nam. His wife ran off on him during his time away and he wouldn't do nothing but play the dogs in Pueblo and Colorado Springs.

And Wes didn't like gambling?

Before he went Witness, Wes played the dogs. But Kenny's losing and always begging money ran him berserk.

But Wes loaned him betting money anyhow?

No, I did. And sometimes he'd ask for pawn bait: jewelry, silverware. He needed to work his racetrack *system* to win back what he'd lost.

No wonder Wes went buggy, Gina. You fed Kenny's habit.

It was an obsession. He had computer printouts, three-by-five cards about them damn dogs all over our house in Gunnison. To work out his *system*, to make him rich.

You fell for that?

Occasionally, he'd win, Mrs. Dennis. But he didn't think to pay us back for staking him. Instead, he'd buy me a TV or Wes expensive hunting equipment. Which dropped him in a hole deeper than his winnings made up for, and Wes would rant about Kenny being an idiot moocher, a big two-ton baby.

Relining Mrs. Callan's eyes, Mrs. Dennis says, "Sounds a dead-on analysis to me."

No. A month before I entered Fitzsimmons Army Hospital, he quit the dogs. Wouldn't run his system at all. That impressed Wes.

But Wes isn't here.

My family's Catholic, and I wanted to be put to rest like a Catholic, but being a Witness made it impossible for Wes to think about my religion without getting angry. It's got nothing to do with Kenny.

But *Kenny's* Catholic. And hates Wes for it. And resents him not being here.

Kenny's *not* Catholic. After Wes and I married, he left. Now he's a Unitarian or some such. He hates Catholics for not giving me communion because I fell in love with and married a guy who'd already been married twice.

"Wheels within wheels," Mrs. Dennis tells the ceiling.

Our first years together, Gina Callan reminisces, Wes had no faith but pro football. But four years ago, a doctor at Fitzsimmons botched the prostate surgery he needed. Wesley nearly died. Some Witnesses got to him while he was suffering, studied with him, poured propaganda on him. He was so far down, he bought it. If the Buddhists or Hare Krishnas had got to him first, Wesley'd be that instead. I sorta wish they had.

You preferred Wes as a Denver Bronco fan?

Yeah. He ignored birthdays, Christmases. Wouldn't buy me a Valentine for fear another Jehovah's Witless would call him, uh, frivolous. Kenny got fed up with *him*.

"I'm almost finished, Gina." Mrs. Dennis takes Gina's glasses from their case, sets them on her client's face, and snugs the stems into her bouffant hairdo.

I went into hospital terrified, the now bespectacled Gina says. I remembered how one of its lousy doctors nearly killed Wes, and *I* was afraid they'd push me to death's door like they'd almost done him.

It's a cliché, Mrs. Callan, but there *are* worse things than dying.

Fear's one, Mrs. Dennis. And when I was really hurting, retaining water and so on, one Army dork—Wes called 'em *dorktors* and they thought he just talked funny—entered my room and said, Ma'am, you're dying. You've only got a few more hours. He didn't ask Wes or Kenny, just took it upon himself to say so.

My God, thinks Mrs. Dennis, appalled.

That knocked me low. Maybe some'd be grateful to be told, but I thought I'd make it and that doctor's words horror-struck me.

What a betrayal.

They'd taken me on and off this and that machine, run tubes in and out of me: I didn't last till morning. Kenny and Wes sat helpless. Being dead isn't half as bad as going sick-scared into ICU and having some fish-eyed Army dork say I was dying.

To herself, Mrs. Dennis wonders, How much more of this can I stand?

Know what scares me now? What disturbs even my death sleep?

Tell me.

Wes'll be okay. He's got his ridiculous religion. But what's to become of Kenny?

He'll be okay too.

No. He never learned responsibility. It was our fault, mine and Ernesto's, but Kenny's gonna pay for it. He's a baby. Still a baby . . .

Aunt Dot, Claudia, and Melinda return from their shopping expedition. Mrs. Dennis and her client hear them coming down the carpeted stairs. The menfolk rise, and Aunt Martha blurts, "Those are wonderful, Dot. They're so unquestionably Gina."

The women crowd in, warning the men to stay put. This is a female matter, putting on her makeup, etc., and Kenny and the other fellas can't see Mrs. Callan again until Aunt Dot declares her presentable.

Mrs. Dennis allows the women's invasion, but feels they're hijacking a torture chamber, not just returning with bangles to adorn their dead.

Melinda closes the door behind them.

"Ta da!" Claudia reveals some beaten-brass earrings with fake pearls in their clips.

"Hooray for clip-ons," Mrs. Dennis says. "She had pierced ears but the holes closed up."

"Clip-ons, schlip-ons," Claudia says. "All that matters is they look like her."

"Big and jangly," says Melinda. "Just Gina, through and through."

The hostess realizes that Gina Callan, who stopped "speaking" when the women entered, is basking in their approval. Finally, she feels good about herself.

"Okay," Mrs. Dennis says. "Let Kenny in."

The men bunch at the door, squeeze through, and approach the casket, Kenny shoving to the forefront.

"Whaddaya think?" Aunt Martha asks. "Isn't that more like it?"

Kenny stares. Repeatedly, his bug-eyed gaze shifts between Gina Callan's hands and her rouged cardboard face. Then he reaches out to Mrs. Dennis and takes her hands.

"This is my mama!" he exults. "You goofballs got it right! She's beautiful again, just like I remember."

"Thank you. Your family helped."

"You found her glasses. Her picture, too."

"An employee found them: Heather Thompson."

"She deserves a raise. I'll get her chocolate. You, too: both of you." Kenny faces the casket and raises his arms in thanksgiving. "This is my mother! God bless everyone here for giving me back my mother!"

Alone again with the bereaved dead woman, Mrs. Dennis sits wearily on her stool.

Wes never came, Gina Callan laments. And Kenny will be totally at sea without me.

"Shut up!" Mrs. Dennis cries, to reclaim the room. "Do you think you're the only damn stiff whose troubles I have to listen to?"

Gina Sekas Petruzzi Callan ceases transmitting. Forever.

"That's better." Mrs. Dennis cups her face in hands. "Who the hell do you guys think you are anyway?"

EXTINCT

Not until my father died
did I begin to mourn the dinosaurs.

Birdlike, Dad lay in the ICU
not much like the raffish guy
who sometimes played peek-a-boo
with his laughing kid
in that first hopeful year
after the Allies obliterated
every hungry competitor
around our smoke-veiled globe.

His forelimbs strapped
by terrycloth tethers
to the rail of his bed,
he moaned around the plastic reed
tapping into the acrid
red backlash from his bowel.
It wasn't hard to tell
my father was warm-blooded,
a failing endotherm,
even if his Roman nose
had become a Cretaceous beak
and the swell of his lips
a hapless dried-out snapper.

Only a gown away from naked,
he still had some gaudy armor:
his doctors, knowing evolution
would have insufficient time
to make the requisite adjustment,
had jiggled gently down
over his incredulous eyes
an ancient football helmet,
a bucket of Big Bird yellow, and
to its dented white facemask
they had expertly knotted
the tight-drawn tube siphoning
crimson from his flooded gut.

Trapped in that polymer cask,
Dad was a stunned ankylosaur
In the defensive backfield
of a slow-motion Sudden Death.
When the screen marking the blips
of his heart's hydraulics
ticked down to a zero hum,
his creature knew extinction.

Not until my father died
did I begin to mourn the dinosaurs.

THREE DREAMS IN THE
WAKE OF A DEATH

i. provocation

Toward morning Lawson had a dream. He saw his late father and himself, as a grown man, standing on the paved edge of a large natural pool. At their backs mingled many anonymous partygoers energized by the mild sunshine, some making preparations for a cookout. Lawson paid no heed, but stared down into the glassy waters. As if he had an underwater, not merely a poolside, vantage, he saw a Labrador retriever, the dog his dad had owned when Lawson was a boy, swimming like a lithe black otter. This creature from Lawson's childhood moved sinuously through the water and rocketed up from the moss-furred bottom to nab in its jaws a plump albino bass.

At this point, Lawson's dream skipped several frames. He had the impression that the dog made several catches in a row, exited the pool without shaking, and carried each white bass to the cooks at the deep-frying vats behind him. Lawson focused, however, on the dog's hypnotic underwater swimming, which ended, fading into another frame entirely, when an alligator twice the retriever's length appeared in the pool and the dog scrambled out.

The alligator also emerged. The dog vanished, into the crowd or tenuous air, while the partygoers continued their merrymaking undeterred. In fact, Lawson and his dad stood calmly at the poolside watching the alligator elbow-walk over the pavement, and at last Lawson thought *This is a dangerous creature, its jaws are metal traps, every person here is a potential victim of its appetite.* That no one showed any sign of panic struck him as totally crazy.

Lawson's father had enough sense to view the alligator's intrusion as a bizarre threat, but instead of warning people, he turned to Lawson to brag *I'm going to kick the bastard in the butt*: a macho boast so typical of his dad in life that Lawson could only gape, though he wanted to say *That's stupid, Dad*, or *Dad, you'll put everyone here at risk* or *How can you kick an alligator in the butt?* Indeed, how could you? That snout-up, elbow-walking reptile had a long, wide, flat, leathery, ridged tail that hid and protected its anus. Did this tail qualify as its butt? Lawson had no idea. His dad was too miffed by the alligator's party-crashing to care. He sidled up and booted it in a part of its tail behind a squat hind leg. The alligator leapt an inch or two on its front legs and swiveled its jaws. Lawson's father skipped aside.

Horrified, Lawson looked on as the beast, deprived of any chance to avenge itself on his father, scooted after the partygoers by the blazing cookers. There, just before Lawson awoke, it seized the leg of a nine- or ten-year-old girl.

ii. shame

A few days later, Lawson had slept for less than two hours when he dreamt again. His father appeared as a handsome thirty-five-year-old man, he as a nine- or ten-year-old boy. His chief private fret back then had been the obliteration of the entire planet in a ponderous ballet of mushroom clouds. This vivid worry discolored every frame of his dream.

In the weeds along the bank of a small river, Lawson and his dad, barefoot, found an old metal boat. As his dad's Lab foraged among the cattails for a musk-rat or jackrabbit, they pushed this boat into the muddy water and leapt aboard. *Let's go musseling*, his father said, skinning out of shirt, shorts, and rumpled military boxers.

Lawson shed his clothes slowly. He had fewer muscles—mussels?—than his father and a tiny pale sex, like a pleated grub. His dad laughed, not mean-spiritedly, grabbed a rusty bucket from the prow, and dove into the warm brown river.

From its bottom, he lifted bucket after bucket of hideous purplish mus-sels. He sluiced them clean of muck and dumped them into the boat. *Arkansas oysters*, he cried, laughing, while standing on the grainy bottom silt. Tepid water lapped him at breastbone height. Although he wanted Lawson to dive in too, Lawson clung to the gunwales. His dad's naked muscles daunted him, as did the shells mounding at his feet like brittle mutant poker chips.

Why're we doin this? the boy Lawson asked.

Bivalve meat for Grampa Cody's razorbacks. Might even find a pearl or two.

No pearls in these ugly things. Lawson kicked at them.

Mebbe not. But with just one, we could drive to Alaska and homestead a place. Get in. You'll blister up there.

Lawson's boyhood avatar refused to budge.

Awright then. His father tossed the bucket toward the bank. Tumbling, it turned into a woman's head, with bright red lips and long blond eyelashes. Lawson felt relief when it vanished among the cattails. Immediately, Dad did a kipping dive, his buttocks glinting in the sun and vanishing into the leathery water. Anxiety consumed Lawson, and the spray showering back burned like welding-torch sparks.

Meanwhile his father swam relentlessly down.

Lawson saw him as if from an underwater perspective: the deeper his father dove the clearer the water became until at last it had the lucid dimensions of a cold cave lake. His dad circled down to a barnacle-grown pub table at which sat three laughing women in gowns of seaweed and organdy. None of the three was Lawson's mother or the divorced Scotswoman with whom his dad had set up housekeeping in Cheyenne.

In the boat Lawson struggled to stand, balanced arms akimbo on the middle seat, and peed a gold parabola into the water.

iii. confluence

A week later, early in the a.m., Lawson had another dream. His dad, a graceful man only when swimming or diving, darted through a tiled catacomb: subway station, public lavatory, or the basement of a vast state library. Carrying his paunch like a compact pregnancy, he ran past turnstiles, sink basins, or filing cabinets, glancing back, incessantly muttering, hurrying to escape his pursuers.

Lawson knew that *he* was one of the latter. A Labrador retriever—the dog his father had owned years ago—tugged him through the echoing spaces on a choke chain. It barked only at intervals, from deep within the ebony vault of its chest. At each bark, the catacomb rang as if from a pistol shot. Lawson struggled to keep up with the dog. Other pursuers, distant and unseen, yelled encouragement to one another and slapped the tiled floor with unyielding leather soles. Surveillance cameras, Lawson understood, were taping the pursuit.

His dad ran up a down escalator and vanished over its lip. The Lab pulled Lawson up the escalator after him, and his fleeing father climbed a long concrete slope toward a granite tower. The tower—a carving, not a genuine building, despite Lawson's first take on it—dominated the otherwise barren cityscape. From its battlements, through its crenels, poured a waterfall. These streams braided into a silvery veil that geysered at street level without spray or runoff. Lawson's father stepped through the waterfall and shimmered beyond it as if frozen.

Dad! Lawson yelled.

The Lab yanked free of Lawson, loped to the tower, and jumped through the waterfall to join Lawson's father. He hitched up the slope after the dog, a sudden flaming pain in one knee. When he was close enough to part the water with his hand, his father's fractured image stared out at him from the roaring backboil.

Come in, son. The water's fine.

I can't!

Then they'll get you too. Take old Sonny's word for it.

Their pursuers would soon arrive. They'd espy Lawson just outside the waterfall and surmise his dad's nearness. They'd shove him aside and reach through the waterfall to arrest his old man.

Lawson's knee ached. That ache had a stabbing counterpart in his chest.

Come on, his father mouthed. Grinning, feinting, he boxed the torrential veil as if it were a punching bag.

Lawson glanced down. The shimmering fabric of his shirt had begun to rain. It melted and ran in self-recycling threads, a tunic of rains. And clad in this shirt, he easily stepped through the waterfall.

iv. coda

A big barking dog awoke Lawson, but at his window all he could see was rain arrowing down in a streetlamp's halo.

THE BALLOON

Balloon Day in Ms. Randolph's class. All her students were about to release into their streaky Dakota sky a balloon bearing a message of peace for whoever found it and took from within it the slip of paper nestled inside like a fragile blossom.

On each leaf of paper, Ms. Randolph had asked them to write a peace slogan, their name, and Rugby Middle School's address. Together, these slips would convey messages only an arms maker could withstand, even if each one was Pollyannaish propaganda:

INVEST IN PEACE.

MAKE LOVE OR MONEY—NOT WAR.

WAR IS NOT HEALTHY FOR SMALL CHILDREN OR INTERNATIONAL TRADE.

THE REAL PRISONERS OF WAR ARE THOSE WHO SUPPORT IT.

WHAT IF THEY GAVE A WAR AND EVERYONE WAS TOO BUSY BEING BULLISH TO BECOME BELLIGERENTS?

WAR IS NOT COST-EFFECTIVE: DEAD PEOPLE DON'T PAY TAXES.

Et cetera.

Thirty kids flowed down the school's steps in a riot of knees, elbows, and rowdy shouts, and rolled along in a sniggering burlesque of harmony to the schoolyard where, every recess in good weather, the boys played tag or softball and the girls jumped rope, or swung, or milled in gossip groups.

"What will you put in your balloon?" Lydia Benkelman asked Brent Sarcoxie, a fellow seventh-grader.

"Air," Brent said.

"I meant, what *message*?"

Brent wanted to boycott Balloon Day. It was a crock. Ms. Randolph was a peace freak. The police action in Mexico, territorial spats with Canada, the shooting over water rights in the Rocky Mountain States. A guy couldn't just make kissy-face noises at such things, quote old folk songs, and pretend nothing was worth fighting for. If you did that, you spat on the bones of brave soldiers like Brent's daddy, who, two years ago, had taken a hand-laser hit in the Minot Brigade assault on Winnipeg in the last big Annexation Tiff. Hell, if you did that, you might as well go to Europe, where lard-bottomed appeasers *talked* out their problems.

Brent ached to reenter the school. He was missing a satellite feed from the Peruvian incursion. For what? Another peacenik balloon fly.

If Daddy was alive, he'd have folks picketing these, uh, festivities.

Ms. Randolph, strapping in a calico pioneer dress, got between Brent and the school building. She towered over him, her ruddy face a no-nonsense stop sign. "You can't go back in before we finish, Mr. Sarcoxie."

"I need to answer nature's call."

"You've answered it twice this morning. You'll last."

"What if I don't?"

Ms. Randolph looked sidelong past Lydia at Brent's pals Tom Killdeer and Johnny Zahl. "I'll buy you a box of security briefs." The boys snorted. Lydia—a pox on her beanpole frame and puppy-belly freckles—giggled.

"He doesn't have a message slip." Lydia tried to stifle her giggles.

"That won't do," Ms. Randolph told Brent. "Every balloon needs a message. Pick a saying from the board. Or write your own."

Brent couldn't imagine sending aloft a message like MAKE LOVE OR MONEY—NOT WAR. It insulted his dad's memory. He said he'd do a message of his own, and Ms. Randolph gave him a notebook and a felt-tipped pen and guided him to a picnic table on the edge of the gravel yard from which their balloons would rise.

"Chop-chop, Mr. Sarcoxie. Chop-chop."

Brent hunched over the notebook, considering. Eventually, he printed a message. Then reconsidered, wrote a fresh slogan on another page, tore it out, and gave it to Ms. Randolph, who read it out loud: "THE BUSINESS OF WAR IS TO BRING ABOUT PEACE. ENLIST IN THAT BUSINESS TODAY."

Ms. Randolph's brow furrowed. His slogan, Brent well knew, had a troubling pool-ball English. But it *was* a call for peace. Sort of.

His teacher handed it back. "OK." But her brow stayed corrugated, and walking toward the helium dispenser around which the other kids jostled, she swished her skirts as if to ward off out-of-season horseflies. Brent wadded up the message she'd OK'd, trash-canned it, tore out his original message, folded it into a small packet, and walked to the helium-dispenser queue. There he chose the only black balloon in a box of multicolored balloons, poked his new slogan through its tight throat, and gave it to a teacher's aide to inflate. Its skin grew into a mother-of-pearl globe, a taut ashen membrane mocking the gaiety of all the other balloons.

"Great!" Ms. Randolph cried. "*Let them go!*"

Brent's classmates let their spheres ascend. Brent hung onto his until nearly all the other kids had released theirs, then held it aloft, made a rude kissing noise, and let it fly. A fleet of tiny globular ships, color by Crayola and Jell-O, arose. Below and behind the armada of colliding balloons, Brent's was a sullen period chasing its siblings into the mottled parchment of a late-spring sky.

What a crock. The only good thing about this was that he hadn't had to read aloud from Hamlin Garland or Willa Cather.

On a Fourth of July seven years later, at an arcade in suburban Bismarck, Brent Sarcoxie was telling a bargirl named Blaisdell about his rotten childhood: Daddy dead in '28; Mamma an image-addict in a home for veterans' dependents in Fargo unable to adapt to her widowhood, and his older sister, Wing, in Helena, Montana, turning high-cost tricks for any flyboy with credit to burn and six or more flak-harassed sorties against the Calgarians.

"Poor kiddo," Blaisdell said. What little she wore kept changing colors, sending shadows and amoeboid highlights over her distracting contours. Soon, memory-stimmed by her sky-blue clinglet, Sarcoxie told her about Balloon Day. How he had hated it. How Ms. Randolph's every lesson and study assignment had made him want to hurl. And how, on the last Balloon Day held in Pierce County, he'd sabotaged her mush-brain peacemaking efforts.

"Balloon Day," Blaisdell said. "Sounds neat."

"Neat? A total waste of time."

"Did people ever find the balloons carrying slogans?" she asked.

"Some got snagged in powerlines. Some popped in midair. But we got back a letter from a farm wife in Divide County and another from an enlisted peace freak at Minot Air Force Base. Nothing from out of state, though, or from the cankers."

"Divide County? Wow. That's like putting a message in a bottle and throwing it into the ocean. A real act of faith. I think that's sweet."

"Ms. Randolph probably didn't." When had Blaisdell seen an ocean? Never, he'd have wagered. "That Divide County woman was a down-to-the-ground patriot. Her hubby too. She wrote Ms. Randolph, our school board, all the media, and the governor. Two weeks later, Ms. Randolph was gone. A retired fighter jock finished out the year for her."

"How shitty."

"It should've happened sooner." Sarcoxie slugged back a tumbler of Bottineau bourbon. "She was lucky it didn't. The Dakotas are hawkish. The North Country Fair: fight for it or flee. The lady was lucky to last as long as she did. If us *kids* didn't yap to our folks about Balloon Day—and I didn't have any folks to gripe *to*—it was because in class she damn-near hypnotized you into treason. Ms. Randolph had a clean Earth-Mamma charisma. Sometimes, but *just* sometimes, she almost made sense."

"Sounds cool to me. Look how great Europe's getting along."

Sarcoxie hacked derisively. "Want to hear how I flimflammed her?"

"I'm envisioning all those pretty balloons flying off with messages of hope. Maybe a few are still up there."

"Cripes, gal. *Come on.*" Maybe she was humoring him, leading him along for tips and after-hours tapas. Well, that was her job. "My message was for the cankers who killed my daddy in Manitoba. I printed it out big and neat: 'WHATEVER LOUSY BASTARD FINDS THIS / MAY YOU DIE A REALLY SLOW DEATH.' That's what *I* sent up, in a balloon the color of a really ripe shroud."

"Good thing that patriotic farm wife didn't find it. She might've asked the governor to give Ms. Randolph a medal. You'd've never got rid of her."

"Hey, don't be smart."

"Nobody ever accuses me of that. And now that you've joined the Devil's Lake Berets, they won't accuse you, either."

Sarcoxie wasn't drunk. He knew an insult when it hit him. He pushed a C-spot at the B-belle, watched her clinglet ripple through a miniature rain forest of hues, pulled his denim beret from his belt, set it at a jaunty angle on his head, and ambled toward the door.

A disabled vet on a stool up front was selling Independence Day banners. He snapped Sarcoxie a salute and asked if he'd like to help a wounded bro.

Sarcoxie returned the DV's salute and handed him a double-tenner. Without taking a pennant.

A month later, huddled against a stealth-copter's bulkhead with six other berets, Sarcoxie prepared to jump into deep woods near the Whiteshell Nuclear Research Establishment. Some Albertan fifth-columnists had done advance work to make their plotted sabotage of the facility come off, but Lt. Noonan had the twitchies. Worse, his nervousness was spreading like COVID cooties from man to man along the jump-line.

Cripes, Sarcoxie thought. Noonan wouldn't be here if his daddy wasn't a Four Star with a chestful of ribbons from the Ottawa walkover.

"Everything's hunky-dory," Lt. Noonan said shakily.

What was hunky-dory about it, Sarcoxie thought, was that Noonan wasn't jumping with them. He was a cheerleader, a stay-aloft with a radio. Fine. On the ground they needed guys who knew what to do and flat-out dog-down did it.

In the August dark, the copter banked, its pilot yelled an instruction, Noonan called out in reply, and *blam blam blam blam blam blam blam* the interdiction-squad members fell toward the black-green shadows of the Whiteshell shield forest in glider chutes.

Ruddering from side to side. Angling across the white-noise rush of a midnight wind. Keeping one another in view through nightscope goggles. Interlinking via throat mikes and earphones. Gyro-orienting in glider-chute harnesses. Slaving like doolies to keep bungholes tight and bellies from evacuating.

A jolt. A dip. A scary separation from the main glider-chute mass.

One of two things had happened. Either he'd been bull's-eyed by a miniwinder or the fabric of his glide wing had torn.

Deadeye ground-to-air marksmanship? A flaw in the synthasilk?

It hardly mattered. With no control over the direction or the speed of his dropping, he was going down. Sadly, this Whiteshell op would have been his first chance to kick canker butt for what the Winnies had done to his dad. Now all he had to look forward to was buying the farm. The wind rippled his denim leggings, his flak bladders pummeling his chest and his back as he careened toward an anonymous fatal nowhere.

Desperate, he tore off his nightscope and flung it into the howling Manitoban dark. His earphones followed. Then his glider-chute and flak jacket flapped off to oblivion like flailing bats. If you're going to die, jettison as much shit as you can. Babies were born naked, and it struck Sarcoxie that the nearer you could get to naked when about to check out the better. His remaining uniform lacked the suppleness to let him double over, undo his boots, and shed them as well but *c'est la vie*. Or *c'est la mort*.

Foliage—needles, twigs, grenade-like cones—basketed him, grabbing, tearing, giving way, grabbing again. The rag doll of his body was snagged and hammocked.

In some of this snapping and ripping, Sarcoxie felt sure, sounded not only ruin for the canopies of the jack pines and balsams that had broken (apt word) his fall, but also godawful damage to his spine, liver, spleen, and lungs. He was dangling at Albertosaurus eye-level (had there been Albertosauruses alive to eye him) near the top of a fir wracked by the slashing of a human meteorite.

Crap, someone said. A croak in the sighing darkness, the sad gulp of a man-sized tree frog. Had *he* spoken? Before he could ask himself again, he passed out.

When he awoke, it was still dark, still cold. The pain awash in all his systems reproached him so bluntly that his consciousness nearly checked out again. How could a guy hurt so much? Where were his hail-fella berets? Was the glow visible through the forest—a vast green patina behind the shaggy silhouettes of the intervening trees—evidence that they'd succeeded in their mission or that his eyes weren't working too well? Who knew? Whenever Sarcoxie moved his head, a blur followed and fireflies danced.

God God God God *God!*

Let me die. *Let me die.*

A specter appeared to him.

A round gray face drifting through the prickly labyrinth of the forest canopy. It had no body, just as he in a sense had no body, only a phantom extension of his consciousness throbbing beneath his neck.

Luckily, the round gray face bobbing toward him approached from a favorable angle. He could watch without too much rubbernecking or visual adjustment.

What did it want? Why was it haunting him?

He tried to cry out but had no voice.

Maybe, plummeting through the tree, he'd punctured his throat, injuring his vocal cords. Nonetheless, the round gray face came on, navigating the fringed lagoons of the forest as if it had eyes in its latex noggin.

But that was impossible.

As well as horrifying because of its absurdity.

Even more horrifying, when the round gray face bobbed only inches from his own, was the fact that he saw a tiny packet of paper folded up in the neck of the balloon: a packet waiting for a hand to reach out, explode the latex skin, and seize it. Sarcoxie was grateful that his hand could *not* do that, for he was a dangling quadriplegic, a dead man, with dawn decades away and nightfall far beyond human reckoning.

SECRETS OF THE ALIEN RELIQUARY

At first, we grossly failed to recognize it,
assuming the displays in the camouflaged temple
relics of their espionage, dandruff from our anxious ids,
the gleanings of a xenophilic curator with eclectic tastes,
or no taste to speak of, an otherworldly magpie
of the inconsequentia and splendor of our species,
a devourer of it all. Later we came to understand
that we had stumbled not into a conventional museum,

but a kind of backdoor bawdyhouse repository
of fetishistic, and thus shameful, alien delights—
not one arising from their own ferrogramineous biology
but rather from a low-percentile, albeit planetwide,
deviant preoccupation, generally discreetly suppressed,
with anything and everything human. Stunned doesn't
begin to describe our mindset passing among the temple's
dioramas and interactive icons, which ranged from the size

of fingernails—indeed, one *was* a fingernail—to that of
an immense holographic projection of a membrane-enveloped
gall bladder, conspicuously diseased, which revolved aloft
like a lopsided glitter ball in a clandestine discotheque.
Who would have imagined that a silhouette of Abe Vigoda,
a pair of gutta-percha galoshes, the scent of halitosis
disseminated via an atomizer, a pictorial chiropractic text,
a large Petri dish of toenail fungus, a video of a Tourette

Syndrome sufferer, or a quaint electronic coupon for a box
of hemorrhoid suppositories would have so reliably tweaked
the private orgiastic impulses of some of these creatures
that they would showcase their favorite libidinous stimuli
in a concealed exhibition hall within an energy field
only a klick from our landing site? Among sentients,
it appears, a pornographic yen is an infallible index:
a potential pacifying bond that we should perhaps explore.

Meanwhile, turnabout being fair play, several of us begin
to find the jut of a Denebolan femoral spur, the lemonish
fragrance of a ruptured ovipositor, or even a coded swarm
of their gill-dwelling symbiotic vermin almost as arousing
as venereal human contact or state-of-the-art handheld
weapons of irresistible concupiscent destruction. What
this bodes for human interspecies relations, I am loath
to speculate. Their reliquary, though, rewards a look-see.

ANNALISE, ANNALISE

For you, said the Independent Parcel Delivery person at his apartment door.

What is it? Dexter Olin had expected nothing. Expecting nothing lent accuracy to his personal forecasts and stymied disappointment.

No idea, said the IPD worker in a reedy voice. I don't check out what I deliver.

Dexter accepted a small brown package and, when the IPD worker left, shut the door and opened the box. In it: a videocassette featuring a gummed label reading *Dexter Olin Unchained*, which stuck to the black plastic like an oval Band-Aid.

I didn't order this, Dexter thought. Who mailed it? He recalled no film with *unchained* in its title except *Hercules Unchained*. Although he didn't much resemble a starving artist, no one would mistake him for Hercules either. He worked as a guide at a local state park, where he led nature hikes and supervised facility maintenance.

Dexter carried the videocassette to his TV/VCR combo and crammed the tape in. No FBI warning preceded the title. White block letters appeared on a cobalt background:

DEXTER OLIN UNCHAINED
starring
* * *Dexter Olin (as Himself)* * *

The tape began. Dexter sat down to watch:

A video image of Dexter Olin comes through his apartment door and falls into the same chair in which he now sat. He pages through the evening paper, rises, fixes a drink, takes a sip, sets the drink down, goes into his bedroom, and reemerges in a soft terrycloth robe. Before the oversized mirror in his living room (which lacked a picture window), his video avatar allows the robe to drop and intently scrutinizes his naked body.

Watching this scene, which he recalled enacting on a dozen recent occasions, Dexter shifted uneasily. Had somebody videotaped him? He halted the tape and searched the room, even checking the wall behind the mirror for a camera niche. Two-way mirrors were not uncommon, but this one, judging by the intact gypsum board behind it, didn't fall into that category. Dexter felt the wall, banged on it, squinted at it from every angle. It remained only a wall.

No one could have videotaped him from inside the apartment, and yet he'd seen himself naked on this tape delivered by the IPD worker. Other folks, all alone, surely studied themselves in a like way, longing for a more attractive set of attributes or taking a secret pride in those they had. Or did they?

If they did, did his behavior derive from insecurity, conceit, or some cold mixture of the two? Was he a freak? A delicious frisson of shame and excitement twinged in him, as if he had spoken an untold yearning to a lover or seen an act both vile and private from an undiscoverable peephole.

But the tape in his TV/VCR unit proved that someone had discovered such a peephole from which to record him in an intimate self-showcase. That was scary.

It also amped up his excitement and curiosity. Others could watch this tape as easily as he, see him stripped to his jacketless soul, and judge him as a spiritual creature as well as one of sinew and bone. This fact seemed to magnify rather than to diminish him. How could the idea of unseen onlookers fail to excite?

Dexter reexamined the package in which the video had come; it had no bill of lading or return address. This absence of any clear point of origin also gave the tape a stimulating aspect, an enlivening mystery. Spies received such unmarked items, even if said agents generally didn't turn up in them as voyeuristic objects of their own espionage.

Dexter dropped back into his chair to reactivate the VCR.

On the tape, Dexter Olin turns before the mirror, runs his hands down his flanks, does a knee bend, puts a palm on the carpet, throws his head back, and stares ceilingward, his ribs as sharply etched as Venetian blinds. His video self has a classicism only marginally compromised by scars, skeletal forearms, the inchoate pudge about his middle. His virilia, which he has always regarded as delicate, nonetheless mesh with this classicism, just Praxitelean enough to avert ridicule if not to summon awe. Arms out, he does another knee bend; then poses upright, shifting his weight from one hip to the other and coyly clutching one shoulder.

The door to the apartment abruptly opens. A lithe figure in a dark green uniform enters. Real-time Dexter started at the video intruder, for he always locked his door after returning from work. His video self, however, sees the visitor over his shoulder, and pivots, concealing himself with both hands.

What the hell are you doing here? *Get out!*

The svelte IPD worker smiles, takes off the teal-green baseball-style cap, shakes out an amber waterfall of hair, toes off a pair of scuffed shoes, peels back the shirt and steps from the pants making up the remainder of the uniform, and stands before video Dexter as a buxom and leggy young woman.

My God, murmured the real-time Dexter Olin. Until now, he had thought the tape a spookily tasty invasion of privacy, not an appeal to the prurient in him. The appearance of this unclad woman altered his perceptions, definitions, expectations. Someone had sent him—or so he hoped—a piece of homemade erotica, a movie to scratch his libido, stroke his ego, free his pent-up sexual energies.

Still want me to leave? says the naked young woman.

No, says Dexter's video self. *No!*

The woman approaches, lifts her breasts into his chest, nuzzles him under the jaw, and, after taking his hand, turns him in a slow-motion pirouette that the tape's anonymous operator artfully developed into a mandala-like montage of carnality and tenderness, the particulars of which the real Dexter watched with a yearning as lofty as earthbound. Each part of his body that could lift—nipples, nape hair, sex, little toes—erected, and rhythmic music throbbed not only on the soundtrack but also in his wrist and throat pulses.

The video images of Dexter and the woman move from his apartment to a drifting canoe to a thundering rollercoaster to a grassy lea to a biplane's lower wing to a trapeze to a hopper car full of swan feathers to a boxing ring to a pristine Mexican beach. The insatiability and stamina of his video counterpart daunted as well as heartened Dexter: he could not remember ever having disported with such a consensual partner or shown such endurance. That was because neither his video self nor hers had the reality of even a noonday shadow, although he'd often wished so hard for such a freedom that in his dreams he could hear chains falling and his blood surging from low metabolic tide to full metabolic flush.

And back again.

The tape was intimate, explicit. He could never show it to anyone, but could keep it in his VCR and mind as a liberator, an imprisoning liberator. He could also rerun it mechanically or mentally to trigger those synapses that skin-to-skin communion so often left unfired. He sighed when *Dexter Olin Unchained*, after nearly an hour, rolled its credits, a scroll of titles and names followed mostly by asterisks:

> Dexter Olin.......... Himself
> IPD Worker...........* * * *
> Director...............* * * *
> Screenwriter..........* * * *
> Cinematographer.....* * * *

The scroll did not halt until the key grip, best boy, caterer, and the cinematographer's girlfriend's hairdresser had all had their asterisks screened. Then the tape rewound with a clunk, a whir, and a final clunk. Dexter wanted to run it again, but someone knocked on the door.

When he answered it, he stood face to face with the IPD worker who'd brought the tape. Dexter reddened, stammered.

The IPD worker touched her cap bill. I need the package I delivered earlier.

Why?

It's not yours. I brought it by mistake.

I've already opened it.

It wasn't meant for you. It's not yours.

Who else could it belong to? Dexter fumed to think that this uniformed woman wanted to filch from him the video dream in which *she* met his every longing. To whom did she plan to deliver it? How could anybody make such a mistake? Her demand was not merely ludicrous, it was an outrage.

It's mine, she said. It belongs to me.

You didn't know the package you brought me belonged to you? Dexter strode to his VCR and ejected the tape.

Hey, you not only opened it—you watched it!

I thought it was mine. And I don't want anyone else to see it. Especially not you. What gall, to ask me to return it.

I've already seen it. I don't want anyone else watching it either, Mr. Olin. I just want it back so I can get rid of it in my own way.

You did that by dropping it off here.

A blunder. Videos make up a lot of my deliveries. It could happen to any-one.

Hardly. I've been twice singled out. You can't expect me to yield the proof, even though I never took part in *any* of that stuff. He lifted the tape. What is this? Computer imaging? High-tech blackmail?

Oh, no. It's real. As real, anyway, as anything you or I ever see on TV.

What absolute bunk. Please get out.

Not without the tape. From what I've seen there—nodding at it—you must have a *degree* of chivalry.

She was half a head shorter than Dexter. What if he grabbed her and thrust her out the door? He tried that, but she karate-chopped his wrist and slid away from his lunge.

You're trespassing, Dexter cried. Possession's nine tenths of the law, and this tape is in *my* hands. *You* gave it to *me*.

Let me buy it back.

There's not enough money in the world!

Must money be the currency of our exchange?

Dexter squinted at the IPD worker. He took her meaning and thought of another form of barter. A frisson of shame and excitement triggered the pulse in his throat. He began to unbutton his park-service shirt. Was what he'd wit-nessed on the tape about to fulfill itself in sweaty reality in his windowless living room? The IPD worker smiled. He stepped toward her, reached out for her cap. When he removed it, he took another step, to kiss her forehead. It struck him then that the removal of the cap hadn't led to an explosion of tumbling amber tresses, that this person had a military butch and an odor of cheap aftershave.

Whoa, said Dexter Olin, straightening. *Whoa.*

I'm her brother, said the capless man before him. Her twin. She was too embarrassed to come back herself. You can understand.

Embarrassment? said Dexter. Sure. Easily.

The form of barter I hinted at no longer interests you?

With her. Not you.

She wouldn't, sir. She had her tape made for an experimental de-inhibiting therapy she's undergoing at the Zacharow Clinic.

High-tech blackmail: I was right then, wasn't I?

Call it a parabolic Freudian slip: she enacted rather than spoke it. She meant to give the tape to Dr. Zacharow, but brought it here through an unconscious mechanism typical of her psychological disorder.

Introduce me to her.

It's too soon for that.

I don't know. You could just as easily assert that it's too late.

Please give me the tape. Show some decency.

Did she have the decency to ask me about this obscene violation of my person?

You don't view it as obscene, sir. And there's too much painful background to recount, to explain why she chose you for her de-inhibiting therapy.

The obscenity lies in her failure to recount that background for me. Not only that, but—Dexter braked.

What?

A pernicious invasion of my life space had to occur to make her tape. It gets me right in the specificity of its anatomical correctness.

A month ago, I visited the park where you work, said the brother. While taking pictures of the nature trail, I also took some of you.

With film that magically stripped me naked?

No. The clinic used my photos and your family's publicly accessible medical records to project a likeness for Annalise's animated therapy tape.

Annalise, Dexter murmured. *Annalise.*

Extrapolation from many different biological inputs and parameters. Beyond our failure to consult, there's nothing sinister about the processes involved.

Lovely name. Truly lovely.

Please return the tape, Mr. Olin.

Dexter slowly rebuttoned his shirt. You can't tell me she doesn't have a duplicate of the tape she accidentally delivered here.

I can't. But—

Then I should have one, too. I *deserve* one.

The idea that anyone other than her doctors and supportive family—by which I mean me, Mr. Olin—might have access to this tape totally mortifies her. More than that, it plunges her into disabling depression.

But we're in it together.

Not really. Annalise lived abroad for six years, in a country divided by old ethnic hatreds, economic disparities, civil war. That's part of the background of her disorder. I'll say no more, except to note that you and she have little in common beyond your simulated presences on that tape. Please return it.

The brother extended his hand.

Dexter, holding the tape to his thigh, stepped back with a growl. Get out!

But you were briefly ready to trade.

I'm not now.

We're at an impasse. I brought no pistol and violence has never been my way.

In your case, Dexter said, that's probably the better part of valor.

Annalise's brother kissed all four fingertips of one hand and touched them to Dexter's jaw, letting them linger for a moment.

Goodbye. Your refusals won't endear you to Annalise or help her toward a cure. You've also forfeited any claim on my affections.

You think I'm sorry?

You're not?

I'm the aggrieved party, but all you can think of is Annalise and nine hundred ways to lay a guilt trip on me. I'll never yield to such tactics.

The brother shook his head and let himself out.

Dexter locked the apartment door—latch, deadbolt, safety chain—and replayed the wondrous tape. He watched it two more times before going to bed, with a growing concern for Annalise and a steady lapsing of desire, not all of it owing to an involuntary climax or sheer psychosexual visual overload.

The next day, Annalise came to the state park. She wore jeans, sneakers, and a sweatshirt, not her IPD uniform, and she found Dexter in a grove of redbud trees shortly after the morning's third official nature hike. A frisson of shame and excitement coursed through him, but he turned to greet her even while trying to ignore the storm of blood to his face.

I'm not the person on that tape, she said. I mean, I am, but I'm also not.

After a beat, he said: Me either.

They squinted at each other through leaf-tangled sunlight, and realizing that he was as worrisome a mystery to Annalise as she was to him, Dexter held both open hands at waist height palms up, questioning.

After a time, she put her palms-down hands into his and stepped toward him with many evolving questions in her eyes.

EPISTROPHY

Julian Wrysodick slumped in his harness as I pushed his three-wheeled chair down the beach through ocean spray and buffeting gusts. His hands sat like crabs on the woolen-clad bones of his thighs. As we progressed, his lopsided gray head lolled. He smelled of witch hazel, camphor, and piss, even as these odors blew by me inland. If only Ferrel Kidd, my uncle Garrick's son and the old man's usual helper, hadn't taken the flu and called me from the Sea Court library to sub for him. If only Julian had bowed to his infirmity and stayed indoors, out of the ocean spray and the buffeting gusts. Winter twilight flapped about us like unsecured sailcloth.

"Rudy, why have you stopped?" Mr. J's voice ratcheted like rusty gears.

"This is crazy, sir."

"It pains me you think so."

"There's a squall blowing up. The winds will capsize us."

"Ferrel would never balk at accompanying me."

What's this *accompanying* business? I thought: I'm *pushing* you. "No balking to it, sir. I'm just noting the inadvisability."

"If I croak out here, you fear a reprimand. Or worse."

"Well, of course."

"You probably should: the wind's indeed tricky." He let me see the custardy white of one eye, the corner of a whiskery grin.

"Then may I take you back?"

"Ferrel wouldn't. He'd push on, right into the buffeting gusts."

"Yessir," I said, honestly peeved.

"There's something I want to see." He pointed a bony finger at a be-duned cape jutting into the chop fifty yards ahead. "Go, man. Go."

I shoved. The old man's chair, designed for all-terrains, even heavy sand, shot forward so that I trotted after, rather than impelled, it: what a buggy. Why fret the ocean spray, the menace of falling night, the buffeting wind? The chair had headlamps on its otherwise useless armrests and vermillion running strips on its tires and sides. To a sand crab, we surely resembled a fiery runaway Ferris wheel.

Ultimately, we negotiated the cape and a shell-studded flat that opened out on a small peninsula of snowy sand, as if a crew of engineers had poured a concrete base beneath its square tip and affixed that slab to the underlying shelf by a method that college-educated pinheads like me would never grasp. As Wrysodick gaped, I rolled him onto the spit, which, from its base up, went like this: concrete subfloor, cap floor of pristine white sand, and, atop this layer tucked into an open-faced shelter of waxed driftwood, the *something* that Wrysodick wanted to see again:

A jukebox!

By now, the sky had given up all its light, the wind was a buffeting dynamo, and the old man had taken on an extra pound or two from his sodden woolen clothes. He no longer stank of hair oil, camphor, and urine, but of something fleece-like and doggy. When I bent to speak into his ear, his bat-fetus face gleamed with memory or fresh contentment. *In the pink,* I thought, for Old Wrysodick now wore the rosy sheen of self-satisfied reminiscence.

"Here?" I yelled.

"Closer: *Roll me up!*"

I would have gladly rolled him into a cast, such as owls regurgitate, and thrown him into the Atlantic, but had mercy and moved his chair. Its headlamps played like spots on the glowing plastic tubes and chromium trim of the jukebox, animating all its curves and sponging the night about it with swirls of emerald, ruby, sapphire, amethyst. The box's console stood five and a half feet tall. Throbbing like a Titan's heart, it towered over the frail patriarch.

"That's the Wrysodick 1440: the first model I put into production after the war."

Which war? I wondered. He meant of course the one we'd ended with atomic bombs, two towering mega-deadly hurricanes.

"When material controls ended, I jumped back into the game," he said. "This beautiful baby was the result."

"You designed jukeboxes?"

"Conceived. Designed. Crafted. Produced."

"Ferrel said you made phonographs, stereo equipment, that sort of stuff."

"A jukebox *is* that sort of stuff, Rudy."

I nodded, invisibly to Mr. J., at the Wrysodick 1440. "Does that work?"

Even shivering in end-game decrepitude, he scoffed at any implication that it wouldn't. This unit had a built-in power source. He told me how to activate it; how to adjust the volume against the booming of the sea and the wind's shrill vocalizations; how to prime the disk player with a slug that automatically returned itself; and how to punch out a favorite from among the twenty-four selections catalogued in rows above the *Wrysodick* nameplate and the wavy arch-shaped tube framing the stained-glass drum of the box's sexy abdomen. I did everything he said, right up to the button punching.

"Punch seventeen, Rudy."

"Seventeen?"

"It's been seventeen years since she died."

I punched seventeen: "Misterioso" by Thelonious Monk. With the box's volume on its highest setting, the notes of this oddly syncopated, quasi-discordant melody banged out like the music of four peeved, jamming skeletons. The xylophone in it hinted so strongly at smart-aleck bone rattling that I shivered even more than Mr. J., now grinning like a cadaver. The vertical tubes on the juke's front outer edges pulsed with the music and our chattering teeth.

"Who?" I asked. "Seventeen years?"

"Irene, my one and only. My beloved."

"Did she like *that?*" I meant the weird Monk music, "Misterioso."

Wrysodick could not see my nod, but easily read my question. "She liked everything on that baby. It's all jazz, all twenty-four disks." Something flew by overhead: seagull, sandpiper, scrap of newspaper. Mr. J. flinched, a jerk of his massive gray head, as this frail UFO fluttered past us toward sea oats and eroded dunes.

Then, like a turtle coming back out of its carapace, he recovered. "Monk on piano, Milt Jackson on vibes, John Simmons on bass, Shadow Wilson on drums."

"I've only ever heard of Monk."

"They recorded 'Misterioso' and a cut called 'Epistrophy'—it's on the box too—in the summer of 'forty-eight."

"Twenty years before I was born, almost."

"Me, I was at the height of my powers."

"Yessir."

"Misterioso" plinked to its conclusion. Three minutes plus of cool sardonic playing that Irene Wrysodick had soared on and that had also levitated Julian. Even after the arm inside the console returned the vinyl disk to its stack, the 1440's sculpted tubes went on geysering. Inside them, in the liquid chemical roiling there, floated tiny grains that clumped and separated again, dissolving and briefly re-manifesting. I left Mr. J. and knelt beside one set of the paired tubes.

"What makes them do that?"

"The chemical in there—*irenex* I call it—has a truly low boiling point." His head lolled. His finger twitched. "Small heaters at the bottoms of the tubes." He chortled. "*Voila!* Instant Technicolor ebullience."

"It's pretty," I said, thinking, much prettier than the ivory collisions of "Misterioso." I fingered the console's ever-present slug out of its return slot.

"Again," Mister Julian commanded.

"Seventeen?"

"What else? *Seventeen!*"

I studied the other selections. I would have liked Sinatra, Dick Haymes, Jo Stafford, Charlie Parker saxing "I Didn't Know What Time It Was" (because I didn't), Ella Fitzgerald on "I Ain't Got Nothin' But the Blues," Dizzy Gillespie's "Lorraine," anything but seventeen. Still, I did my duty by the old geezer and hit seventeen. Thelonious plunked, waves crashed, and the wind flung shrapnel against the gleaming backside of the 1440's driftwood lean-to and out into spray and buffeting gusts.

"Irene loved this spot. We put her to rest here."

Obediently, I peered into the dark: "Where?"

"Inside my machine. We cremated her. Her bones went into a box and the box into a small compartment of the 1440."

"I thought with cremation you got ashes."

"You get *cremains,* Rudy, lots of ash and some charred bone fragments. The latter we boxed and stashed in the Wrysodick."

"What about her ashes?"

"Most we put into the cedar box with the bone fragments. A sprinkle, though, went into the jukebox's bubble tubes."

"The bubble tubes?"

"Sure. She dances in those things. She inhabits this place."

"Ferrel never told me."

"I'd've fired him if he had. Nobody reveals my eccentricities but me."

A beat or two later I asked, "Is it legal? Interring someone in a jukebox?"

"My wife, our property, our choice: If it isn't legal, nobody'd dare tell me."

Once again, "Misterioso" plinked to its off-key conclusion in the deafening salty gusts. Meanwhile, Irene Wrysodick, or a gritty part of her, danced in the bebop tubes of her husband's incandescent music box.

On our way back to Mr. J.'s house, he lurched heavily against the straps in his chair. A heart attack, the coroner said. No autopsy confirmed this assessment, but as stipulated in his will, a cremation was followed by a memorial service at the jukebox beach site. Ferrel got me invited by arguing that the person in whose presence the patriarch had died—no one, by the way, ever accused me of neglect or negligence—had a *right* to attend. Who, after all, had last spoken to Julian Wrysodick? Who'd seen his definitive death throe? Who'd wiped his mouth of sputum in the ocean spray and buffeting gusts?

At first, I hadn't wanted to go. But Ferrel said that Emily Singleton, the eldest daughter, had mixed the cremains of her dad with those of her mom and spooned them all into the cedar box inside the 1440. Some of Mr. J.'s ashes had gone into the bubble tubes, there to blend with those of their children's beloved mother.

And so the ceremony, consisting of a text from First Corinthians and several appropriate jukebox numbers, genuinely moved me. I began to love Julian Wrysodick and the woman who had predeceased him by seventeen years. I even discovered a happy, if well-concealed, lilt in the Thelonious Monk piece "Misterioso."

After the funeral, Ferrel Kidd and I stopped by the Sea Court Public Library for some work I needed to do at home. We sat down at a table in the community meeting room to talk. Ferrel is two years younger than I, a card-carrying member of Generation X. At events other than funerals, he galumphs in outsized jeans, granny glasses, and a Fishbone baseball cap worn backwards. I still hadn't adjusted to him in a chalk-striped charcoal suit with visible suspender straps under his jacket.

"When I die," I told him, "please put my mortal remains in a jukebox."

Ferrel raised his ashen monobrow. "Rudy, they don't make Wrysodick

1440s anymore. Hell, they don't manufacture Wrysodick boxes at all."

"What about a competitive model?"

"A Seeburg? A Rock-Ola? A Wurlitzer? None of them really suits."

"But I'm snowed, Ferrel. Think of something that *would* suit."

"What's snowed you?"

"Its beauty. The fact that Mr. and Mrs. Wrysodick still continually jazz each other in the rainbow-colored tubes of his namesake machine."

"Yeah."

"Beats going into the cold clayey ground or a random scattering at sea."

"Maybe," Ferrel said skeptically.

A few months later, Tropical Storm Eliot struck the coast and wreaked havoc. Buffeting and collapsing every building on the Wrysodick estate, the storm raged in gusts, soared inland roaring, and junked the jukebox tomb of Mr. and Mrs. Wrysodick. Soon after, Ferrel and I threw in to buy plots in a modest Sea Court cemetery.

A blue note to end on but the discordant truth.

DEAD POET PARABLE

A woman writes an ode
whose every caesura
her night-sweating child
stresses with a cry.

A seraph with draftily
scissoring wings
edges into their flat.
You may keep her, he sings,

for the legacy
of a beloved poet—
that poet's lyrics
or your girl. Select.

After scarcely a thought
the woman says, *My daughter.*
The seraph departs,
leaving a ruby feather.

Months later, fresh voices
break on a naked strand.
The girl runs into them,
high-stepping, clapping hands.

Ignorant disciples
of the disappeared canon
gather on the shingles
to revile her, and mock.

One throws crab shells,
driftwood, beer bottles,
but many others assent
with missiles of their own.

The hurt girl stumbles,
chokes on scouring salt.
Over the operatic combers,
the spectral poet grins.

MIDWIFING THE WORLD

*"In the beginning was the Word,
and the Word was with God, and the Word was God."*
—John 1:1

Before the Light: total darkness. Unspeaking, Sirena slogged about like a pregnant waterspout. Moselle, Zoe, and I feared she'd splatter us against the cavern walls or splash off into unknown grottoes and vanish.

Anchovy-breathed, Moselle said, "Her footfalls betray her. Each step echoes like an orca's leap."

Zoe and I listened: Sirena's tread *did* sound different. Nearer. Indeed, she bumped us bodily. Zoe seized her and would not let go. "Feel the grease on her belly," she said. "A sign of her readiness." When I touched the fleshy globe hanging above me, a briny sweat clung to my fingertips, reeking of cod liver and krill.

"Ah," I said. "Sirena smells like a rotting dinghy on a tide of eel innards."

Moselle and Zoe chuffed like porpoises trying to restrain her but Sirena broke away, and Zoe hurried after crying, "Help," so Moselle and I joined the chase. A trio of pilot fish, we soon flanked Sirena.

"To the birthing slab," Moselle urged us.

Blindly, we tugged Sirena to that slab and shoved her down upon it. She forearmed us—*smack! smack!*—and sat back up, but we forced her flat again.

Moselle and Zoe pinioned her arms whilst I crouched on her haunches, inhaling an odor at once like damp sand and coelacanths. When Sirena's water broke, the flood swept me away, only faintly glinting as the water tumbled.

"*Abra!*" Moselle and Zoe cried.

I fetched up drenched against a craggy wall. Retching and hacking, I groped back to the birthing stone. "H-h-here," I gasped.

"Bless you, Little Abra," Zoe said. "Bring us the book."

"The b-book. Why?"

"For its weight," Moselle said. "And its solace."

"Hurry, child."

I splashed grumbling through darkness sniffing for it. Despite the stench of dying crabs and barnacled limestone, I nosed its scratchy scent. The book weighed half as much as I. I toted it, stooped over, to my sisters, who laid it open on Sirena's belly. Two thousand blank pages in binders of cumbersome slate.

"*Push!*" Moselle and Zoe urged our mistress.

I said nothing but one of my sisters snatched me up and set me astride the tome on Sirena's abdomen. She jerked like a hooked marlin. I held on like a parasitic merwitch. Even as Sirena fought, Moselle squatted between her legs. I put a bracing hand to Moselle's heretofore unseeable face, smelling from the book no trace of sentience. Sirena's spasms, however, spoke to me even through the dense heavy slate.

"It won't come," Moselle told us.

"Then we must cut it from her!" Zoe shoved me and the book to the cavern floor.

My indignant wail bought no sympathy, for Zoe had released sight upon creation with a barracuda fin. She'd sliced that fin across Sirena's belly and slashed again across the membrane of her uterine wall, cuts that freed Sirena's wavelike *and* particulate child.

"*Light!*" Sirena spouted.

That re-blinding light rayed from the rents in her flesh like negative squid ink, dazzling and drunk-making. It pierced and flowed, showing the dripping hollows of our cave, embedded shells, my sisters' huge stunned forms, hints of coral and palm fronds beyond our cavern door, bathing everything in . . .

. . . the opposite of darkness.

The cuts in her body still agape, Sirena arose yelling "*Light!*" and knocked Moselle and Zoe down. She then lurched into the world, geysering glory and trailing an umbilical cord, now with a wrapper of electrical tape about it and a plug at its tip.

Moselle and Zoe leapt up to pursue her and her new appendages, sallying out into vivid sunshine.

And I? I crawled out from under our slate-bound wordless book and trembled half-blind in the holy glare of eternal day. Until then, never having known the full extent of my ugliness, I blinked in wonder against the terrible brightness.

Later, with *real* squid ink, I compile a wordlist on the dry fronds of a new book, not in A-to-Z sequence but as chance and my mood determine. I flip back and forth and write whatever I like whenever I choose. Light makes my task easier, but also more open to scrutiny, my own and others'.

Never mind. I like my illuminated pages, but I like even more the words upon them. Words like *waterspout, kelp, porpoises, coelacanths, merwitch, barracuda, uterine, slashed, rents, fronds, geysering,* and *holy glare.*

Occasionally, Moselle and Zoe call to me from beyond my cabana, urging me to join them, and even as I scritch and scratch, loading my tiny book, their petitions really do tempt me toward the light . . .

MENARD'S DISEASE
(BIBLIOARTIFEXISM)

M enard's disease, or Biblioartifexism, subjects its sufferers to the delusion that they have written (i.e., recomposed word for word, line by line, albeit in a fresh context) a classic literary work by a well-known writer.

This rare ailment takes its name from the French symbolist poet and belletrist Pierre Menard. According to his friend Jorge Luis Borges, Menard produced "perhaps the most significant writing of our time" when he duplicated the ninth and thirty-eighth chapters of Part I of *Don Quixote* and a fragment of Chapter XXII in Bayonne, France, between 1918 and 1939. Although no one but Borges could distinguish these pages from their counterparts in Miguel de Cervantes' masterpiece, Menard argued that reconstructing a novel that came spontaneously to Cervantes demanded more labor and subtlety than did its original composition. It further required a full suppression of his own personality: his tastes, aesthetics, and metaphysics. Indeed, this symptom—a total lack of existential affect—typifies all final-stage Menardians, rendering them, paradoxically, at once megalomaniac and bland.

Without exception, sufferers of Menard's disease present to us a tangible artifact—an actual copy—of a well-known literary work as their own achievement. They offer it, whether Cervantes' *Don Quixote*, "The Nine Billion Names of God" by Arthur C. Clarke, or *Gone with the Wind* by Margaret Mitchell, as if they had written it by excruciating protocols of self-denial and reenvisionment. These protocols, they contend, have alchemized the popular original into its consummate hypostatic text, thus mysteriously transforming it.

Clinicians may initially mistake Menard's disease—not to be confused with Ménière's disease, a disorder of the inner ear—for *plagiarism*, which it resembles no more than a hangman does a hangnail. Others misidentify the tangible symptom of the disease—the literary artifact that the afflicted one produces, as a sufferer from gout patient produces kidney stones—as a *parody*. Typically, such misdiagnoses further madden the patient. Caring physicians must scrupulously guard against them.

Besides the eponymous Pierre Menard, other sufferers of Menard's disease have included Carter Scholz and Robert James Waller. Scholz's own literary case history, "The Nine Billion Names of God," recounts his devastating extended bout with the disease, but, remarkably, does not reduplicate the famous Arthur C. Clarke story on which he fixated. (Scholz has since more or less recovered.) Waller, however, does reproduce, in all its fatiguing banality, the text of a best seller, *The Bridges of Madison County*, which Waller wrote in a state of self-possessed delirium. (Clearly, this last example stalks the borderline of psychiatric orthodoxy, but Menard's disease also tiptoes that ill-defined pale.)

Another unconventional sufferer was Norman Spinrad, who channeled the toxic anima of none other than Adolf Hitler to recompose a lost science-fiction novel of the unlamented führer, *Lord of the Swastika*. The flamboyant Spinrad's psychosis had progressed farther than Menard's, however, and its virulence led him to the self-aggrandizing chutzpah of titling Hitler's novel *The Iron Dream* and releasing it under his own name—with *two* title pages. Like Scholz, Spinrad has since benefited from remission, although his disease periodically erupts in otherwise inexplicable forays into the electoral politics of the Science Fiction and Fantasy Writers of America (SFWA), a periodically dysfunctional literary organization.

Untreated Menard's disease usually leads to greater delusions of genius and/or popular acclaim. (Accordingly, the sufferer becomes insufferable.) So rarely does this orphan disease manifest, however, that major pharmaceutical houses fund no research to produce ameliorative drugs. Therefore, treatment includes subjecting patients to public humiliation. Outdoor readings of their allegedly transfigured texts and barrages of rotten vegetables often restore equilibrium after three or fewer applications. Sadly, this treatment may *reinforce* the delusion of surpassing genius. Consequently, death proves the longest-lasting efficacious therapy. One caveat: Legal proscriptions and penalties generally counterindicate murder.

Although it has yet to assume epidemic proportions, Biblioartifexism strikes a few more authors every year. Yes, plagiarists and parodists have long abounded. Some romance writers—usually, the only female sufferers of the syndrome—have imported colleagues' words into their own texts with no clear improvement to their work or conspicuous damage to their sources. But Menardians prefer grander substitutions, and specialists predict more outbreaks as literacy fades and celebrity fever soars. Hence, health-conscious citizens must beware of future "reenvisioned" editions of James Joyce's *Ulysses*, Harper Lee's *To Kill a Mockingbird*, and possibly even David Sedaris' *Me Talk Pretty One Day*.

—Michael Bishop, M.D., author of a new edition of
The Journals of Sarah Goodman, Disease Psychologist

THE ALZHEIMER LAUREATE

In 20—, American writer Dominic McLock of Black River Falls, Wisconsin, received belated acknowledgment of his genius when the Swedish Academy bestowed on him that year's Nobel Prize for Literature. A photo of the cherubic-looking writer sitting at his antiquated Apple wearing a Russian cap, gutta-percha galoshes, and a candy-striped thong became poster fodder and sold millions of copies worldwide.

After toiling in obscurity for at least thirty years, the darling of only a fanatic proprietary cult, Dominic McLock now rose to stratospheric heights of international fame. Predictably, every remotely literate bumpkin claimed to have discovered his multivolume masterwork, *Chronicles of a Laminated Tomorrow,* an epic comedy of manners and technological innovation, back when its first installment, *The Lost Cursor,* issued from a shoestring publishing house that sold eighty-six copies before plunging into unlamented bankruptcy.

In his late fifties when *The Lost Cursor* flash-in-the-panned over the literary landscape, McLock kept writing. He found other supporters—mad bibliophiles and eccentrics—to urge him on and publish him, and *Chronicles of a Laminated Tomorrow* grew by an installment a year for the next two and a half decades. Sales rose modestly. Each addition to McLock's *Chronicles* attracted new acolytes and more nominations for obscure literary prizes: The Frickle Hambly Award, the Hypertext Medallion, the Enemies of Aesthetic Mediocrity Citation, etc.

As sequel followed sequel, each work had not only a quaint hardcopy avatar but also concomitant lives as video artifact, CD-ROM, eBook, podcast, computer game, continuously mutable wall hangings, psychedelic lozenges, and sheath-free talking birth-control aids, or *water-soluble fertility coins* (depending on the bio-state or procreative tenets of each consumer). Each avatar of McLock's *Chronicles* advanced, deepened, and glossed every other chapter in its revolutionary meta-structure. *Pixilated Pixels,* from 20—, sold well enough to appear briefly on the *New York Times* Bestseller List (in a footnote, as a likely up-and-comer) and became a glib catchphrase on a popular radio wranglefest. A dozen or more young McLock wannabes (at that point in his career, only a recluse would have wanted such limited notoriety) strove to emulate his style, voice, tone, and jolting impact on the collective unconscious of the five thousand or so dilettantes who actually read him.

If McLock had any precursors, said the one national critic who paid him any heed at all, they were bona fide inventors like Proust, Joyce, and Eliot, who left in their wake not flourishing schools but thunderstruck, largely impotent gangs of admirers. In many ways, pontificated this critic, McLock "subsumes Proust, Joyce, and Eliot in his own sensibility, extending their socio-psychical criticisms in the astuteness of his encompassing judgments and the radical virtuosity of his vision." (*Say what?* moaned even the people who read this pedant, a group smaller than that who followed McLock.) No matter. McLock's follow-up to *Pixilated Pixels, The Monitor and Merry Mack,* which some view as cryptically autobiographical, was remaindered in all its forms within six months, plunging the author back into the ironclad obscurity to which he and most of his loyal readers had grown accustomed.

Years passed, and Dominic McLock continued to manufacture a title—no one any longer called his productions "novels"—a year, each complex, idiosyncratic, and abstruse. In Europe (mainly among Florentines, Swedes, and Parisians), translations of the first twelve installments of *Chronicles,* in a single indexed package, sold in staggering numbers and convinced the mover-shakers of their various literary establishments that the provincial clods of the US had again snubbed a homegrown genius. They touted his work as inventive, sad, funny, and trailblazing in its cagy profundity.

Meanwhile, back in Black River Falls, McLock added briefer, more runic book-length chapters to his masterpiece, episodes so dadaesque that the only American critic once receptive to his *oeuvre* confessed, to legions of the ignorant and/or blasé, that the "scalding brilliance" of McLock's latest work had left him panting to keep up, baffled past insight, and humbled by his efforts to decode what McLock had "so incandescently shaped."

Today, most literary historians—American, European, South American, East African—agree that Dominic McLock would have received the Nobel Prize a mere five years after the release of the indexed package of the *Chronicles'* first twelve books, if not for the hidebound conservatism of many of the Academy's most intellectually decrepit members. As a like crowd had once repeatedly denied Jorge Luis Borges the laurel, these same reactionaries, or their heirs, repeatedly blackballed Dominic McLock, who bore their snubs with a dignity that may well have sprung from his total indifference to their opinions or deliberations.

By 20—, though, the last of McLock's detractors (Academy members who did not know a hard drive from a drive train, a hypertext card from a hypnotist) had died, and the appearance of the arcane thirtieth book of his *Chronicles*, charmingly titled *Yoyo y Yo,* at last provided the impetus for his admirers in the Academy to bestow on him the award.

When he flew to Stockholm to accept the prize, Dominic McLock was eighty-nine years old. The citation for his Nobel commented favorably—fulsomely, some said—on the uniqueness of his vision, the teasing opacity of his style, the gnomic delicacy of his wit, the prophetic sweep of his social criticism, the sureness with which he grasped and illumined technological matters, and the futuristic catholicity of his taste in product packaging.

McLock tottered up to receive his award and recite his acceptance speech. Along with his plum-and-ivory tuxedo jumpsuit, he wore the same furry hat and galoshes that later appeared in the poster commemorating his victory. (He may also have worn a candy-striped thong, blessedly hidden by his jumpsuit.)

Once at the podium, McLock delivered neither the shortest nor the longest Nobel address on record, but surely one of the most striking. It consisted only of a conjugation of the English verb *to fuck* in its present, past, and future tenses. Briefly, it appeared that McLock would also essay either the corresponding perfect or conditional tenses, but he halted, shouted, *"Boom boom bosilac,"* and bowed.

This address was received in what one attendee called "appalled silence," but after her own tentative effort to initiate some tension-breaking applause, the silence soon evolved into persistent clapping, cries of *"Bravo!"* and *"That's the way to tell 'em, Dom!"* and a tsunami of photographic activity.

McLock's address had scored a surprise TKO.

Under the inspiration of the Nobel, the laureate returned to Wisconsin and wrote many new chapters of *Chronicles of a Laminated Tomorrow*. His publishers, also under the impetus of the award, issued them in all the various media long after they ceased turning a profit: a failure owing to the fact that each new addition to the writer's belatedly celebrated masterwork seemed more gibberish-ridden and incoherent than the one before.

Except as poster boy and media-landscape book-talk staple, where his shrill cry "*Boom boom bosilac*" acquired shibboleth status, McLock was abandoned not only by the general public but also by many of his once staunchest fans.

New medications slowed his descent into total babbledom, but he refused gene therapy and eventually died alone, wearing the outfit in which, as a kitsch poster figure, he still decorated the walls of dozens of die-hard dilettantes worldwide.

The last "words" on the screen of his Mac, preserved in the museum that had once been his house, are "*Y y y n y.*" Now Dominic McLock sleeps his eternal sleep in a family graveyard outside Black River Falls.

The site's custodian, once chair of the Dominic McLock Booster Club, tells visitors that the laureate, during his final month, wrote his own epitaph, which one may read on his mammoth salmon-colored tombstone:

Hickory Dickery
McLock,
Dominic Celestine
Dead at 100
A Century unto Himself
What gohz aboot cumz aboot!

HER CHIMPANION

i.

She ordered a Chimpanion from a Senegalese sidekick corporation and received it thirty-two days later. It flew steerage in a suborbital cargo craft, the *Rorqual,* and then was maglev'd to her over the mountains from Edmonton. Never having seen snow, not even in hi-rez, it peered about the white-epauletted shoulders of the coastal depot like an unsuited sodbuster manifesting on an airless escarpment of Olympus Mons.

ii.

Her Chimpanion was undoubtedly male, enunciating a pidgin patois of Frenchified Anglo in a belch-riven bonobo accent. She laid a finger to his trembling bottom lip and bought him a pair of ski pants. He answered to Valentin and wore the ski pants abashedly, hobbling beside her toward their transport pterosaur like a shaggy James Whale hunchback.

iii.

Through the better part of a bitter year, Valentin afforded her Chimpanion-ship. As she spread-shot estimates of last summer's krill chill and the clear attrition of dependent sea-going species, she heard him swinging from the larder's caribou hook or pounding tattoos on ice-plugged water barrels. During breaks she tenderly groomed him or read to him from Dr. Goose's *Chimp with a Limp* or Goodall and Peterson's *Visions of Caliban* as Valentin twirled a braid of her coal-black hair on a crooked index digit as purple as sunset.

iv.

In November he caught pneumonia. She feared *his* sun would set. The virus did not respond to antibiotics and to her surprise she found that an ape could sweat, manifestly at night, through the buffer of his pelage and the icy acetate of his pajamas. Then something *worked*: a bitter pill with the commercial sobriquet Bonobax, and Valentin got better—only to succumb to viremia, a detonation in his heart of the first lung-monkeying virus. She wept for his lost Chimpanionship, his calibanesque playfulness, and maybe his soul.

v.

The next time she ordered an Animal Sidekick, she insured it for a cool million creds and requested a Penguin Pal.

TIRED

One morning, Gordon Pointer got an e-message from the left-front Goodstone tire on his elderly Callisto sedan. He had bought the car used a decade ago and retrofitted it for the mindful interstates of the Piedmont metrosprawl.

Gordon abhorred palmflips, infraspecs, logomaniacs, microserfs, lapcops, and digital Kleenex, but he lived at the computerminal in his Callisto, journeying between office foci to talk with other human fossils and did not quail at sitreps from his lead tire. Intermittently, after all, Gordon also heard from the engine computer, the door locks, the trunk light, the fuel tank, and the brake drums . . . although seldom with such self-effacing politeness as from Adam, the lead Goodstone.

<Gordon,> epistled Adam, <an internal sensor reading of my surface topography indicates alarming altitudinal decay and thus severe frictional reduction of my tread. The highways and your attachment to them have worn me down to narrow fraying belts, the smoothness of a baby's bottom. Replace me, Gordon. Soon.>

Unlike the archsurvivalist computer HAL in an old Kubriflick, Adam *sought* his own removal and replacement. In this brave new century, technology had acquired not only self-aware smarts, but also a type of self-abnegating helpfulness—altruism?—that boggled its human beneficiaries. Gordon did *not* want to junk Adam. He *liked* Adam, and buying four new tires in an age of labor moratoria and management-production shortages would cost a debilitating seven thousand omnidollars.

Driving to Brasstown Bald for a summit with MultiPrinz & Stru's CIO (chief itinerant officer), Samantha Gams, Gordon e-asked his lead tire:

<How many kilometers do you and your mates have left, Adam?>

<None.>

<You're jiving me, right?>

<You've ignored many warnings, Gordon, each more tire dire than the last. I might shred and pavement-plow you at any time. So might Beatrice, Charlie, or Doreen. Go to the nearest Goodstone dealer and swap us for a brand-new Alice-Bob-Carol-and-Danny set, say. Or my next e-caution could end in mid-sentence.>

This prophecy scared Gordon. He braked, carefully, and halted at the base of an incline for runaway 42-wheelers and got out to inspect his Goodstones.

A flock of ruby-throated lizards whirred up from the gravel and swarmed into the dead loblollies on the hillside. The sky glistened a headache green free of fluorocarbon and dietary-product-extract pollutants, a faintly throbbing antihistamine atmosphere that had confirmed his decision to keep traveling as TyrannoCorps' southeastern sales rep.

Breathing painfully, he held a fist against his chest to prevent a cough: anything to keep the rubythroats from re-whirring through the evergreen stumps. Other travelers passed his sedan without slowing their autopiloted vehicles. They rarely even cut their eyes to assess its antiquity. Gordon had bought it because it ranked as a least-frequently-stolen vehicle, just behind Yugos and battery-powered rickshaws.

Kneeling at each wheel of the car in turn, Gordon examined the treads of his Goodstones, installed when his odometer had read 386,472 kilometers. On every tire, a gray crosshatching existed where hard syntherubber should have shown. An onionskin transparency replaced what had once been firm black tread ridges. Adam had not shitted him. Only luck had kept him from dying in a road accident, for road deaths had risen every month since last year's Congressional ban on airbags and impact gels, after clandestine lobbying by auto makers and emergency-room managers.

On his left-wrist e-pad, Gordon tapped <Thanks, Adam; a hearty thanks indeed.>

<Wait!> beeped Doreen on the e-pad screen. <I've still got tread. How can you *consider* junking me with Adam and his e-roaded cohorts? Think of the omnidollars you could save by keeping me another three thousand kilometers.>

Sotto voce, to no one in particular, Gordon said, *Good Lord.*

<Come back around,> said Doreen, <and recheck me.>

Gordon schlepped around the Callisto to do as his right-rear tire had suggested. A trucktrain whooshed past, rippling his tunic, but he kept his feet and noted that Doreen did look less ground down than her mates. Hmm.

An anomaly, given that he'd installed these tires at the same time, but *not* a bad anomaly. Three replacements *would* cost less, and Doreen would signal her impending failure well before it endangered him, especially if he rotated her to Adam's supervisory slot.

<Okay,> Gordon e-told Doreen. <You can stay.>

<Charlie and I resent the exception you mean to make for Doreen,> Beatrice e-zapped Gordon. <We came as a team and should go as a team. Besides, the reduced wear of Doreen's tread signals your failure to check and repair your car's wheel alignment and suspension system, not any superiority in her manufacture. Had you only been more alert, Gordon, we might all have lasted another five thousand kilometers.>

"Oh Lord," said Gordon aloud.

<You didn't rotate us as per the manufacturer's suggestions,> e-sniped Charlie. <I've spent my career as a load bearer and travel facilitator at this same left-rear location. Even had you kept your chassis in repair and all of us in alignment, we *still* would have worn irregularly without periodic rotation.>

<Look, it wouldn't have made much difference!> e-jaculated Gordon. <You all have finite lives as tires, and if you wanted quasi-immortality you should have petitioned Goodstone to fabricate you as rocks!>

Another trucktrain blew past, rocking the Callisto frighteningly. The sky writhed above the bowl of the hills like hot guacamole. Even as Gordon took a sliver of satisfaction from his sarcasm, he regretted it. Arguing with artifacts of post-millennial capitalism seldom redounded to the consumer's benefit. Far too many "helpful" products held grudges. In the end, they repaid you with shoddy performance, recrimination, even betrayal.

<You think yourself a wit,> Charlie e-countered. <A member of the Algonquin inner circle. Well, Gordon, we are *not* amused.>

Gordon looked about the in-leaning hills in resigned panic. He dared not drive on to Brasstown Bald. His Goodstones had exfoliated too much tread on hundreds of long hauls for TyrannoCorps Unlimited, and he could no longer trust them. Indeed, given this tiresome roadside spat, he must fear that they might deliberately dump him.

He fetched his valise, locked the sedan's doors, and began walking.

<I'll sue!> Charlie e-shouted. <I'll engage a corporate attorney to slap you

with a multibillion-dollar proceeding for abuse and neglect!>

<I'll join him!> Beatrice e-promised. <You never maintained us well, but I never thought you a *calculating* scoundrel!>

<Till now!> Doreen e-said. <I've got a lot of travel in me yet! I'll sue you for ecological indifference, alienation of affection, and abandonment!>

There followed on Gordon's e-pad a series of pound signs <# # # # # # #!> that indicated either weeping or unconstrained rage.

In the green day, Gordon hiked up the median between the road and the shoulder of the runaway-truck incline. He rued not only his wisecrack but also his abandonment of his otherwise reliable car. The Callisto had not e-messaged him from its engine computer either a farewell or a reproach. Only his disgruntled tires messaged, overloading his wrist screen with maledictions. Several yards from the summit, Gordon unsnapped the e-pad and prepared to hurl it across the highway into a vale of sweetgums and gnarled loblollies. A glance at the device stopped him, for its screen now blinked with an almost wistful shimmer.

<Goodbye, Gordon,> e-said Adam, ostensible speaker for the Goodstones. <I've enjoyed my chance to serve you.>

Gordon tried to thank Adam for this sentiment, but Beatrice, Charlie, and Doreen weighed in with competing rebukes, contradictions, and curses, all brief but hard to read. Gordon, cursing, flung the e-pad into a close-to-hand shadowy ravine.

That spring, on his apartment balcony, Gordon showed Samantha Gams a small garden at the hub of a well-used tire. This makeshift planter boasted lamb's ear, salvia, zinnias, and radiant orange Mexican sunflowers.

"They're really pretty," Ms. Gams said. "They'd look better, though, if you'd set them in a painted window box."

"Maybe so," said Gordon, gripping his left wrist, "but I'm absolutely certain that Adam would have approved."

AN OWL AT THE CRUCIFIXION

As
I stood
on
Golgotha
among
the grieving
women,
an owl
at the
Crucifixion
perched atop the blood-fouled tree. It spread its wings in imitation
of the dying Man. When the earth shook, it fled crying from so much hurt
into the desert where He had wrestled with Temptation. I fled with it,
as a spirit. And when the owl hid itself in a hole in the waterless
rock, I
hid, too.
And when
it opened
its parched
throat to sing,
as of old,
like a lark,
or a nightingale,
but all
that spilled
forth was
a frail
shriek, I
shrieked, too.
and so
the owl and I
crouched
in our small,
dark holes
in the tall,
hot night,
heedless
of the cool,
bright music
that would
peal
a little
later.

SEQUEL ON SKORPIÓS

i.

Yeshua, an old man with tangled nose hairs and rotten teeth, has died. I lay two of Caesar's denarii on his eyes to blind his death stare. Soon in this Ionian island's ferocious heat his body will release the first odors of corruption.

Many people believe that Yeshua died forty years ago on a cross on Skull Mount outside Jerusalem. Many others believe that two days later he rose from his tomb, not as a ghost but as a death-changed cutting of God's selfsame vine. In truth, Yeshua did not die on that cross and had no call to come alive again. Our plot entailed bribing two Roman soldiers and so much risk that even now I marvel that we succeeded.

In our hovel on Skorpiós the dead Yeshua hardly resembles the young rabbi whom the soldiers scourged that day, pressing a mock crown onto his head and marking his back with flails. The crown's thorns and the flails dripped with an opiate I had boiled out of a wilderness lichen. This opiate helped him stand the pain of crucifixion and lapse by the slowing of his heart into a limpness akin to death.

One bribed soldier argued against breaking Yeshua's legs. "He's gone. Why waste more effort?" When another legionary said, "For the fun of it," our soldier, to stymie a worse assault, speared Yeshua beneath the ribs, delivering another dose of opiate. This sustained his deathlike slumber until Sunday morning.

On Friday evening, Joseph of Arimathea arrived with an oxcart and several women to Skull Mount, to take Yeshua from the cross. I also came, in woman's garb, and wrestled him into the cart. Later I carried him into the garden tomb. After I laid him there, Mary, Mary of Magdala, and Joanna massaged his body with spices and bound him in clean linen strips.

Tonight, Yeshua's aged corpse has nothing of his younger self's poignant beauty. (What foolishness, seeking to reform the corrupt Judean religion by shamming a death and a return!) In its fleeing slumber, his crucified body had appeared ready to soar out of itself on viewless wings. How did so lovely a man dwindle into this grizzled wreck? In this wise:

On that far-distant Sunday, Joseph and I crept into the tomb through a hidden tunnel. When Yeshua awoke, we unwrapped his body, robed him, and led him back out to a juniper grove a thousand paces away. From there Yeshua fled, ultimately reaching Nazareth in Galilee. Earlier some soldiers had moved the tomb's stone—for a rumor had spread of an attempt to steal the body—and found nothing inside but Yeshua's discarded wrappings.

Later, on a Galilean mount where the rabbi had given a celebrated sermon, we feigned a resurrection event. Even more people believed. When the Romans came to investigate, Yeshua and I hiked to Tyre, boarded a Greek merchant ship, and yielded the preaching of his gospel to an army of beloved acolytes.

ii.

Cephas, the brothers Boanerges, the man once named Saul, and many others carried our false good tidings (believing them implicitly) to the Gentiles, to every major city on the jagged northern shore of the Middle Sea. Soon colonies of Yeshua's followers pocked the coastlands, suffering their pagan neighbors' scorn but spurring many others to believe. Yeshua, whom some of these early evangels would have known even in disguise, avoided his old comrades.

We settled in a village on Skorpiós. I made and sold rare medicines. He worked wood or fished, but nearly undid us by urging baptism on annoyed pagans and casting his cryptic parables before them like pearls. And then a fishing accident left Yeshua unable to move any body part but his eyes. If God had chosen him (as Yeshua had always said, even during our Passover ruse), why had this evil paralysis befallen him? I could not believe that God would so malignly humble his anointed son, but my affection for Yeshua led me to serve him as physician and slave. I fed and cleaned him, often turning him to prevent pallet sores. Beyond assisting his ruse, however, what had I done to render myself the mortal Yeshua's keeper?

Observing me at work, an islander asked why I did not simply abandon him and return to Palestine. I recalled his summonses to visit the sick, go to the prisoner, and clad the naked, and I stayed. The pleaseless dignity of his gaze had seized me. Heal yourself, I begged him. Meanwhile, my ministry to him stretched into years. I sometimes prayed he would die, but his eyes kept me from withholding food, gentle rubdowns, the occasional clumsy story.

Travelers to our village told me of the spread throughout Asia Minor, Greece, and Italy of an odd Judean sect embracing a Savior who had died but now lived again, an emblem of eternal hope. I said nothing in rebuttal, for, eating and eliminating, Yeshua mocked this hope every time I put unguent on his sores or fresh ticking in his pallet. Sadly, my faith in him had fled long ago, even before the accident at sea.

iii.

This morning, in his seventy-third or -fourth year, long after most chronic invalids have ceased to breathe, Yeshua died in fact.

I have leisure to write. The dead do not rise. Even worse, God does not preside.

Yeshua's corpse, its aroma unbearably high, sits propped against a wall in mute witness to God's silence. I should bury the man, but that act has no urgency, even in this heat. Does it matter that our lives have no sequel, that we sleep rather than soar?

Tonight, as Yeshua's corruption mounts, mere oblivion seems a gift.

iv.

God forgive me, I burned him on the beach. I made an oven of stones and torched his tenantless body. The smoke climbed both sweet and foul into the twilit sky. His skull failed to burn. Even more disturbing, so did his heart.

If only in the here and now we have hope in Yeshua, we who loved him are the most pitiable people on earth—as I, a slave in bondage to a lie partly of my own devising, have known for years. And now

coda

Yeshua has manifested to me. Without opening a door, he stood before the table in my hovel cupping his heart in his hands. He laid it on my table. He looked like an old man, but one in perfect health with a lovely bronze nimbus about him.

He said, after years of invalid muteness, "Blessings, Lebbeus." And vanished as quickly and startlingly as he had come.

I do not know what this means.

But Yeshua's heart rests on my table, and I did not visit the beach to fetch it here. Nor, akin to those from whom Yeshua once cast out demons, have I gone mad. Meanwhile, his heart smells sweet, less like braised flesh than new roses, and what I begin to know is that I must open my own to its fragrance.

OUTSIDE THE CIRCLE

God beheld the human component of Creation and suffered to behold it:

Whaddaya mean, you didn't give it to me? Gloria asked. You think I spend my mornings selling myself to VD-ridden creeps on Bonner Street?

Bruce shoved her aside and slouched into the kitchen for a beer.

When Cleary reached the stoplight, a squeegee man appeared from nowhere and slopped a bucket of dirty water across his windshield.

As the squeegee man mopped the mess this way and that with a soiled bandana, Cleary pounded a fist on the inside glass.

Don't! he yelled. I won't pay! Not a dime!

The squeegee man smeared bugs, grease, and road clay all across the cloudy slope of the windshield. Lifting a wiper blade, he popped it off its track.

Cleary opened his door and leapt into the intersection. You stupid—

Who's stupid? The squeegee man swung his bucket, clipping Cleary in the temple and drawing blood. Then he pulled a tiny handgun, shot Cleary in the neck, and hopped in behind the steering wheel. He squealed away before the light changed, leaving bucket, squeegee, and Cleary sprawled on the concrete like street-festival debris.

Horns blared as a hard-eyed preadolescent boy darted over to turn Cleary's coat pockets inside out and scavenge through their contents.

*

Mortar rounds fell whistling into the city at unpredictable intervals, dislodging plaster and roof tiles, buckling walls, and engendering snowstorms of choking brick and gypsum dust. Pandemonium. Chaos. Desolation.

Paula ran along the street with a vinyl pail of fish heads and entrails for the bears at the Metropolitan Zoo. She ran stooped over like an arthritic grandma, greeting both acquaintances and strangers scurrying past her along the urban canyon called Sniper's Alley.

At the zoo, under snow-furred mountains on the city's edge, the animals were starving. Hungry refugees had butchered many of them, but the bears remained: shaggy, slat-flanked, and bewildered.

Paula called to them from the iron railing in front of their concrete habitat. The largest bear recognized her voice and lumbered from its den for a taste of trout. As Paula lifted her pail, a sniper on the mountain shot her through the temple, and a mortar shell burst nearby, mutilating the bear.

Glistening fish heads and guts flew, cyclonically.

Please step away from the doors, droned a robotic voice. *This train is leaving the station.*

Amid a host of people traveling to the international concourse, Markham backed deeper into the car to clutch a support pole. A man in a green peacoat hurried by him and sidled through the fast-closing doors. Before stepping onto the platform, he dropped a battered shoebox.

Hey, Markham called to him, you lost something! But the doors had closed and the car was moving. Upon hitting the floor, the shoebox had split and acrid steam hissed from the rent, flowing out yellowly into the train.

In the car ahead, a like fog was spreading and ten or twelve passengers toppled or slid open-mouthed to their knees. The fog grew yellower, more acridly biting, swaddling Markham so fully that he could no longer see. When someone fell against him, he too toppled, and when the train reached the international concourse, it was a morgue on rails.

Over a Pacific atoll, an ascending vermilion fireball blotted out the sun and vaporized a flock of cormorants.

*

Beholding the human component of Creation, God summoned the seraphim and charged them with improving matters by developing an Eleventh Commandment.

Today I delegate that task to you, God told them and departed.

Raphael, Michael, and the other six-winged seraphim immediately began to kick the issue around, brainstorming.

The most conspicuous early results—at least in the US—were a hurricane, torrents of rain, ravaging tornadoes, and the seventh One Hundred Year Flood in a decade.

Okay, guys, Raphael said. Lay out what you've got.

Thou shalt not elevate thy cholesterol, Michael said. The key is good health. Folks in fine fettle don't stick shivs into their neighbors.

Floss, said Eurael or Uzziel (for all seraphim have similarly euphonious names). *Thou shalt floss*. Religiously.

Okay, Raphael said, eyebrows raised. Keep 'em coming.

Thou shalt not take offense too readily, said Heybael. Think of the grief *that* causes.

More. Give me more.

Thou shalt never speak evil of Israel, said Pompael.

Thou shalt sue the unrighteous, said Barrael.

Thou shalt cleave to brand-name products and spurn cheesy substitutes, said Itzstael.

Wait, Raphael said. Aren't we unproductively narrowing our focus?

What's wrong with the old Sinai Ten? asked Eurael. As well as I see the importance to mortals of a hearty floss, it still—

—sticks in your teeth? asked Raphael.

—grates that they don't observe the first Ten. How will an Eleventh help?

I got it! cried Itzstael: *Thou shalt keep the Original Ten!*

The seraphim regarded Itzstael as if he had just let go a seraphically impossible explosion of body odor.

Eurail scoffed: That goes without saying, it's a built-in given.

Sure, said Barrael. Would anybody with any sense say, *Thou shalt not kill*, and then add, *I really mean it, Don't kill?*

Speed it up! Raphael urged them.

I've got one, said Eurael. I like it, but I'm reluctant to hazard it.

Say it!

It's simple, said Eurael: *Thou shalt not do violence in any situation, ever.*

Too simple! Barrael cried. Creeps would take advantage!

Yeah, said Pompael. Weapon-wielding nutzos!

And what *is* violence? said Barrael. Who defines it? The courts? The churches? Our families? Is karate violence? Is pinball? Is pear-peeling?

Let's amend it, Michael said: *Thou shalt not do violence ever, except in recreational sports or upon inanimate or sentient-free objects.*

Nonsense! cried Barrael. What garbage!

When God looked in again, he found the seraphim striking one another with hands, feet, and wings, so he closed the door and withdrew.

And with the escalating brouhaha in the meeting room as background noise, God again looked down on the human component of Creation:

I don't *know* how I got it, Gloria protested. I swear to God.

And to Dr. Parker's exasperated chagrin, she began to weep.

The suspect's headed toward West Gunther, Sergeant Lomax told headquarters over his patrol-car radio, and he's really highballing it.

Give chase, Lomax.

Lomax turned on his flashers and siren and accelerated.

At West Gunther and Elm, the squeegee man cornered on two wheels and plowed into a group of kids playing street stickball.

Later, tossing amid his bedclothes, Lomax could still hear their screams.

That spring, the last bear in the besieged city's zoo stuck its head out of its concrete den. Nobody remained in the city to feed it or up on the mountain to snipe away its life.

Cowardly gas assaults had spread to so many parts of the world, said the news anchor, that they'd become as common as L.A. smog.

Children slept with insect-like gasmasks strapped to their bedposts. If they had bedposts. If they had gasmasks.

Ground Zero lay everywhere.

God stood outside its circle's immense circumference considering various ways to step back in.

Part Three

�♄

LAST NIGHT OUT

LAST NIGHT OUT

Some will fail to understand that on the evening before our attack, M and I visited the strip club not as a last vulgar gift to the animal in us but as a way to bolster our scorn for the reputedly innocent people we planned to kill. This strategy worked every time that we paid our cover and ducked inside. The smells of spilled whiskey, warm beer, and male rut never fail to replenish my outrage; they also firm my wavery sense of righteousness, may God forgive me.

On this Monday night, few other patrons vied for the bartender's attention. What would you fellas like? he said.

A blonde young woman in crimson cowboy boots and a glittery red thong strolled the high counter behind the bar, dipping her shoulders, twisting in time to the techno-rock. In the dark mirror behind her, her image mimicked her dance, and M's pupils dilated to reflect both images even as he squinted against the ungodly offense they embodied.

Come on, fellas, the bartender said. Order up.

My friend wants a Manhattan, I said.

And you?

A Bloody Mary.

You got it, the bartender said. But your pal there don't much look the Manhattan type.

M smiled, only with his mouth. I'm *not* the Manhattan type, he said. But this is a special occasion.

I leaned toward M, who eyed the strolling girl with a hard-to-read hunger. Even after more than a year together, he startled me with his odd enthusiasms (bluegrass music, salt-water taffy) and cruelties (as when he told a ticket taker at a movie theater that she should lose some weight or expect lifelong spinsterhood). Please say no more, I told him.

A *very* special occasion, M said more loudly.

Tattoos of blue barbed wire circled the bartender's upper arms. A hot-white pearl gleamed in his right earlobe. No kidding? You get promoted?

Tomorrow I get promoted, M said.

But you're partying in advance.

M clasped my neck and drew me next to him, the heat from his nostrils warming my jaw. Tomorrow, he said, we *both* get promotions.

Not that I'm unhappy to serve you fellas tonight, the bartender said, but most folks wait till *afterward* to tie one on.

I broke from M's grip. The woman in boots assumed a vulgar hoochie-coochie crouch. Rolling her shoulders, she winked at me.

Circumstances do *not* permit us to wait, M told the barman. *Carpe diem*, as you people sometimes say, Bubba.

The bartender's ruddy face darkened. *What?*

Seïze the moment, seize the day, seize the nation, said M, returning the muscular New Yorker's glare.

Please, I said. Our drinks.

Through the smoke haze and the pulsing air, the bartender studied me as if I had dropped from the moon. Of course. One Bloody Mary and one Manhattan. He looked at M. You want a marshmallow in that?

No, thank you, M said. A pearl, maybe.

The bartender stared at M, then swung his grimace toward me. The longer I talk to your annoying pal, he said, the more doubts I have about what he's got in his coin purse. You follow, little man?

M produced his wallet and riffled several crisp bills under the big man's nose. My friend and I have jobs. Good jobs. High-paying jobs. We fly airplanes.

Pfaugh. The bartender turned away to fetch our drinks.

Unbelievers all about us, alone in our pocket of obedience, M and I sipped what he at last brought us and watched the show.

Good women obey, M said. Give them money, they do just what you ask.

I thought, Good women guard their modesty because God demands it, but these make money showing what the obedient hide.

M stuffed bills into my hand and nodded at the runway woman. Buy a harlot. Before noon tomorrow, virgins will surround you.

Soon, my money deep in her boot, the blonde slid along my thighs at a table in the nightclub's center. Nearby, M had his own girl, and the techno-music gave both women a strong beat by which to shimmy and beguile.

May God forgive me, I am but a man, and I roused.

Nearby, M laughed in pleasure and contempt, his responses joined like twin infants with one bitter shared heart.

Perhaps I shuddered, for the blonde straddling my knees tilted her head and put a finger to my nose. You don't really like me, do you?

I gave you money.

Yes, to do what I'm doing.

Why do you do it? Does money have such value?

She barked a laugh and looked at me coyly. Call me Marie.

I made no answer.

Or you can let me move on to a man who will appreciate me.

A man who appreciates you would never let you come here. He'd beat you before he let you—

Let me what?

Shame yourself and your family.

Ah, a God-squad do-gooder. Is this a Save the Strippers thing? Did your church take up an offering so you and your best bud could fish for our frail womanly souls?

I ignored these impertinences.

I'll tell you why I do this. God gave me this body and dropped me into this city. When I had no idea what calling to follow, He appeared in a dream and told me that if I asked for work here, the boss would hire me, and in two years I'd have enough money to attend nursing school. You know what, sweetie? I just about do.

God told you to strip for school money?

As sure as I sit here. I've had visions off and on since I was eleven.

You've deluded yourself.

No more than you and your noisy friend, coming in to win my poor lost girlfriends and me for Jesus.

You badly mistake our purpose.

You badly mistake mine.

The bartender and club bouncer were nowhere in sight. I shoved *Marie* off my lap and told M to end his frolic and hasten with me from their satanic pit.

M waved me off, but I persisted, and finally he slipped his naked succubus by giving her more money and a copy of *The Recital*.

Thus bolstered, we left. Soon we would bind the hands of women more modestly clad than these but no less deluded.

In the ruins of the fallen towers, an ash-quilted fireman came upon a copy of a charred document in an unintelligible script. He passed it along to a law-enforcement agent and trudged back to his group's unending search for bodies.

THE MOCKINGMOUSE

asked [a biologist specializing in behavioral ecology] whether there could be mouse versions of the mockingbird—mockingmice—which mimic the songs of other animals. . . . After a pause, she said, "Maybe a mockingmouse, yes, that seems possible. But who knows?"
—Rob Dunn
"Singing Mice"
Smithsonian (May 2011), p. 22

In a California pine stand
amid the needles and the bark mulch,
a band of deermouse tenors,
Peromyscus Pavarottis,
piped their seductive night songs.
There I knelt with my handheld recorder to do the experiments
I'd planned: a bacchanalia

of midnight eavesdropping
on the ultrasonic love songs
of a hidden rodent sex club—
melodies strained like aural honey
through the DNA strands of these
petite Casanovas. I wanted their gland-
driven serenades siphoned from the air
and canned, saved for decipherment

so that every behavioral ecologist
across our mouse-miked land might
one day fathom the mysteries
of *Peromyscus* mating cries and maybe
understand the dumbstruck longings
of the *human* heart. Sound-starved and
libidinous for answers, I returned
to our Monterey County lab to listen

to the lovelorn arias of tiny
beasts not unlike me, in the grander
cosmic scheme. Through my headphones,
at speeds so slow they lowered
the pitch of these rutting squeaks
to the register of the late Johnny
Cash at his most rum-belly and macho,
I heard your singular solo, a four-note

theme in a wooing *basso profundo*
that made you sound not like a mouse
but a petulant humpback Romeo.
I strained to comprehend, to lend
to your succinct but sea-dunked carols
a meaning that would pour Christmas on
my soul and Revelation on the world.
And the Spirit leapt upon me. Something

in your digitalized decrials opened
the doors of my ears and I had my Pentecost,
if not my tuneful yuletide. You'd crooned,
"Have you no shame. You are no man.
Go to the damned. Leave me alone."
Thus mocked, I shut down shop and drove
cross-continent home to play Carolina
bluegrass on my plangent tongue-tied banjo.

PURR

I am not, in the argot of townhouse dwellers and soccer moms, a *cat person*. But when I call on Paige, I feign a curmudgeonly tolerance of the fat miaower who shares her flat.

You see, I hope to leave with Paige on my arm and to return after fajitas and a fandango to the carnal reward for which my courtship charade works as lead-in. *There ain't no such thing as a no-strings smooch*, as a frat brother of mine used to say, and he knew whereof he spake.

At the door, Paige greets me with a kiss and two pats to the cranberry-colored lapels of my leather carcoat: Roland, you goof, you're twenty minutes early.

Visible over her shoulder in the galley doorway stands the huge incontinent feline on whom she dotes with a self-mocking adoration that I deplore. Swishing his flag of a tail, her tom eyes me with spooky emerald peepers. A fine Cassandra Wilson CD plays in the background.

Get a drink, Paige says. I'll finish dressing.

I'm not thirsty. And you look dressed to me. I try to slide a hand into her robe.

Whoa! To you, I'd look dressed in a Band-Aid. And she leads me to a green leatherette lounger with a built-in footrest.

Sit. Ten minutes. Then we'll paint the town.

Ten means thirty.

She shoves me down and, levering the footrest up under my calves, gives me a glimpse of cleavage

Ten means ten. Relax. Listen to Cassandra and dream a little dream of me.

Paige must have Cassandra mixed up with Mama Cass. Meantime, her hefty grey-and-white tom, which she calls by the moniker G. K. Grimalkin, advances toward me like a puffer in a gulf. He appears on his last fins, a feline *fugu* full of a toxin that makes his breath precede him like sardine-cannery fumes. He is as wide as an old sea lion and sadder in his decrepitude than a disarmed octopus.

Even sadder is the fact that he *likes* me. He has *always* liked me. His purr, with which he preens and wheedles, has the subaqueous burr of a broken torpedo propeller. G. K. purrs as he nears. He painfully hoists his squat forelimbs, scrabbles at the footrest, and hangs there gazing up the Himalayan slope of my legs and torso. I give back my most granitic Mount Rushmore visage, but it dissuades him no more than would a filet of mahi-mahi.

G. K.'s so cute he kills me, Paige says.

He's such a chub, he can't get up here. Thank God.

Now, now. And to G. K.: Poor widdle Gwimawkin. *Juss wed me wift wu onto wuvwe Wowand's wab.*

No, I tell her. Don't.

She acts on her baby talk and lifts G. K. onto *lovely Roland's lap* anyway, where he settles like a cannonball wrapped in the pelage of penicillin mold. He revs his broken-propeller purr into a drone riven by raspy sleep-apnea gasps.

Well, aren't you the pair? Paige pats my arm, scratches G. K.'s big noggin, and heads for her room. Be sweet, boys.

When she's gone, G. K. and I eye each other like moony freshmen at separate tables in a high-school cafeteria, I less moony than he. The engine in his throat runs at its highest burr, and his eyes drop nictitating membranes through which his emerald irises peer. *Sold!* I bark, startling the tom. My imperishable soul for the immediate return of my lap!

G. K. crooks me a Cheshire-cat grin and kneads my thighs. Through my trousers, he rubs my flesh as a baker would a dough ball, working his claws to the syncopations of his purr. Stop! I tell him. Knock off the one-note commentary.

G. K. studies me through slit eyes, then ratchets up his kneadiness and the volume of his purr. He rolls more *R*s than Long John Silver. He digs me deeper than Dizzy Gillespie: burr and purr, delve and dig, a cross-sensual litany of aural tactility. It doesn't hurt, and G. K.'s motor has a mesmeric effect. You're getting sleepy, it alerts me. You're sifting and drifting, floating and boating, falling through your body to a sublevel of Lethe you've never visited. Yes, I can sense that darn cat sinking into me, intermolecularizing with my very blood and being—

Roland! Paige's voice calls me back, but not for long. G. K. doesn't pause, either with his paws or his bronchial purring, which soothes because its volume overwhelms me, so that the deeper he digs the deeper into his nerve-laving la-la-land I slide. How comforting the persistent background hum. How gravity-free my down-trending self. How impenetrable the foggy veils of ganglia through which I grope or fall.

Down, down, down. Glide, slide, glide.

The fog's edges grow darker as my id pushes into the vast gray grotto where my needs become another's and the night sluices away my identifying dross—

Roland!

Who can hear the siren? And who do you hope to be when you've stalked to the bottom of Grimalkin's well and that filmy notional curtain drops behind you—?

My eyes flicker open. I have a much higher vantage. I don't feel myself. At all. I feel *better* . . . but some aspects of my vision—its acuity in the interior twilight—have dulled in the past few minutes. No stentorian purring assails me. In fact, the strains of Cassandra's vocals lick sweetly where recently a magnificent purr held sway. A weight depresses me, though, one that my freshly alert state guides me to call *dead*. This weight's inertia, the end of a need to rub my knees, confirms the aptness of that word: *dead*.

Paige, fetching in a black dress, casts her shadow over my recliner. A fond sound tries to form in my throat, unsuccessfully. A look of alarm shines upon her face, and she reaches toward me tentatively, alarming me too.

Puh, I say. *Paige*. I deserve kudos for framing that syllable, but I earn none. Her fingers touch my middle, my *new* middle, and linger, stroking.

Roland, what did you do?

I b-b-beg your pardon, I say, with difficulty.

"Something's happened to G. K. What did you do?"

"Fell asleep. Just f-f-fell asleep. He put m-me to sleep, clenching and unclenching his claws, and p-p-purring."

Paige lifts the weight from me and holds it before her in both hands. Its grey-and-white bulk hangs before her like an obese *beaver* still in its pelt, a limp organic pendulum. I love this woman. I must act now with more than human cunning.

I d-didn't k-k-kill him, I say. I just k-kept him c-c-company whilst he p-purred.

Paige squints into poor Grimalkin's face, which I can't see. He's not quite dead, she says. His eyes just flickered. He's breathing faint fishy breaths.

Paige, he's s-seventeen, and he's had a str-str-stroke.

She sets the feline body back into my lap, gently. How do you know *that*?

It st-stands to r-reason. I stroke the alleged stroke victim as Paige sets him down.

Not the stroke diagnosis. Roland. His age.

D-Didn't you t-t-tell me?

I'd tell my cat's age no sooner than I'd tell mine.

Then I g-guess I g-guessed. She regards me skeptically while our hands jointly pet the oblivious cat. Anyway, Paige, he'll never fully recover. He's m-much too old, and the stroke, going b-b-by his limpness, hit him h-h-hard.

She stops petting G. K. and takes my chin between her fingers.

I've never heard you stammer. What's going on?

I try to speak clearly: I'm upset. I love old Gilbert Keith as much as you d-do.

Paige, kneeling by the lounger, evinces a sad but radiant smile. You must. You checked out what his initials stand for. She strokes my cheek. Now what? she says, widening her eyes.

Think of the kindest solution you c-c-can, I say.

Sleep, I suppose. Euthanasia.

Yes.

It's Saturday evening. No vet on call. We can't wait till Monday, Roland.

Her inclusive *we* sounds propitious.

I have a p-p-pal, Paige, an amateur entomologist who has chloroform at h-home. We could take G. K. there.

How far is it?

The northern suburbs.

She objects to taking G. K. into the October cold, to having him die somewhere other than her apartment. Given his neo-comatose state, I could put him to sleep in minutes by pinching his nostrils until he painlessly, *virtually* painlessly, expires. Paige recoils from this suggestion. I refrain from pushing it, but do point out that she could sit with her palm on G. K.'s head, as his nurse and keeper, until such time as a final shudder signals his demise.

She lays her face against the imposter's back to consider this proposal, and I exert my frail male will, my frail male *human* will, to maintain a modicum of bodily decorum. Although chronologically older than a few moments ago,

I am again a prime procreative specimen. Paige looks up.

What you must do, she says, do quickly.

I lean forward, kiss her forehead, and obey.

As I do, a great purr gathers in my chest. I suppress it, knowing that I won't have to do it long, for with my love of loves I've embarked upon my tenth and most promising life.

—for our son Jamie, on whose notes this story is based

MIRIAM

On the night of the blessed infant's coming, things got complicated. Miriam felt her fetus lodged athwart her birth canal: prelude to a disaster of which the archangel had given no warning. *Don't be afraid*, he'd told her, *for you've found favor with God.* She had no certainty of that favor now.

"The baby comes cross-wise!" Despite the awkwardness of his hands, Yosef turned it slightly and so brought it forth. Yeshua, or The Lord Will Save, came forth dead, mocking the name that Gabriel had told her to bestow upon it. Now Herod would have no call to massacre all the male babes in this donkey-run village.

Yosef placed the blue child on a stone beside the straw on which Miriam still lay twisted. He beheld it with resentment and wonder, then put a hand to his chest and opened his mouth like a suffocating fish. Then, eyes bulging, he toppled to the cavern's uneven floor.

"*Yosef!*" Miriam cried. And: "*Yeshua, my Yeshua!*"

A bald villager named Gideon took pity and saw to the old man's burial and that of the stillborn Son of God. He sold the spavined animal that had carried her to this place and found her a small room in the crowded caravansary. Too late, thought Miriam. Too late.

Gideon fed her figs and bread, and in three days she tried to join some Galileans who had heeded the Quirinian census on the road back to Nazareth. Men looked askance and women muttered behind their hands. Because she had no protector, she often overheard the name *Jezebel* or the epithet *whore*.

Again, Gideon rescued her. On a tall whey-colored horse he returned Miriam to the hill cave in which Yosef and Yeshua had died. What did he want? Her heart misgave her. But if Gideon hoped to rape or murder her, she would tear at him like a wounded dog.

But in the cave he expanded and glowed, without growing larger or brighter, and Miriam recognized him as Gabriel, the angel who had erroneously announced the advent of her lost son and a mysterious unending kingdom. His voice, when next he spoke, twinned or tripled so that he sounded like a small choir:

Rejoice, Miriam, for you among women are most favored and blessed. The Lord stands with you, His might a cloak about your shoulders.

"No," said Miriam. "Tell him to get somebody else."

Gideon, or rather Gabriel, dimmed a little. *Hear me, child. I bring good tidings from the Highest.*

"No. I gave my all. It didn't work. Why would God wish me to suffer nine more months of doomed hope and another fruitless labor?"

Miriam, hush and obey.

"God or demon, He has no right. If He wants his Son to wear the suffering flesh of a mortal, let some other suffering mortal do His work: a woman whose womb will release, not strangle, His beloved get."

You misapprehend the Lord God's new design.

"Why did His first design go awry? Did I anger Him somehow?"

No, no. Satan pranked your womb. Now the Highest must answer.

"By making me His cow again? Why not undo that heartbreaking prank and let His little Son live?"

Gabriel raised his arms, which now bore snow-white and indigo plumage, and thereby threw her into shadow.

Enough. The Lord God wishes to anoint and transfigure you, Miriam. He no longer wishes you to bear His Son, but to step forth from this cave His only inspirited Daughter, the Messiah of this age and all the following.

Miriam's breath stopped . . . but eventually began again.

And the brief career of Miriam Messiah had no parallel. Biding her young womanhood in Nazareth, apprenticing as a weaver, she fabricated garments of such perfection that teachers and magistrates alike clamored for them. She traded for lessons with the rabbis and for dispensations from public officials for starving neighbors, but showed no more preference for the rich than for tax gatherers or shepherds.

At length, after increasing in learning, wisdom, and stature, she left her master weaver to proclaim to Galilee and Judea the kingdom of heaven. From as many trades, denominations, and peoples as would hear, she called disciples, both women and men, always with the suspicion that she was not only shadowing her stillborn Son but also extending His lost ministry. She provoked resentment among the hidebound and hostility among the powerful by disputing with the learned outside synagogues and, once, in a court welcoming to women near the Temple. She made bad wine sweet, broken bodies whole, and a host of frenzied minds serene.

Hecklers—Jew, Roman, Samaritan—she disarmed with sage and gentle words. Homilies and epigrams, she dispensed with the skill of a venerable apothecary. Demons she cast out with the ferocity of a God-fueled warrior. Healings she administered freely to almost anyone. The arrogant, avaricious, and cruel she rebuked with authority but also with tenderness. The pious, smug, and hypocritical she shoved to the walls of their delusions and asked them questions that stripped them of the virtues they thought theirs by birthright or seizure. And so they accused her of slander, blasphemy, unnatural acts with her bemused disciples.

"I am Daughter of Wisdom," she said, "Queen of Nations, Mother of Faith, Sister of Spirit and Peace. Whosoever would know the Most High's heart need but wrap herself in a robe of my weaving and live within it as if within her own skin. We are fearfully, intricately shaped in Sophia's womb and emerge from it primed to glorify both Her and Her all-embracing Partner, El Shaddai."

These sayings and others enraged Pharisees, Levites, and teachers of the Law. Just as talk of her as Israel's Consolation and of a strange coming kingdom unsettled the Roman colonizers; and an advisor to the Emperor warned the procurator of Judea to help the Jews suppress this untoward female abomination and threat. Then Dorcas betrayed her, and Miriam was seized, tried, convicted, scourged, and harried along the Via Dolorosa to a destiny that flickered in her awareness like that of a Son she'd never fully known.

Dorcas fled with her silver, but Jew and Roman alike agreed that the heretical Miriamist movement required a quick joint response. During Miriam's trial, they arrested and sentenced to death many of her disciples, even picking out eleven women to die with her on Golgotha, the Mount of Skulls. This seemed just, given the women's defiance of traditional proprieties and strictures and their maddening loyalty to Miriam. No mild insurrection, it summoned a harsh rebuttal, and neither the procurator nor the high priest had any qualms about crucifying eleven women with her: the Romans made few gender distinctions when punishing slaves or foreigners, and once, at Ashkelon, a ruler named Simeon ben Shetah had ordered over seventy sorceresses nailed up for their presumption and apostasy.

So, Miriam staggered out of the city behind the black Cyrenian carrying her cross. Much of her hair had been snatched away, and blood had dried on her countless stripes like holly-berry husks. She looked up.

On the small dome of Golgotha, a forest of crosses thrust skyward in double rings about its apex. From each cross hung a woman who had accompanied Miriam during the nearly three years of her God-sparked evangelism, but she could not easily identify them because the soldiers, at the behest of Hebrew priests, had affixed them to their crosses face-first, out of some warped notion of executionary decency.

Still, Miriam knew their names: Abigail, Bilhah, Chloe, the twins Dinah and Rachel, Esther the Matriarch, Merab, Naomi, Shunamite, Zilpah, and Esther the Maid: all dying for her and the Sisterhood of Heaven.

To her cross, the soldiers nailed Miriam facing front and naked but for a blood-streaked loincloth. They'd lifted her stake at the top of Skull Mount, the highest tree in a glade of such palings, and they diced not for her garments, a woman's contemptible things, but for the right to break her legs and to expose her totally once she had died. Further, a society of Jewish women, none Miriam's followers, prowled the uneven slopes offering drugged wine to the sufferers, but Miriam refused this kindness and her crucified disciples were not positioned to receive it, so at length, alternately laughing and cursing, the soldiers chased these sad do-gooders down the hill and back into the city.

"Father-Mother," murmured Miriam, "why have You forsaken us?"

But One was resurrected; and Dorcas, in lifelong atonement for her betrayal, traveled and preached and healed and wrote, so that, eventually, Miriamism overcame the world, and much in the world that was stupid, arbitrary, and cruel inevitably, gradually, lost its foothold.

NO APPETITE FOR COMMUNION

Dropping to her knees between Mama and brother Brent, Dotty realized she had no appetite for communion. Her hands formed a palms-up cross so that Reverend Hart, moving along the rail in robe and stole, could lay the Host into her palm and say, *"This is my Body, broken for you,"* but Dotty felt cramped both by her fellow communicants and the obligation of taking her Savior's sacrifice as bread. As food.

Nausea roiled in her like bath water circling a drain.

Ushers had once directed fifteen or sixteen persons to the rail, where they comfortably awaited the elements, and from which they arose without cracking the rail, even if they used it for leverage to stand, but now ushers counting off more than twelve had no concept of the altar's length or the bulk of their congregants. Indeed, whoever had sent Mama, Brent, and Dotty up had so poorly estimated the space necessary for today's communicants that a small fifteen-year-old girl, Dotty herself, felt like the runt in a litter of enormous piglets. Well, that was an uncharitable thought, even if a glance behind Mama and another behind Brent confirmed its aptness, so Dotty fisted her hands, depriving her pastor of a place to put her bread.

"Dotty," he whispered, "do you wish to receive today?"

She shook her head, aware of Mama's sidelong gaze and Brent's gulp of disbelief, or maybe admiration. After a rustle of vestments, Reverend Hart tore off a crust for Mama and moved on.

At home, Mama tore into her: What did Dotty mean, mortifying her so? What kind of example did her behavior set for Brent? Mama had never been so ashamed at a worship service or *any*where. Tactfully, Dotty did not say that Mama's gluttony at covered-dish dinners and her kamikaze attacks on the Golden Corral buffet were surely as worthy of shame as Dotty's own declination of

Christ's body and blood at the rail.

Instead, she said, "Hunger strike. I'm on one."

"Why?" Mama asked, and Dotty said, "For the starving people in the Sudan." On the evening news, she'd seen skeletal black kids and emaciated women in colorful robes squatting in camps, bereft of hope, flies sipping at their eyes and nostrils. Maybe those images, which Mama had also taken in, would prompt her to connect Dotty's scruples today to her loathing of so much self-indulgent Christian flab.

Brent, only eleven, said, "The bread and juice don't count as *actual food*. They're *soul food*. You should've taken them."

As she'd done at the altar, Dotty shook her head. Folks out of harmony with neighbors and family couldn't accept the elements, and the immoderation of other congregants, including Mama and Brent, disgusted her. They lived to eat instead of . . . well, vice versa.

Dotty decided not to eat at all until Mama, Brent, and some other over-stuffed church members realized that her outrage at the calamity in Darfur had a homegrown equivalent in the gluttony all about her. She couldn't say that, of course, because Mama'd smack her, Brent would sulk, and other folks would deride her as a stuck-up little bigot.

People who dissed the *weight challenged*—never say *fatty* unless you wanted a crippling body bump in gym class—were as bad as race baiters, anti-Semites, and male-chauvinist swine. Even Dotty believed that, but sometimes the helpless ire of the natural-born skinny person whose space a person of larger dimensions has invaded rose up in her unbidden and she *snapped,* or, at least, collapsed in on herself, finding her wells of charity vinegar-tainted and her live-and-let-live reservoir drained toward empty.

That evening, as a provocation, Mama made lasagna in a deep metal pan. Then she and Brent chowed down as Dotty looked on, a glass of water at her elbow, her lips set in a moue of defiant saintliness.

Mama said, "Holier-than-thou nitwit!" Brent made crude lip-smacking noises, and even the cat got mozzarella-laden noodle scraps, over which it purred like a miniature jet engine. Temptation didn't storm Dotty's defenses though, and on Monday she avoided both breakfast and an inevitable spat with Mama, who left to clerk at Buy-&-Bolt twenty minutes before Dotty entered the kitchen.

During lunch at school, Dotty worked on a research paper in the media center, where she ignored her queasy gut by focusing on a website devoted to reindeer herders in Lapland. That afternoon, she purchased some Gatorade at the IGA—drink was okay on a hunger strike, wasn't it?—and cautiously sipped it perched on the window ledge of the laundromat across the street. She didn't go home for dinner at all, but caught hell from Mama when, dizzy, she wandered in around eight and dropped to the settee to watch a moronic reality show.

"You missed the news," Brent said. "You've been on a hunger strike for thirty-two hours, but those folks in Sudan are *still* starving to death."

"I know that!"

"You're just going to add one more to their number. For what?"

Dotty eyed Brent, thinking: It would hardly hurt *you* to miss a freaking *month's* worth of meals.

"Maybe you could yank three or four boxes of Chips Ahoy out of that locker in your room and send them over. You'd survive their loss just fine."

Sweetly reasonable, Brent said, "A hunger strike makes no sense if you don't tell anyone about it."

"You and Mama know, and it makes bushels of *spiritual* sense even if nobody else knows or cares but God."

Dotty lived on water, Sprite, Spearmint gum, fantasies of murdering the media-center Balloon People (as she called two chubby kids working there) for reminding her each day of the Flabbifying of America, and on midnight dreams of food, glorious food, please, sir, could I have a ton? But as her strength dwindled, she stopped watching, reading, or talking about the news from Darfur, a nightmare land in a death-haunted fairy tale. And one evening, frail as straw, she pulled on an old purple shawl of her mother's, looked into a mirror, and beheld the pale ghost of a grim Sudanese woman.

Mama begged and threatened. One night, Dotty awoke to find the nozzle of a turkey baster in her mouth, and Mama struggling to squeeze a milkshake fortified with raw egg into her. Dotty spewed it out, knocking Mama aside, and fled to the bathroom, where for seven minutes she vomited air and bile.

Stretched out supine on the floor, she prayed for deliverance. Brent shouldered the door in. Then he and Mama knelt and laid hands on Dotty, to pray with, for, and against her. Feeling her soul detach, she panicked, for she really had no wish to die.

The next morning, she ate. A soft-boiled egg, a few dry Cheerios. Later, white rice, a spoonful of egg custard, a cup of sweetened tea. Later still, scraped toast, an apple slice, banana pudding, and, yes, some hazelnut-flavored coffee. Mama beamed, from beam to beam.

Dotty recovered.

In less than two weeks, she looked healthier than she had before her quasi-secret hunger strike. She befriended the weight-challenged people in the media center, advised Brent about a Social Studies paper, and twice cooked her family's supper.

At her first church service after her strike though, Dotty closed her hands when Reverend Hart approached. She would not, could not, receive the elements. She had her reasons, reasons different from last time, but even if nobody else understood why she lacked the slightest appetite for communion, well, God surely would.

THE LIBRARY OF BABBLE

More by accident than by design, I took my twelve-year-old son to the Library of Inescapable Cacophony, which some call the Library of Babble (an off-key tribute to a late literary blind man). But our field trip proved helpful, instructive, to us both, even if I could not have foreseen that outcome before our visit.

My wife Libretta and I had named our son Palabro to heighten whatever verbal skills our DNA had provided him, but he had just shamed himself during a music program at his school. Although only the narrator, at one sensitive point he pulled a yam-shaped ocarina from his jacket and blew three notes so piercing that the lenses of Head Mistress Adoba's bifocals broke and two chorus members suffered burst eardrums. Earlier that week, these same female students had said no to Palabro's efforts to enlist them in an ocarina trio, so I admired, to *my* discredit, the skill with which he'd directed these retributive notes.

No one, a friend of Palabro's later testified, had ever before heard an ocarina produce such knifelike piquancy. Sadly, though, Señora Adoba called me from my labors at the Institute of Document Purification to escort Palabro home and discipline him. She was too distraught to do it herself, and Libretta could not do it because she had flown to the capitol to work on an epic opera about the life of the supreme maestra of Enigma del Sur, Angelina Puig-Otálora, who grew to adulthood here in Adivinanza, second largest city in our small homeland. My punishment of the boy, I confess, consisted of haranguing him about the importance of the editorial work from which his misdeed had called me and of taking him to La Casa Rosita for a lunch of yam fritters and marmalade-basted flounder. (That would teach him.)

After we'd eaten, we strolled to the greensward on which the Library of Inescapable Cacophony sits, a swatch of land where, a year ago, skinny POWs from Guacamayo tried out radical soccer strategies under the eyes of our Olympic coach, Robert Hansen, an ex-patriot Swede. The Library, which Señora Angelina meant to rebuke those institutions whose inhibiting **SILENCIO** signs had plagued her girlhood, startles me every time I see it, as would any structure whose design suggests a fusion of the Sydney Opera House and the coppery bells of three huge Sousaphones.

The fame of this facility has spread from little Enigma del Sur throughout Latin America (and beyond), but no one in our culture-loving family, despite Palabro's many pleas to take him, had yet visited it. Libretta's work keeps her away from Adivinanza for months on end, and, frankly, I feared what I would find there.

What I feared, I feared with reason.

The Library of Babble always validates the aptness of its name, with flashing signs requesting **NOISE,** for the colored bulbs around these signs sound strident xylophonic notes in dissonant runs, and exuberant human noisemakers stand on pedestals, pose in galleries, or play on stair landings. These folks include woodblock ensembles, dueling typists, and masked persons in tinfoil suits running about with petrol-powered leaf blowers.

This never-ending din occludes thought, invading the aural cavities and flushing from them all the lees of coherency or serenity. One's blood pressure soars. Migraines and a menacing sense of intellectual bankruptcy flood one's being. The impulse to flee from overlapping dins, to press one's skull between one's palms and scream like the anguished figure in Edvard Munch's famous painting assumes the weight of obligation. It never departs.

Palabro, I tell my son. We must go.

He seizes my wrist. No, Papá, no.

In rapid succession, he nods at a tuba player turning a passage from *Don Quixote* into flatulent *oom-pah-pahs*; a woman in a blue bikini using a jackhammer on the fifth-floor gallery to dislodge a wavery fall of marble dust; a Masai warrior and a ventriloquist figure of a baby baboon crooning a "duet" of "Bésame Mucho" in two distinct voices; a foursome of New York gang-bangers tap-dancing on garbage cans that they wear as shoes; and a pig, which a matron with a bonfire of red hair holds like a bagpipe, squealing "Amazing Grace" to the prompts of her syncopated squeezes. That I can *hear* such distinct rackety phenomena at all derives, I suppose, from the focus I've learned as an editor at the Institute of Document Purification.

Ecstatic, Palabro shouts, Why, Papá, have you never brought me here before? Why, I ask myself, have I brought you today?

We head into the stacks at my instigation, for I hope the banks of shelves and their books and periodicals will act as baffles and thus spare me a debilitating, largely premature, deafness. It takes only moments to realize, however, that every book in this Library talks—indeed, *babbles*—and that I can't escape amid the stacks or, for that matter, anywhere else inside.

Palabro, bless him, expects fresh wonders in the stacks: self-propelled whistling stools; shelves that reposition themselves at a button push; wandering librarians who yodel, belch, or crepitate. Now, of course, Palabro believes that he should get disciplined more often. The stacks have an annoying volubility that calls to the boy. He pulls out a book, cracks its open, and averts his face as a cardboard bandstand pops out and Slavic voices braying the lyrics of two-hundred-year-old polkas vie with the bleats, moos, and neighs issuing from a nearby mis-shelved tome on animal husbandry.

Proctors in caps and bells sidle past prattling a gibberish in which they urge us (as we interpret their gestures) to add to the sonic pandemonium. They pantomime "gargling air." They cramp their hands in their armpits, whistle the themes of such Westerns as *She Wore a Yellow Ribbon* and *The Good, the Bad, and the Ugly*, loudly rebuke silent patrons, and give the most reticent mutes noisemakers: juice harps, tissue paper and combs, maracas, castanets, inflatable paper tongues that, when blown, unroll like tiny royal carpets.

This is maravilloso! Palabro yells.

This, I think, is hell on Earth.

My head is the size of a weather balloon. Stray phonemes ricochet inside my skull like rapid particles of sleet or cholesterol. So far beneath the innate dignity of my age and station has all this demonic noise driven me that soon I will drop gibbering to my knees, like a teenybopper at a concert of iconic rock holograms.

Palabro! I bark. Enough! I can take no more!

At which point the hands of a ghostly marble Angel grasp my shoulders, and a glassy dome or bell descends over my torso, seals about my waist, and hovers in the aisle for a timeless moment that discloses Palabro frozen before me like his own picture-perfect effigy. Inside this dome with me, the Angel announces: Fulgencio, the Library of Babble has a purpose other than to enmadden you. Do you believe this?

Sí, I say. *No*, I correct myself. *Ai, ai, ai*, I wail in indescribable pain: a scarab in a bell jar dense with chloroform and hundreds of jangly echoes.

The world teems, the Angel tells me. It bulges not only with objects but also with their noises. The Library of Babble, like every other such institution, is a training ground. Do you follow me?

I do, I lie.

The Angel, the image of Angelina Puig-Otálora, vanishes. The dome rises. And Palabro awakes into his resilient self, shaking the maracas of his fists like a self-absorbed pop star. I understand *nada,* or maybe a bit more than *nada:* that the Library of Maestra Puig-Otálora is something smaller than a late payback but larger than an angry little girl's joke.

Heedless, delirious, Palabro drags me from the stacks to meeting rooms in a separate wing. We see a Poetry Slam, where people with mynah-bird puppets turn their own muteness into Joyful Noise. They rhyme in Finnish, Swahili, Esperanto, or Penguin. Also in Tagalog, Basque, Tamil, Lakota, Mongolian, or Bushman clicks reminiscent of the sounds of the Library's ubiquitous typing-pool.

We visit a Mock Oratory where people mock-pray and a Mock Parliament where people mock-debate, at intolerable volume levels and ecstatic cross purposes. In a Music Room we play every kind of drum, electrified bagpipe, trumpet, trombone, flugelhorn, flute, dulcimer, guitar, sitar, banjo, and nail gun. Meanwhile, my hearing deteriorates.

Now, each noise wheels over me like hurricane surf or the brushfires of holocaust. Even our son will not escape our visit unscathed. A boy's ears demand tender treatment, for nothing larger than an elbow, or a jillion decibels, should ever cave-crawl their canals. At length, I point to *my* ears and, by miming a five-seconds-into-the-future flop to the ground, demonstrate to him that I can take no more. My body will buzz with fuzzy internal hums for weeks. He not only sees what I have mimed, he *empathizes*, puts his arm through mine, takes me to the door of the Library of Babble, and guides me down the Maya-temple-like grade of its endless front steps.

Gracias, hijo mío, I tell him. *Muchísimas gracias.*

De nada, Papá.

I forgive him for breaking Señora Adoba's bifocals and discomfiting the eardrums of two haughty but otherwise innocent girls who would not join his ocarina trio. (Libretta will scold him more severely later.)

Exiting the Library, I find that little of the noise inside the structure seeps out into the plaza. Yes, a low persistent drone hovers about, a sound more like that of a small air-conditioner than a relentless clatter of pots, pans, and colanders.

This discovery heartens me.

I know a secret, Palabro says, squeezing my hand.

No fair to say so but fail to tell.

The Library of Babble isn't equal to the universe, Papá.

I never thought it was.

All the Libraries of Inescapable Cacophony in Enigma del Sur, my boy proclaims, fail to equal our universe. Nor, Papá, do they correspond to any abutting universe.

Ah.

So, we may visit the Library of Adivinanza with no fear of entering a closed labyrinth.

How has one trip to this Racket Pit taught you so much?

Palabro grins. Rather than answer, he tugs me toward a pond far enough from the plaza that Silence fills the afternoon like fragile unscored music.

We sit on an iron bench near the pond.

In it lolls a ten-foot alligator of bronze and leather. In it, also, stands a red-winged heron on a single wiry leg. A cyclone of midges hovers above the shallows, and the insurgent Silence of this spot recharges my heart.

Bless you, I tell Palabro.

He produces his ocarina.

I recoil, but he puts it to his lips and coaxes from the yam-like flute a melody so fair—a medieval plainsong? a folk ballad of Enigma del Sur? an air from the summer in his soul—that it tastes like ripe oranges and soothes like a peaceful breeze.

Indeed, through his ocarina come Palabro's vivid breaths and the notes of God's harmonium. How long my young son plays I cannot tell you, but not even Pan himself pipes more hauntingly.

Tomorrow when I report for my duties, before I turn to any other task, I will purify *this* document.

—for our son Jamie, on whose notes this story is based

PHILIP K. DICK IS DEAD, A LASS

with dark hair said. Her tears flowed wholesale,
remember? Phil wrote like a relentless dentist,
drilling the pocked enamel of reality to expose
its beautiful decay. Midway through the wood
he popped fish-shaped paranoia pills, chewed
the holy fat of messianic redemption, & chased
the godly lot with pot after pot of hot black
coffee, all of it decanted from percolators whoop-
whoop-whooping their projective derangements. Beer
furred his tongue. Mars floated mauve in his
eyeballs. The smell of ozone-depleting aerosols

wafted from his armpits, ubiquitously. When Anwar
Sadat died, he scarred himself with a can of Orange
Crush in spontaneous homage. He took courage
when Linda Ronstadt sang "Different Drum" & no
bleak umbrage if a buddy crooned, *"Una cosa me da
risa—Pancho Villa sin camisa."* He was fully sane
in Berkeley, Fullerton, & Santa Ana. He was crazy
in California. Kafka had nothing on either Philip
K. or the latest demented broadcast from Radio Free
Albemuth. (Oh, to be a Blobel!) If he wakes as
a Brobdignagian beefsteak tomato to orbit Papa,
an angrily expanding sun, take cover. "Not 'rekal'

but recall," the receptionist corrects him. He
readies himself for Papa's apotheosis with a jolt
of Nov(a)cain. He essayed suicide because Elijah
left him. *"There is nothing worse in the world,*
no punishment greater, than to have known God
and no longer to know him." To eulogize Phil
properly, recall from the post-apocalyptic junkyard
a menagerie of maimed automata—ersatz sheep, a robot
German shepherd, a naggish simulacrum of Secretariat—
and a crew of pertinacious little people, from Lumky

to Isidore to Tagomi, then set them singing until
they entropically abort. As calm as caffeine, Phil
fled aboard a talking taxi to Sri Lanka, suffered
in remainderdom, elbowed Norman Mailer for a side
of macaroni, was rediscovered, restored to print,
cultified, read, reread, & queried. If we want
him to digest it, we'll have to eat his celebrity
for him. The ambulance that hauled him to hospital
babbled beneath its wailing like his long-dead baby
sister while a blue-zillion rusty percolators whooped
in aromatic chorus for the conveyance of his soul.

—for Phil, dead on March 2, 1982

CH-CH-CH-CHANGES

i. All Saint's Eve in Tokyo

Eleven-year-old *Big D* had four years on me, and I wanted his approval. I joined his trick-or-treat posse in the American housing enclave there in Tokyo.

He and his same-age pals wore cowboy outfits and packed low-slung six-shooters, as did I. Instead of a red bandana, though, Big D sported a flamboyant polka-dot bowtie. I grabbed his shirt and showed him my scrawled hold-up note:

"Give me all you Babby Rooths."

"It's 'your,' not 'you,'" he said. "And *Babby Rooths* make me puke."

But he let me tag along and later allotted me a generous lot of our Halloween haul.

ii. A Lesson outside Seville

You next meet him in a dependent high school outside Seville, Spain, in your art class, where everyone calls him *Degas* for his depictions of ballet dancers and racehorses. Despite this nickname, he eschews that artist's colorful palette for sketches in various shades of blue, using pencil lead or chalk.

Mrs. Clytemnestra Samaras, your art teacher, likes Degas so much that she makes him class monitor, almost an instructor's aide. You, and others, assume that she esteems his suave looks and gaudy lavender scarf as much as she does his sketches, but you still don't much mind that. After bringing in a pewter stein of blue pencils, he ceases to apply himself so obviously to his own art and goes from table to table correcting your and your classmates' efforts.

"Rub out this grackle," he says of one of your studies, making a blue mark beside the ugly bird.

"Rub it out?"

"If you agree, I mean."

"And then what?"

Degas makes a blue check elsewhere. "Put a peacock in full display here. You'll create balance and more interest."

After brief doubt, you do as he says, and your peacock stares out at the onlooker with an oblique enchanting ferocity.

iii. Renovations in Chautauqua

Dai had always wanted his own house, perhaps one that he built himself from the ground up, but not necessarily. After all, he'd built many structures in the past, either storage sheds or warehouses, each with its own purposes and symmetries, its own architectural eloquences and enduring specific satisfactions. Even the neighbors in nearby dwellings had noticed and lauded these efforts, either after standing at their doors and peering in or during intensive guided tours of their open or labyrinthine premises.

He had a knack for visualizing a full-grown red maple from the imaginary winged seed cradling it, and he could share this vision with others through such basic but vital tasks as spading, manuring, watering, and pruning: the essential down-and-dirty work of cultivation.

Still, he wanted his own house, not a metaphorical tree for gilded nightingales to croon in, but a dwelling that would shelter, nurture, and solace him, a retreat for the body, intellect, and spirit. He found such a habitation in Chautauqua, New York, already intact but in welcome need of renovations that would reshape it according to the dictates of his unique desires. Where some builders would have used gypsum board or oak, he used clothbound books and manuscripts of antique linen-based paper. Where some decorators would have used caladiums or ferns, he used woodcuts from books or shiny dust jackets, stripped out or off, and twisted into origami fans and foliage uncannily akin to flourishing plants.

Thus, Dai tore out the stairs going from the foyer to his second-floor study and replaced them with steps made of encyclopedia volumes, sets of the complete works of Seneca, Dante, Shakespeare, and Stapledon, and multivolume indices to all the science fiction magazines printed before the advent of electronic periodicals and eBooks. These had solidity. A person could stand upon them. Or a person could kneel on them, unlatch a higher step, and peruse at sweet leisure an alternate metaphysics and the secret mechanics of metamorphosis.

For these reasons, Dai lived on the stairs, which seemed to him beaches, steppes, terraces, foothills, mesas, and mountaintops all at once. They lifted him up. They ferried him down. They grounded his every climb and every descent. One day, he would discard them for a chair-lift, an elevator cage, or a swami's lariat, as the spirit led, for in this old house he and only he decreed every change of needful validity.

iv. Enraged Red Octopi on Mars

Moist tentacle-bearing red aliens of daunting height and strength fell upon Mars because they liked its climate and camouflaging dust.

Its surgically adapted human colonists at first meant little to the invaders because their shelters were hidden crevice dwellings indistinguishable from the terrain, and because the bipedal settlers gave off so little heat or luminescence that the octopi (a stupid but inevitable name for them, even if they had only seven appendages) couldn't detect them with their bio-mechanical alien-specific sensors. Only when actively roaming the scarlet planet's surface did these ETs finally realize they weren't alone: an outrage that ramped up their ire and led to the first earthling-octopus skirmishes leading to all-out war.

DiCorso, the colonists' foremost surgeon, had equipped his people with gill-like slits for filtering the Martian air and with lungs as large as industrial bellows to distil and distribute its oxygen throughout the settlers' systems. A few other doctors aided DiCorso, who specialized in those cases requiring greater diagnostic expertise and surgical skill, until *all* of them had to treat laser burns and/or sucker-inflicted hickeys that only the most hardened physicians could consider without revulsion and utter self-dissociation from their victims.

Even DiCorso, who often saw to suction-cupped patients, would return to his rock hovel seeing phantom victims but glad for his lack of appetite. Sadly, the longer the octopi stayed on Mars the more attuned they grew to human spoor and the more adept at tracking down, flushing out, battling with, and hurting the gone-to-ground settlers.

Finally, a battle on the foothill slopes of Olympus Mons, the tallest and largest volcanic peak in the Sol system, ensued, mainly because so many of the colonists' warrens honeycombed these foothills and had seemed to afford such reliable shelter from dust storms, meteor showers, and every other imaginable disaster, except perhaps titanic eruptions of the dormant volcano and epic floods of magma, lava, and other superheated igneous slurries. After all, Olympus Mons had not been active for millennia, and no one could have foreseen the advent of these land-crawling cephalopods of colossal physique and hateful disposition.

Anyway, on this peak the enraged red octopi took the offensive, not with the laser tubes, now exhausted, that they had initially used but with rocks that they snatched from the ground and hurled with devastating accuracy into the settlers' hidey-holes. The aliens projected these rocks like David, or like Dizzy Dean, Rapid Robert Feller, Warren Spahn, Sandy Koufax, Bob Gibson, Juan Marichel, Tom Seaver, Greg Maddux, Randy Johnson, or even Reezy Faludin (the all-time strikeout king of the first Interplanetary League), except that every cephalopod warrior seemed to channel each of these storied human cowhide hurlers in its seven-limbed body and Mars' thin air offered minimal resistance to their dumbfounding pitches.

These pitches enlarged the settlers' burrows and ricocheted about inside them like spit-spun shrapnel, meanwhile beheading, disemboweling, or delimbing the crevices' squatters, who fought back with plasma hoses that bowled over and quasi-fricasseed many of their assailants. At the end of that bleak day, hostilities ceased (mysteriously, unless outright fatigue and despairing nausea had interposed), and DiCorso ventured from his unscathed lair to assess the damage to friends and foes alike. He took a giant breath and scrutinized the landscape. Many wounded colonists had left their dens and sprawled about in various states of impact trauma, including dismemberment and, if yet alive, psychic brokenness. The octopi lying on the slope had fared little better, resembling mutant boiled tomatoes or large copulating polyps in a burnt marinara sauce. The dead required burial and the living treatment.

Able if bemused settlers emerged to help, and DiCorso instituted a program of triage for *all* combatants. He organized grave-digging teams. Other human techs pushed halogen trees about the battlefield to throw light upon it, and DiCorso got busy. He used lots of anodynes, mastics, and reels of invisible nylon fishing line to treat both his human and his cephalopod patients. Despite unalloyed looks of disgust or horror, he employed detached alien tentacles as surrogates for human limbs, and vice versa. And, at the end of that Martian night, he did litter checks on his surviving patients and pronounced them fit for additional future living . . . if the goddamned octopi would only take their antagonism in tentacle, so to speak, and convert it into unmitigated amity.

A gigantic wounded cephalopod spidered up the hillside and grinned problematically at DiCorso. "Your name for us isn't our name," it squeaked in an accented brogue. "But even in your barbaric tongue, the proper plural for us isn't *octopi*, but *octopuses* or *octopodes*, the latter of which derives from the Greek *oktō*, 'eight,' plus *pous* or *pod-*, 'foot.'"

"Thank you for that helpful redaction," DiCorso said, and he and the cephalopod shook hands and shook hands and

v. Adventures in Time and Space

an author with whom *Dai* had been working at Simon & Schuster flew in from Atlanta, Georgia, at the publisher's expense, to reside with Dai in his house in Chautauqua, New York, while they took the visitor's manuscript in hand (in the early 1980s, many literary persons still used typewriters to compose their works) and turned it this way and then that to see how to best hew from it a commercially viable novel.

M——, a writer with four other flawed books behind him, settled into the guestroom but soon emerged for a tour of Dai's house. The stairway of books that M—— had seen in passing but not scrupulously examined now captured his full attention. He marveled at its construction, its constituent "bricks" (in reality, books with latches that one could flip to access their contents), and the rarity of many of the volumes neatly arranged within it.

Dai watched as M—— opened a copy of the American hardcover edition of J. G. Ballard's *The Atrocity Exhibition*, a printing that the outraged publisher had had pulped in its presumed entirety rather than release to the world to his company's imagined eternal scandal. (Later, another firm issued it as *Love and Napalm: Export USA.*)

"Incredible," M—— said.

"I call that one a wonder," Dai said. "A wonder it survived at all."

Dai led M—— into the kitchen, opened the box holding his fifth novel, and set it out on the table in piles of several chapters each. Its story alternated between chapters in the present and others in the past, with a coda set in the future, but Dai didn't think that the arrangement of these chapters worked as well as it might, and he had stuck tabs on them so that he and M—— could juxtapose them in ways lending greater urgency to M——'s storytelling.

Reordering the chapters proved time- and space-consuming. Both men wound up on the linoleum floor shuffling and reshuffling the chapters like big floppy playing-card decks. A hunting scene in 1958 now preceded a hunting scene in the Pleistocene; a scene of graphic eroticism in modern Spain followed one between the protagonist and a female hominid 1.5 million years ago.

Later, both Dai and M—— had cricks in their backs and smudges on their knees, but M——'s manuscript felt much more supple and compelling, and both men slept well in their beds.

vi. A Perfect Game in the Keeler Dome

Despite never having heard of the "Interplanetary League," you now "catapult cowhide" for the "Titans" on a moon of Saturn in Huygens City in the Keeler Dome, an inflated bubble with o- and g-levels like those occurring naturally in the "Houston Astrodome."

After the Battle of Lower Olympus Mons, an "intern" named *Degas* admires your rock-tossing prowess at a "peace gala," an event celebrating the end of hostilities between hole-humans and your own noble cephalopod clan. He then "touts" you to his brother in Huygens City as a "virtually infallible prospect." This "touting" leads to your "drafting" by his "franchise," your "engaging" Degas as your "agent," and your "signing" with the "Titan Titans."

You owe Degas. He saved your life after the hole-humans plasma-hosed you. He put gunk on your burns, disposed of your dead striding tentacles, gave you human "legs," and redid your throwing limbs with cephalopod-adapted "Tommy John procedures." A work of Degas' art, you are a talented "Frankenstein" "monster." An hour ago, you threw a "perfect game" for him in the Keeler Dome.

Degas ties a purple "paisley" "cravat" below your beak and hugs you hard. "My boy," he chortles: "You are totally one of us now."

vii. Goodbye to All That

In Tokyo, I join a writer's panel, "Editing Yourself for Readability and Profit," whose other members include a romance editor, a fantasy editor, a Pulitzer Prize-winning novelist, and a comely scarlet cephalopod named *Big D.*

Big D wears a bowtie, like a flesh-colored orchid with measles, and talks at length about the necessity of creating for one's readers a continuous vivid dream using simple but nonetheless colorful language.

I counter that sometimes it's OK to make the reader work to parse the meaning of a fictive dream, but when Big D lifts a tentacle and rumbles, **"DELETE!"** I immediately dematerialize—

—for David G. Hartwell, on his seventieth birthday

THE MAKING OF KID DIBAUDA

Kid Dibauda lived in a small Florida panhandle town. Because he dug crime fiction, he often sang its dialogue aloud, in tones as lucid as a silver piccolo's. At sixteen, he left school and flipped a coin. Heads, he'd hitchhike to the Big Easy and scat-sing jazz in the French Quarter. Tails, he'd Greyhound to the Big Apple to ask a mob boss for work as a hitman.

His coin spun to a standstill: *tails*.

In Manhattan, the Kid told people he hoped to earn a living taking out the rivals of gangland lords and garroting stool pigeons.

"You?" said a news vendor. "A stick of spaghetti wearing a cap?"

Days, Kid Dibauda prowled Central Park. Nights, he flopped on sidewalk grates. He was cop-hassled and harlot-beset, but he sidestepped fatal victimization and never lost heart. In the subway, he busked for change with a coffee tin for a bongo drum while crooning calypso tunes. His first day he made $7.54.

Next morning, the Kid found a dingy bookstore and bought a stack of pulps, *Nefarious Capers*, for $6.44. An ad on one issue's back cover electrified him:

Become a Made Man, Deep-Six Your Foes, Attract a Moll,
Bask in Gangster Glory! Send a Dime to 1332 Necrostrasse, NY, NY!
Be Certified a Titan of Crime!

The Kid bought an old city map for a buck, mazed his way to 1332 Necrostrasse, and knocked hard on its padlocked door.

An unseen woman inside cried, *"What?"*

Yelled Kid Dibauda, "Certify me a hitman!"

"Put a dime in the padlock!"

The Kid obeyed, the padlock opened, and the voice told him to remove the lock and come on in. The door swung inward at the base of a towering stairway.

A huge woman peered down at him from the second-floor landing, her rusty black dress taut across her pillowy breasts and fender-wide hips.

"Toss me the padlock!"

He did.

She caught it in her mouth pouch and spat it into a humongous handbag. "Hey, boy, you ever poured gasoline on a puppy and set it afire?"

"Oh, no," Kid Dibauda sang.

"Drowned some kittens?"

"Never," he crooned.

"Pulled the wings off June bugs?"

"Oh, no! Oh, no-o-o-o-o-o-o!"

"You'll never make a Titan of Crime. Forget a bona fide hitman."

"But I gave you my last tarnished dime. / Your refusal is surely a criiiiime!"

The woman bent a slip of paper into an airplane and launched it down the stairs. It dive-bombed into the Kid's mouth.

When he tongued it out, she said, "What'd you expect for a dime? Scram." It was a bus ticket to New Orleans.

A year later, the Kid headlined a Bourbon Street nightclub. He had placed second in a talent competition, landed a recording contract, and made a well-received CD. Seven of its cuts still got airplay.

A sign in front of the club announced,

"Presenting Kid Dibauda: The Hit Man."

DR. PRIDA'S
DREAM-PLAGUED PATIENT

Of course, Dr. Prida, I sleep during the day in a storm pit or canning cellar (whichever term you prefer) beneath the pantry of a country Victorian home in a quickly modernizing county in a Southern state whose denizens display little belief in, and less tolerance for, beings like me. I lie in a rotting johnboat on a slab of plywood atop two sawhorses, and my diurnal companions, in the clayey darkness beneath the prosaic brightness of day, include spiders of several species, spotted camel crickets, and bewildered moths, whose wings often fleck my lips and forehead with their chalky powder. The darkness attracts and soothes not only these unlovely insects but also the rarely sated longings of my forfeited soul. *Selah*.

I'm here this evening, Dr. Prida, at the urging of an early mentor and under protest, but admit that your couch-side manner and bone-china complexion?—is that last observation sexist?—have much palliated my initial prejudice against this visit. Perhaps it will lessen my anxiety, counteract my depression, and give me an incentive to explore the perilous extremities of night, dawn, and dusk with a bravado I previously lacked.

You know, I like your chignon. And the flush at your throat derives, I believe, from the lamp beside your wingback, not from the somatic manifestations of a quickened pulse. After all, with that Chopin nocturne playing in the background, your office has quite a calming ambience: indeed, the security of my canning cellar, without the ever-present dankness.

How charmingly you chuckle. All right, *laugh*. But by *chuckle*, Dr. Prida, I meant no derogation of your femininity. Shakespeare had a character?—Edgar in *King Lear*?—declare that *ripeness is all*, albeit in a different context. I place more value on specificity, whatever the circumstances, and am like to remark a person's looks and actions, not to mention speech, with more apprehensive detail than does your usual machine-stamped client. (No offense to lockstep clones.) Let me also remark that when you frown, beautiful tiny wren tracks bracket your eyes.

My dreams? You want to know what sort of crooked dreams I have lying in my great-grandfather's johnboat in my great-grandmother's canning cellar? What would any sane and cogent professional expect? They appall me, these dreams. They make the plush beneath my fingernails engorge and the flesh of my scrotum tighten. My languid heart accelerates, my flaccid lungs assume the groaning liveliness of bellows, my back arches, my agitated body balances on the achy points of my shoulder blades, coccyx, and heels. A low-level, galvanic current courses through my chest and abdomen and streams discontinuously, maddeningly, from a shifting locus in my brain to my fingertips and toes. An onlooker would suppose me electrified or an epileptic suffering a disruptive, shackling fit. If only I could awake.

Their substance? Relate the substance of my dreams? Specificity? Certainly. You want from me only what I pride myself on providing: namely, facts: namely, details; namely, the distillation of the synaptic impulses informing my visions into words that recount and evoke. Very well. How can I deny you? How transgress against the eminence who made me this way, and who sent me to you, by withholding that which, fully aired and processed, could end my torment? But, Dr. Prida, I hesitate, from conscience as well as shame, to subject you, a learned woman, to the dreadful aberrance of my sleep-engendered imaginings. I hesitate to alarm, repel, violate, perhaps estrange you. I cringe from disclosing the heinous constructs of my id, whose depravity only a god or a child could visit without life-altering damage.

You scoff? Well, go ahead. As young as you look, you claim to have practiced a good fifteen years? You've heard—as confessions—the laments of anorexics, adulterers, pederasts, fools, bigots, self-mutilators, poltroons, traitors, murderers, and blasphemers? Nothing I might say, no shameful act I might reveal, could dent your therapist's armor, much less pierce it and render you, a queen of unshakable aplomb, a gibbering parody of your degree-bearing self? Very well, I'll speak. Note that I warned you. Remember that I hold the kernel of innocence at your venerable core in higher regard than you do yourself . . .

Three days ago, in my johnboat coffin amidst pseudo-fetuses of canned tomatoes and squash in ill-shelved Mason jars, I dreamt three devastatingly twisted dreams. That I survived even one, that I outlasted all three, amazes me,

Dr. Prida. The first alone would have unmanned thousands of diurnal sleepers of my aggrieved persuasion; indeed, shocked them to insentience and left them easy prey for brown recluses, camel crickets, and mice. Forgive what must sound like boasting, but I know the Achilles' heels of my colleagues as well as I do my own, and my first dream let fly its arrow at that portion of *my* psychic anatomy and hit it square on.

The dream. Get to the dream. I'll tell it as starkly as it inflicted itself upon me: I awoke—not in reality, but in the washed-out opalescent landscape of my vision—and struggled from bed into a chamber of undivided white: white ceiling, white floor, white walls, white bedstead, white clothes-tree, and, upon this clothes-tree, white clothes for the ten-year-old boy that, in dreaming, I had become. I dressed, for I'd awakened naked and the stinging brightness of my chamber required a rapid adjustment to prevent my going blind. Shuddering at the touch of each item, I donned a pair of schoolboy briefs, a ribbed white undershirt, a pair of white-duck trousers, a starched white dress shirt, and a hooded white sweatshirt, whose hood also afforded me some shelter from the ruinous brightness.

Head down, I groped my way back to bed, found some white cotton sweat socks on the white feather pillow, and pulled one of them onto my pallid toes, over my albino instep, and up and over my leprous left ankle. The sock had no end. It covered my calf, knee, thigh, groin, and, by some inexplicable geometric convolution, my midriff, torso, and neck, so that a last I was wrapped in a snowy full-body strait-stocking that clung to my entire body mercilessly. When I screamed, still asleep, this first dream unraveled . . . without, however, releasing me to the dank but comforting reality of my great-grandmother's canning cellar.

Ah, my recitation has left you speechless, Dr. Prida. I get it. What could more reliably silence a psychiatrist than the image of a helpless child pent in a tenacious white strait-stocking? You smile, surely to convey by a compassionate look that not even this horror upsets you, that I may speak freely, with no inhibiting fear of your outrage or censure.

All right: my second dream, which followed the first after an interval of mental chaos, erupting into my apprehensive awareness in the workaday vicinity of noon. Unsurprisingly, this daymare centered on eating. As a young man of twenty-five or -six, I sat in a Victorian kitchen before an immense porcelain tureen of potato soup. Beside this tureen resided a large white platter hosting a grilled sandwich of mozzarella or provolone cheese, a hardboiled egg, and a scoop of macaroni pasta with almond slices, water chestnuts, and shards of sun-bleached celery. On the table's white Formica surface, a tumbler of skim milk stood like a miniature Doric pillar. Nauseated, I spooned soup, nibbled at the sandwich, bit off tatters of egg, sampled the pasta, and sipped the milk in a repeating sequence that my dream self could not halt. The peristaltic action of my throat continued without letup or interruption until white tears fell into my soup and a lambency-shot fog clotted the kitchen, applying a gauzy clamp to both my esophagus and my second dream.

You smile again? More comfort for a troubled client? More compassion for a deviant dreamer? Of course. What else do we pay you for, Dr. Prida? Who else can we turn to? But you see why shame mantles me and my conscience gnaws. But having gone this far, why not disclose my third most aberrant horror show?

Listen, Dr. Prida, as you have listened to the others, and withhold your outrage and its inevitable articulation until I've purged this psychic poison. Know, though, that it has a narrative arc absent from the first two dreams and an additional character: a *story*, as opposed to the static imagery of my inchoate earlier visions. Further, if my mentor had not found me in the throes of an abreactive post-dream spasm and hurried to help me, I might have ceased forever. The word *forever*, at least in this hypothetical projection, has more finality than I, or any of my anonymous half-, quarter-, or no-blood siblings, can bear.

Listen:

As a man of forty (my apparent age this evening, Dr. Prida), I stand at an altar in a white tuxedo and trade vows with a woman twelve years my junior in a traditional white bridal gown. She gazes at me with a nonjudgmental gentleness as rare as midsummer sleet. After the wedding and a grand reception in a country Victorian house colored ivory and cream—from interior dome to transoms to louvered shutters to wainscoting to balusters—we ride in a bone-hued limousine to a white-marble villa on the top of a mountain of quartz and milky chalcedony. Here, in the last light of the afternoon in a high-windowed room overlooking a valley carpeted with white mums and pale gardenias, we consummate with no bites or strangle marks the promise of our vows and lie in each other's arms until we move again in the same tender way and thus traverse the entire self-negating night to the doorstep of morning, whereupon my real body, here in this pit, began to thrash in dread-stricken protest against the conventional harmoniousness of such a wholesome union. And, as I've already told you, I might have died forever but for the timely intercession of Gregor, your undying father.

Yes, smile. Smile wider and come to me in your black-velvet slippers. What pretty white teeth you show, such fierce incisors, my sweet Dr. Prida, and such a way with wordlessness that perhaps we need not ever speak again . . .

DID YOU WANT TO TALK?

Did you want to talk, Cremins? At this hour? Do you have no idea of the havoc that interruptions wreak upon my focus? And after our four-year history, do you still consider me merely a *teacher* of writing? Has my reluctance to talk about my work left you wholly ignorant of its scope? Any idea where I published my most recent micro fiction? No? And has no one told you of my latest satirical screed against the upstarts whose ravings crop up all over the Internet nowadays? Why wouldn't a wannabe like you, Cremins, follow his mentor's output? Ever heard of the online mags *SnapStory* or *Strip-Mining the Spirit*, the literary journal of the Community College of Tupelo? Do you know how often the editors of these reviews ask me to guest-edit special issues? Can you imagine the high degree of stress a *professional* deadline induces in an artist like me?

You're kidding, right? How can you compare a due date for an English 102 theme to the deadline for a new story, or for an *entire issue* at a venue like *Wind Chimes*? Do you totally lack imagination? How, fanboy, do you propose to write if you can't frame even a muzzy mental image of the tasks that succeeding requires of you?

Are you going to hang in my doorway forever? Why not take a seat? Would you mind moving those books? Cripes, do you think dumping them on the floor manifests the respect that firsts of Henry James and Walter Pater deserve? And why would I care if you hold them in your lap? Is there road tar on those skinny jeans you apparently never change? Cremins, why this wild look? And *how* did you get up here? Wasn't the building locked? And how did you know I'd be here? You aren't stalking me, are you?

Spies? Do you think me such a milquetoast that crying, *"I've got spies all over campus!"* could possibly amuse me? Can't you tell adult wit from infantile crapola? What's on your mind? Another source for your senior thesis? Advice about your latest sorry stab at a relationship? An upward nudge to the louche D plus you finagled as a sophomore in my O'Connor seminar? Did you know that at any point during our tenure here a full professor can adjust your grade? Have you set your never-washed backward ballcap on my doing just that for you? Again?

Why so riled? Why would I insult you, Cremins? What do you mean, *That's all* I've *done since you got here*? Do you look upon me as the rabid tormentor of a supersensitive David Foster Wallace wannabe? Why not spill it, Trevor?

You're messing with me, right? Did you know that I've sat on the Honor Council at this institution for the ethically disabled for a decade? Do you think me unable to distinguish between writing my own story and passing off a lack-talent's crude tale as mine? Which one do you claim I stole? Where'd you see it? What proof do you have? Is that it, that flash-fiction printout with *my* byline? Why would I ever say that *you* wrote it? Are you out of your paranoid mind? Would not a more likely scenario be that you liked *my* story so much you committed it to memory? Can you really see me risking my reputation copping your work even if I viewed it as . . . brilliant? Haven't you heard of inadvertent plagiarism? Did you know that Beatle George Harrison once inadvertently borrowed the tune of a Motown hit, "He's So Fine," for his hit, "My Sweet Lord"? Can't you see you've pulled a Harrison with my short-short, "Did You Want to Talk?" Where's the proof your story antedated mine's publication in *SnapStory*? How could anyone, anywhere, credit your claim of precedence if you can't prove it?

Hey, do you know how much that chair cost? Will raking Raymond Carver's photo off my wall turn your self-serving falsehoods into truth? Will breathing like a beached marlin reset your erratic drug-sped metabolism?

Cremins, didn't you pass Dr. Sleigh at work just down the hall? Do you know that our security guard brings thermoses of coffee up here for all us night owls? Don't you think it kind of him, looking out for dedicated faculty members working late? Would you please step back, Mr. Cremins? Don't you understand the consequences of letting your confusion lapse into rage? Do you really want blood on your hands, your conscience, your permanent record? You know our state still has the death penalty, don't you, Mr. Cremins?

Say, didn't you come up here just to talk?

SEEVY

First, the kid didn't look like the rest of us. It didn't have to do just with his being poor. Cottonwood, Kansas, had lots of poor kids. Ellie Smyrles came to school in cotton dresses mud-stained from life in a riverside shack with her parolee dad. Doug and Drury Croup dug potatoes every fall and every spring helped their sharecropping kin plant pole beans, cucumbers, squash. They missed so much school that Mr. Bissell, our truant officer, swore he knew the Croup twins better than he did his own terrier-faced children. When the Croups did show, they sat cave-mouthed and fish-eyed from field work and filched sleep, and Mrs. Bonds, Coach's wife, our teacher, often knelt beside their desks to keep them awake and help with their homework.

No, this kid, Cezary Vrtiska, didn't look like us. He wore matching shirts, pants, belts, socks, and shoes: all red, all brown, all burnt-orange. He doused his flyaway dark hair with a bitter barbershop tonic. His given name sounded like "So-sorry," and his last name like that of a sci-fi critter from Mars, maybe. Together, both names sounded like a curse in Czechoslovakian, if that's a language, so we shortened them to his initials, C. V., and turned them into an amusing funny nickname, *Seevy*.

Anyway, who could even say Vrtiska?

Seevy hated sports—maybe because he stunk at them—but dashed around our fenced, mostly gravel playground at recess like a turbo-fueled chicken, so, chasing him, we also called him *Chicken*. But we never caught him, knocked him down, or got lucky enough to see him slip in the gravel and tear a hole in his snazzy red pants. Although he threw like a girl and swung a bat like a spaz, he had speed, toy-top balance, and a jackrabbit's ability to *jink*. When he outran or ducked away from us, our lips twisted and blood muddied our eye whites.

Despite his unusual matched clothes, Chicken Vrtiska came from a family as poor as Ellie's or the Croup twins'. He had just three ugly outfits, and they all reeked of sad little-boy sourness, the predictable result of a lot of recess running and his foster parents' lack of a washing machine. Seevy suffered, we figured, not just from poverty but also from limited smarts. Maybe his daddy had shaken him like a dice box as a baby or the kid had eaten leaded paint chips off a windowsill. He claimed to know stuff he didn't, popped off wild-hair answers, or, if confronted with crap outside his intellectual ken, sang nonsense songs. Once, noting this fact, Donnie Hollis said, "Seevy must mean sieve-for-a-brain!" And everyone but our redhaired Mrs. Bonds howled like hungry wolves.

Really, most of that school year, I didn't think that much about Chick Vrtiska. He'd come late, showing up in October from Hungary, Bulgaria, or What's-the-matter-stan, when we were writing our all-nation Social Studies reports, drawing import-export charts or flags, and waxing in their colors with crayons. As for me, I was trying to show Billie Jo McCutcheon how much smarter, cooler, and artier I was than my rival, Malcolm Richards. So poor Chick, poor Seevy, flew really low under my social radar.

When spring came, I played on a midget baseball team coached by Mrs. Bonds' husband, Ron. I wanted to play shortstop, like the Dodgers' Peewee Reese, but Coach Ron put me at third because I had a slingshot arm and no fear of hard liners smacking me in the kisser. At school one day, Mrs. Bonds said, "Ron thinks that one day he'll see you taking our county high-school team to a state championship." Well, I ate that up like grade-A ground chuck.

But I didn't spew it around. Even at ten, I had a code. Folks in Cottonwood called me Good Kid or, when speaking of my sports skills, Whiz Kid. I liked those nicknames, but didn't want anyone to put reverse English on them so that they swelled my head several hat sizes. Only I could keep that from happening, by clear thinking and straight-arrow acts. That was my code. It earned me gold stars, real or make-believe, all through sixth grade.

Then Mrs. Bonds paired Seevy and me on a project drawing famous writers' portraits—tracing them, actually, and coloring them in—and free-drawing illustrations for their poems and stories. Seevy couldn't draw a *stick figure*. Or a *circle*, even if you laid a quarter down and asked him to pull his pencil around it. Malc Richards liked to joke that he couldn't "draw water from a faucet or a Radio Flyer down a fresh-paved sidewalk." And everybody but our racehorse-legged Mrs. Bonds laughed like Canadian loons.

After school I told her, "Seevy won't do a thing. He *can't*. I have to do it all.

And all he'll learn from that is it's good *not* to know how to do anything. And that's just not—" Flummoxed, I stopped.

"—fair," Mrs. Bonds finished for me.

"No, ma'am, it's not."

"Show him how. Work with him, as I do with the twins."

"Doug and Drury have brains."

"Chick's parents died in Eastern Europe. He's living with an aunt and uncle in a country he never expected to visit, much less grow up in. If your places were switched, you might appear stupid to many people, too."

No, I wouldn't, I recall thinking.

Seevy's reputation for dumbness derived from brain damage, outfits only a clown would model, and no athletic talent but the ability to run like a cheetah, but if *I* ever got stolen away to Transylvania, or wherever Seevy hailed from, I'd fit in so easily they'd vote me class president my first month there.

I never knew where Seevy got off to after school: a farm outside town, a rundown house *in* town? He never rode home with anyone, and I never asked him home with me, even if, once there, I could have tutored him in stuff: Edgar Allan Poe's spooky tales, how to draw a marlin jumping high and flipping water from its fins. Anyway, I had baseball practice afternoons, and my parents liked it better if, on weekends, I went to the Hollises' or the Richards' to play rather than asked their sons to drop in on us. Mom and Dad liked their off days *quiet.*

Seevy and I got a *B-* on our Lit project. I refused to do his work—the drawings—so we turned it in half complete. Mrs. Bonds graded us that easy because she wouldn't penalize me for Seevy's shortcomings and because Seevy did finally contribute *something*: a carved dried apple with cottony hair and white threads for a mustache, all set atop some shellacked pipe cleaners, an object that—*ta da!*—he identified as Mark Twain. That *B-* pushed Malc ahead of me for the six-week period and taught Seevy nothing except that Mrs. Bonds rated kindness higher than she did holding a goof-up accountable. I ached with my grade and got ragged for having to partner with Seevy. Mrs. Bonds could have chosen anyone for that role, but she chose me, Gary D. Rawson, and for my poor English grade, my mom, a *Reader's Digest Condensed Books* junkie, bawled me out royally:

"Come on, Gary, hunker down and bear up."

And I did, through mid-May. Then Mrs. Bonds told us, while Seevy was out with strep throat or tending his sick aunt, that she had decreed the last day of school Seevy's birthday. We should buy or make him a gift. His actual birthday fell in September, but Seevy had not arrived in Kansas until October, so we must adjust for that fact, just as we did to honor the "unfortunate" (grin) children whose birthdays fell during our "boring" (bigger grin) summer vacations. Okay, I could handle that.

Or Mom could. Ordinarily, she gave me a sports book for the boys or bracelet charms for the girls, and I did nothing but carry the wrapped item to school and hand it over. On Freedom Day itself though, I got all the way to our playground before realizing, just as Seevy entered the school, that I'd forgotten his gift. Worse, even after reminders, I'd put off telling Mom about my need for one.

So, at fifteen minutes before first bell, I laid my book bag on a teeter-totter and ran like Seevy, cutting through yards, flowerbeds, and a pocket park to our house. I fingered a key out from under the door mat and clomped inside. My folks had long since driven to McConnell Air Force Base in Wichita, so I scurried around looking for anything that would qualify as a quasi-heartfelt offering. I couldn't take any of my folks' stuff, but maybe I'd left a usable item in an odd place. My room held no sterling sacrifices though, so I wound up foraging through drawers, my toy chest, shoes and sporting-goods crap on my closet floor, back-of-closet shelves, even the dust-bunny forest under my bed. Then I spied a likely item hanging over my bed and cut it down with my pocketknife. I seized an old hatbox from Mom's closet, fit my gift into it, taped facial tissue to the box, and raced for school again. I figured that if I did this regularly even poor Seevy might pop a hamstring trying to escape me during any future playground chases.

I begged a hall pass from Principal Larkin to proceed to class, set my gift on Mrs. Bonds' desk, and sat. The boys had mock-cheered my entrance, but Seevy had paid no heed, his gaze locked on the highest branches of an oak tree outside a window, or the blue sky beyond it. Mere trivia—not classwork—took up the morning, and Malc whispered to me across a pair of desks, "Jeez, Gare, they might as well have let us out yesterday."

Then Mrs. Bonds told Seevy we had a surprise for him: "Today's your birthday." This had to be explained, but when he got it, he twinkled like a Christmas ornament. We circled our desks around him and one by one went forward to hand over our gifts.

None were Magi-worthy, but not many qualified as paltry, ranging from movie-theater tickets to sacks of groceries to a cellophane-wrapped fruit-and-cheese basket to matched-trouser-and-shirt outfits to a battery-run toy robot to a 400-piece jigsaw puzzle to a science kit with (my God!) a plastic microscope and test tubes. Oh, there *were* more ordinary gifts: a baseball book by John R. Tunis, a water-color set, and so on, but my gut queased and my soul sought a hidey hole even as I rose to force my body forward to give Seevy my gift.

"Gary, we'll save yours for last. You made a special trip home for it."

"*Mrs. Bonds,*" I pled, but amidst the paper crinkling and popcorn crunching, she ignored me. When she finally did wave me up, Seevy sat cross-legged in a treasure trove like unto Ali Baba's. I took the hatbox over and set it in his lap. Seevy peered up through olive-black eyes. I glanced aside. He removed the tape from my wrapping, set the crumpled tissues aside, smoothed them out, and piled them by one knee. Then he revealed my gift: an old Revell model airplane, a B-17 Flying Fortress missing its propeller, tail rudder, and most identifying decals, as if German fighter pilots had shot it up over a Nazi munition factory. Seevy lifted it by one of the threads from which I'd hung it from my ceiling, its nose pointing down, and everyone could see what a wreck it had become since Daddy and I assembled it two years ago with airplane glue and brittle plastic tabs.

It swung before my classmates like a stiff dead swan.

The birthday boy bit the threads off the B-17, took its fuselage in one hand, and yanked the Flying Fortress this way and that over his head. Then he landed it on the folded tissues, stood from his lotus pose without using his hands, and hugged me about the waist.

"Thank you, Gare. Thank you very much."

The party rolled on. Seevy never again touched my assembled model. But he also ignored the other gifts in favor of eating popcorn and looking through Ellie Smyrles' and her girlfriends' Social Studies reports.

A little before noon, Coach Ron enlisted every ballplayer from Mrs. Bonds' class to carry Seevy's birthday haul out to his truck for transport to the Vrtiska place. "Many hands make easy work," he told us.

Afterward, when I got back to our classroom to clean out my desk and gather my books, Mrs. Bonds said, "Have a good summer, Gary," after which her back spoke more eloquently than any rebuke.

THE GRAPE JELLY
AND MUSTARD METHOD
OR, HOW TO WRITE SCIENCE
FICTION, MAYBE: A SHORT PLAY

ROIG: A Radically Old Involuntary Guru in a humanoid robot body
COA: A Chimpanzee-Ostrich Amalgam with augmented intelligence
SOAs: Sundry Other Amalgs[1] in a host of unlikely combos

A planetarium on the Moon's dark side. On its stage: ROIG, a dormant toga-wearing robot with the downloaded mind of a dead science-fiction writer. ROIG's animatronic persona is a white-haired ectomorph[2] with a bump on his nose.

COA, a hybrid of Bongo the Chimp and Big Bird (albeit purple instead of yellow), enters the planetarium from a door on its top tier, thus activating both the planetarium's interior lights and the comatose ROIG.

COA canters down the steps and mounts to the stage. ROIG regards this weird monkey-bird with wary but kindly concern.

ROIG: I won't ask how you got in. Programs won't resume until 2100 hours tomorrow, Greenwich Mean Time, but I *will* ask, "What are you doing here, my dear amalg?"

COA: You're the expert, Mr. ROIG. So: How can I write science fiction?

ROIG: Read.

---

[1] *Amalg*: abbreviated Moon term, short for *amalgam*, meaning, in this context, an intelligence-augmented creature combining two disparate types of terrestrial fauna, extinct or extant.

[2] *Ectomorph*, says *The New Oxford American Dictionary* (New York and Oxford: Oxford University Press, 2001), is a physiological term designating "a person with a lean and delicate body build. Compare with *endomorph* and mesomorph" (540).

COA: But I do. I also watch TV shows and movies, even documentaries.

ROIG: Read more.

COA: I'm a visual learner. I like hands-on stuff too, now that I've got my wings, and hands with opposed thumbs!

ROIG: But read still more. Then sit down, or stand at a lectern, and write. And never forget to read.

COA: Read what, exactly?

ROIG: All the best of what's been tagged SF, whether *Speculative Fiction, Super Fantastika, Science Fiction,* or *Sci-Fi.* Read from Aldiss to Atwood, from Ray Bradbury to Octavia Butler, from C. J. Cherryh to Arthur C. Clarke, from Samuel R. Delany to Gardner R. Dozois, from—

COA: Wait! How far do you plan to go with these ABCs?

ROIG: Only to *"from Zamiatin to Zelazny."* But I could have added in *"from Harlan Ellison to Suzette Haden Elgin,"* or, a bit later, *"from Le Guin to Lem,"* with more to follow.

COA: Sir, I snuck out of my zoo-dorm. If I'm gone too long, they'll grok my absence.

ROIG: Then let's start: First, never believe the Insidious Lie that a Grand Whiz-Bang Idea—antimatter, cryonics, faster-than-light or time travel, or any other SF cliché *or* novelty—makes up for dull characters or clumsy plotting and prose.[3] History proves that you can commit screenplays or fiction with all these faults that will *still* reach audiences, but—

COA: But what?

ROIG: All such novels, stories, and movies *stink.*

COA: That's harsh.

ROIG: No, because it's not just true of SF, but of *all* genres: mysteries, romances, thrillers, detective stories, pictorial novels, Westerns, or "realistic"

---

[3] See "Who Was Rex Jatko?" by Gordon Van Gelder in *SFWA Bulletin* (December 2018), 22-27, in which Van Gelder quotes a November 1954 letter from Theodore Sturgeon, author of *More Than Human,* to John W. Campbell, editor of *Astounding Science Fiction,* noting that, in his office in 1939, Campbell told Sturgeon, *"Never forget that stories are not about ideas; they're about people"* (23).

Given Campbell's reputation as a generator of ideas for many of *Astounding*'s contributors, this statement may sound out of character, a contradiction of his own editorial stance at the magazine, but Sturgeon wanted Campbell to acknowledge that even *he* accepted, on a visceral level, the primacy of strong characters in science fiction . . . and in *any* fiction.

mainstream narratives. In all of these, even the last, something odd or life-altering must occur, to lifelike characters (human, animal, vegetable, mechanical, or hybrid) against well-visualized backdrops in clear but distinctive language, to repay a reader's time and attention.

COA: Sounds like a lot of work.

ROIG: *Writing* requires work, but good SF asks no more of its practitioners than do good spy stories, Westerns, or literary novels. Regard no genre as inferior to any other; good writers can create masterpieces, or *near* masterpieces (to be finicky about it, as critics often are) in any format. Think rap musicals or puppet-show tragedies. Whatever their genre, medium, or audience, the real goal for all artists is Quality.

COA: I sneer at none of those categories, sir.

ROIG: Then you've learned a lesson that many struggle to internalize. I have hope for you as an artist in any genre you choose.

COA: But I *want* to write science fiction.

ROIG: Ah, we've come full circle. Keep in mind that SF includes many subgenres, from time-travel tales to anthropological speculation to alternate-histories to off-world adventure stories to dystopian nightmares—and more. You've chosen a field offering great freedom of exploration (as do all the others, ideally) as well as freedom from boredom in your researches and the extrapolations that pop into your head.

COA: How do I start? With people, weird inventions, strange images of other worlds, or sentient beings unlike you or me?

ROIG: Note how the writers who inspire *you* set down their stories. Learn grammar and syntax, mechanics and punctuation. Master it all.

COA: Yuck.

ROIG: Yuck yourself, monkey-bird. If you don't master them, your writing will teem with distracting mistakes, and you'll eject your readers out of your lovely starship heading to Vega back into every-day reality, and you will have failed those readers.

COA: You're the expert. Give me a trick for writing SF.

ROIG: Tricks? I can't tell you much that's specific to SF writing, monkey-bird, beyond paying heed to science reports, new findings about human origins, new treatments for diseases, or recently discovered planets in other solar systems: *tricks* that should be second nature to an aspiring SF writer.

COA (*looking about*): Hurry, sir. Soon, our keepers will arrive.

ROIG: All right. Here's a technique any writer may use, but that's a main-stay for writers of fantastika. I always—

COA: Wait! That's the second time you've said *fantastika*. What is it?

ROIG: A good term for subgenres of fantastic literature, including not just SF but fantasy and certain types of horror, surrealism, and slipstream work. The critic John Clute made the term popular in a 2007 article.[4]

COA: All right, then. What about my SF-writing trick?

ROIG: I call it the Grape Jelly and Mustard Method. It's not solely an SF trick, but an easy way to stop thinking in clichés.

COA: *Tell me!*

ROIG: Once, a *long* time ago, my friends and I threw fondue parties and heated pans of peanut oil over cans of Sterno, then stuck raw meats or veggies on skewers into the oil to cook them.

COA: Yuck, again.

ROIG: Now it sounds pretty awful to me too. But we'd dip our cooked morsel into a sauce and eat it. Our dips included steak sauce, ranch dressing, melted butter, and an off-blue sweet-and-sour sauce that I liked . . . back when I had taste buds.

COA: I still do. Was that sauce, uh, grape jelly and mustard?

ROIG: Yes, but *well mixed*. I admired the maker's courage in mixing those two items as much as I did her sauce, and I applied her method not just to cooking but also to writing.

COA: What exactly was this method, applied?

ROIG: The hope of blending two or three unrelated topics to create a memorable story. Who could imagine that grape jelly and mustard would taste so good together? Who would believe that turning the Frankenstein creature into a minor-league first baseman during World War Two would earn its amalgamator both readers and some mild critical acclaim?[5]

---

[4] Clute, John. "Fantastika." *Encyclopedia of Science Fiction*, www.sf-encyclopedia.com/entry/fantastika. Accessed 01-03-2019.

[5] See, for example, *Brittle Innings* by Michael Bishop (New York: Bantam, 1994) or in its newer, modestly revised edition (Bonney Lake, WA: Fairwood Press, 2012).

COA: That doesn't sound very ess-effy, sir.

ROIG: Some critics, monkey-bird, see *Frankenstein* as the first *real* SF novel.[6]

COA: Don't you have better examples?

ROIG: How about putting our knowledge of quasars, the farthest known astronomical objects in our universe, and the Christian saint, Augustine of Hippo[7], into the same story?[8] After all, the real Augustine had never even *heard* of quasars.

COA: That might work as SF. But *how* would you do it?

ROIG: By researching quasars and St. Augustine and then linking that old guy to objects as remote to his knowledge as they are in astronomical distance from our galaxy. You'd make his effort to understand quasars credible and its results as life-changing as the religious conversion narrated in his *Confessions*.[9]

COA: That sounds *really* hard.

ROIG: Yes, and that tale's author, a young avatar of myself may not have fully succeeded.

COA: Aren't there easier jumpstarts for good SF or fantasy writing?

ROIG: Sure, but I figured you already knew them.

COA: Maybe, but I want to help other wannabe writers in my zoo-dorm learn this stuff, too.

ROIG: Ah, an altruistic teacher as well as a future SF writer.

COA: Please hurry, sir. Our keepers approach.

ROIG: Ask questions and point to answers in the stories they inspire. Ur-

---

[6] See *Billion Year Spree* by Brian Aldiss (New York: Doubleday, 1973) and/or *Trillion Year Spree* (New York: Atheneum, 1986), a revision-expansion, with Dave Wingrove, of the earlier volume. In both books, Aldiss makes this well-known case for Mary Shelley's *Frankenstein* (1813).

[7] Augustine, Saint (b. 354-d. 430 AD). Full name: Aurelius Augustinus.

[8] See, for example, "For Thus Do I Remember Carthage" by Michael Bishop in *The Universe* (New York: Bantam Spectra, 1987), 209-224, edited by Byron Preiss; or in Bishop's collection *At the City Limits of Fate* (Cambridge, MA: Edgewood Press, 1996), 127-149.

[9] *The New American Desk Encyclopedia* (New York: Signet Books, 1984), 97, notes that Augustine of Hippo composed his autobiographical *Confessions* between 397 and 401 AD. Over time, *The Confessions* have had many translations, adaptations, and editions.

sula K. Le Guin, author of *The Left Hand of Darkness*, called this approach a "thought experiment."

COA: What question did she ask in that book?

ROIG: What a world would be like if all its humanoid bipeds were neither just "women" nor just "men," but could be either fathers or mothers at different times in their lives. She was asking *what it means to be a human being*, not just what it means to be a male or a female of the species, and she wrote a classic work of SF working out the answer to her own question.[10] How's that strike you, monkey-bird?

COA: Being part chimp and part ostrich, pretty close to home. How did it strike you?

ROIG: *The Left Hand of Darkness* made me ponder that question, too. So, while alive in the flesh, I also struggled to dramatize that question in a novel or two.

COA: Which ones?

At that moment, a rush of warm air flows from the planetarium's highest tier, followed by Sundry Other Amalgs (all intelligence-augmented): a Raptor-Goat, an Elephant-Octopus, an Otter-Sloth, a Pangolin-Elk, a Dodo-Dalmatian, a Hamster-Hartebeest, and far too many others to name. They bumble onto the theater's top tier and dash, galumph, trot, scamper, scurry, flow, or canter down its steps to the stage on which ROIG and COA have been powwowing. Speaking in and out of turn, the SOAs confess that they ambushed their robot overseers in the zoo-dorm to keep them from dragging COA back to his cell. Then they hurried to join COA's session with ROIG. Wannabe SF writers, they are anxious to digest what COA has already learned.

ROIG (*shouting above the din*): It's simple! Read all you can! And brainstorm with others like yourselves!

COA (*shouting back*): But we're none of us alike!

ROIG: That's true! It's also *not* true! And it's glorious, either way! None of you resembles any other much, but you share a common ambition! That's glorious! So, rejoice in your alikeness *and* your diversity!

---

[10] See *The Left Hand of Darkness* by Ursula K. Le Guin (New York: Ace Books, 1969), which originally appeared as an Ace Science Fiction Special in paperback, but which has deservedly had many subsequent reprintings and editions in both hard and soft cover.

The SOAs, COA among them, lift a cheer that resounds through the domed building like the conclusion of Beethoven's Ninth. (Or a bad movie.)

ROIG: And now, my monkey-bird, my pachyderm-cephalopod, my ant-eater-ungulate, etc., etc., I'll treat you to a planetarium show many hours ahead of our usual lunar schedule. *(Crowing mightily):* **Let there be stars!**

The planetarium's interior lights dim. Its ceiling becomes the canvas for a moving skyscape of planets, satellites, meteors, solar systems, nebulae, novae, galaxies, black holes, even quasars, all in light-riven dance as these astronomical objects collide, collapse, unmake, remake, die, and revive for as long as the Star Maker lasts and/or resurrects and begins again . . .

ONE-RHYME SONNET ON THE MUTABILITY OF HUMAN FAITH

By Muni Ben-Ami (1876-1942)

> *Alas! I am a harvester of dying fruit,*
> *A drinker of the dregs of bitter wine,*
> *When nothing springs from the land to eat . . .*
> *The good have left our holy earth;*
> *Not one saint clings to the altar horns.*
> *A bloodthirsty remnant slaughters its own,*
> *And even the young poison their begetters.*
> *—Micah 7:1-2*

Through unending wastelands of sun-cracked clay,
    We pilgrims stagger on our dire way.
We gulp swirling dust and choke down cracked hay,
    Petition old landlords, and sometimes slay
Their run-amok chickens, which every curst day
    We rend in secret or in starved fury flay
To red gobs, then bend to God, our hearts a-splay,
    And with ash-coated tongues pretend to pray.

Like penury, hate, or that mange-draped stray,
    Hunger—whate'er we do—will maddeningly stay;
It sweeps our raw guts like a barracks bay
    Emptied of meat by its plebes' lethal play.
Walking each wadi, struck numb with dismay,
    Here plod we pilgrims on our dire way.

YAHWEH'S HOUR

Mercer always showed up at the Dadd Tower & Lodge to watch "Yahweh's Hour." In these Patchwork States of America, Overman Troy B. Dadd's evangels had chosen the *Flam Channel* to air the show. Watching it at 8:00 p.m. on Thursday was mandatory for almost everyone, especially ex-cons, so it always had a one-hundred-percent rating for its time slot. Every other network went off the air.

At the grand ballroom's door, Mercer received his sized lobe-link crown, fitted it to his skull, and, elbows in, headed with other attendees toward the huge screen at the far end of the room. Many tables had filled, but midway in, a jaundiced-looking man yielded his place, which Mercer took. Then Mercer petitioned a weary-looking Chicano server for a beer and eyed with distaste the glowing screen.

"I hate TV," said a burly man next to him. "I'd dig ditches before I'd watch most of the crap they shovel, but I *love* this show. Wouldn't miss it for a scrub in the tub with First Lady Aaliyah."

"If you miss it," Mercer said, "you die."

"Well, there's that, but thanks to Overman Troy's sponsorship, I can hardly wait for my weekly sixty-minute God fix."

"Forty minutes, tops." Mercer's disgusted look slapped the man dumb.

Three years back, after the first season of "Yahweh's Hour" (replaced each summer by reruns of "So You Want to Be Filthy Rich?"), every penitentiary in the land had released, on Overman Dadd's pardon, any prisoner who had slain an "enemy of the state." Which was how Mercer had escaped a life sentence for beating to death a "godless transgendered teen" ten years before Dadd's ascension to the overmannery.

Mercer had been glad to walk free, but unlike the clod next to him he loathed "Yahweh's Hour." All he ever recalled of it later was its ads for Discount Daddcare, Troy Dadd University, Daddillac Escapade Limos, and Overman Troy's Casinos & Spas. These roughly five-minute ads came at ten-minute intervals after each God torrent, phosphor-dot hurricanes of mind-fogging vagueness. During them, attendees supposedly drank glory from God's aura. No one knew just what these storms embodied though, because conscious memory failed, and recording, or trying to record, a God spot was *verboten.*

Thursday's timeslot worked for the show, said Overman Dadd and his suck-ups, because more viewers stayed home on Thursdays than on weekends and God had no desire to piss off pastors, priests, rabbis, or any other regime-certified clergy who passed collection plates Friday through Sunday.

The *Flam Channel's* animated devil-cherub danced, an ad for Discount Daddcare broke open Mercer's musings, and when the devil-angel next jigged, a hard flat glow from the screen frosted eyeballs and slowed brains.

Like everyone else there, Mercer succumbed.

In this first blitz, he felt tied to the Deity, raged against that tie, and endured a host of imposed emotions: surely, only milquetoasts and madmen sought a mind-meld with God. As an inmate on a prison yard seeking to skip a "Yahweh's Hour" an entire season ahead of Dadd's controversial amnesty, he'd had a vision of hell that spoke to his adolescent anarchism: Dadd as God, God as Dadd, *smoke everywhere:* Dadd is to God as Muhammed is to Allah.

After that warning, he never avoided the show again. You got one chance. If you tried for two, you triggered a stroke and slept with worms.

God is love, *Mercer consoled himself, still awash in roiling mother-of-pearl images.*

If that was so, why did everyone else about him submit to this irreligious crapola? Yes, you had to watch—no, hallucinate—*these segments, but who but God decreed that you must yield your entire being to these blurry spiritual fugues? By this belated point though, even quasi-stimmed, Mercer had begun to frame an answer . . .*

A Dadd University spot started and ran, and as captives around him semi-awoke, Mercer bolted upright and pondered.

Then, as the ad faded to black, a God-lit nova flung everyone back into stupefaction: all but Mercer, who blinked the starburst away and edged toward epiphany: Since the first season of "Yahweh's Hour," Overman Dadd's assets had quadrupled, his pals had prospered, and his self-aggrandizing agenda had taken root. But some of his pardoned followers had recanted their crimes and asked forgiveness.

In its phosphor-dot storm, "Yahweh's Hour" was now disclosing that this development greatly irked Overman Dadd, even though his rarely consulted Deity approved it.

Through a storm-dispelling lens, Mercer looked down upon his victim in a high-way overpass outside Tyre, Georgia, beholding the kid's battered skull and a face warpainted with congealing blood.

And this act, which had defined Mercer for the country but which had charmed the sensibilities of Troy B. Dadd, he now regretted. Once, he'd seen the waif at his feet as vile human waste (as Overman Dadd still did), deserving of no sendoff nobler than that of flushing dung down a toilet, and Dadd had pardoned him for the glory of God and also for that of Dadd himself, with whom the latter motive had held the higher priority, a fact seldom remarked by his disciples. Or his children, as Dadd called them . . .

A third commercial spot kicked the crowd out of its hallucinations into more activity than it had shown emerging from earlier God fits, perhaps because ads of Daddillac Escapades toting revelers over the Golden Gate Bridge, through New York's China Town, or along the Blueridge Parkway stirred everyone's blood.

A buzz arose, bowls of cashews landed in front of patrons, beers were sipped, and the doofus beside Mercer raised his hands evangelically.

"*Hallelujah!*" he cried.

Mercer turned to him. "Okay, what'd *you* see?"

Still groggy, the man replied, "Maybe my ship's coming in. How 'bout you?"

"Nothing like."

"Then you just ain't seeing things right."

The devil-cherub icon pranced about the high screen, an alarm buzzed, and beers and tapas vanished from tabletops as the night's third deific eruption flowed like lava over every chained mind. Indeed, Mercer saw fires like those that, last summer, had beset every forest in the far West through the ballroom as well as the smoky grottos of his own cranium.

Under the overpass outside Tyre, Mercer's avatar knelt beside his victim's long-dead doppelgänger and touched its shiny face.

Wrong pronoun. Wrong place. Wrong time.

Wait. The pronoun might be wrong, but not the place or time, which were right for what Mercer was doing, for in this place and time an atoning harmony held sway, but if he dallied, the flames all about Tyre and environs would overwhelm and incinerate the kid and him like ants in a firepit. Mercer spoke an apology, scooped the broken body into his arms, and lurched toward the roadway.

Harmony, *he thought,* but no hope.

Headlights brighter than the scary all-embracing glow bored through smoke and flames toward them from the south. A limousine. A white limousine bearing down, scattering as it came the polluted atmosphere around it.

The vehicle halted beside Mercer and his victim, ticking: a hot hunk of metal shedding heat through quick contractions and expansions. It had no saintly white-clad driver to welcome and usher them aboard, but two of its passenger-side doors opened out like unfolding wings, and Mercer placed his mutilated victim on a seat behind the leather benchseat and slid in next to the empty place where a spectral chauffeur should have sat.

And off they sped anyway, to escape the surrounding devastation . . .

God's firestorm faded to black as a commercial spot for Overman Troy's Casinos & Spas shook everyone awake for more flash rowdyism and lobe-link adjustments before the last quasi-quarter of "Yahweh's Hour."

But Mercer couldn't move. He hunched on his chair just as he had perched in a Daddillac Escapade in the vengeful fires of the Overman's impersonations of an Entity that Dadd tried to ape, incompetently.

"Was it better for you that time?" the doofus beside him asked.

"Yes."

"How so?" The other guy took a gulp of his Yuengling.

"I shaped some of its content myself."

The burly man frowned. "That ain't kosher. You gotta go with the flow."

Mercer shut his eyes and waited for the spot to fade, which it did quickly, as usual, and after an indoor sheet-lightning flash, the ballroom's watchers again fell under the spell of, well, who exactly?

In Mercer's case, not the megalomaniac sponsor of "Yahweh's Hour," but the wounded saint within himself.

The limo ferried his victim and him through fire after fire, cross-continent, to a locale in the Pacific Northwest where the kid had grown up, differently. It finally stopped at an upland cabin by a cordwood stack where a man in a watch cap, dungarees, and worn sandals looked up as if at an alien visitation.

Mercer scooped the nameless kid from the limo, let both doors close automatically, and walked with the kid's body toward the scowling man. The limo eased away into some scraggly reemergent evergreens.

"What in hell you want?" The man approached. "And who in hell's that?"

"Your daughter." Mercer knew in his gut that the child had purposely morphed from boy to girl, but the man stared at the ruined being a while, then glanced in outrage between the body and the interloper holding it.

"The hell it is, Sambo! That's our boy Garrett. If you've brought him back for us to bury, you're out of luck. We got shut of him long ago."

"I'm here to confess I killed her."

"Him!" the man insisted. "Why in holy fuck would you do that?"

"I served time for doing it, but Overman Troy pardoned me, and I—"

"Then God's grace on him and cold ashes on you."

Mercer narrowed his eyes.

"Get gone and take that mangled piece of shit with you."

Mercer lifted the young woman higher, in supplication, but her father, scoffing, limped away, up toward his family's cabin.

Stunned, Mercer lifted the young woman, and whatever truer name she'd called herself in life, higher, and her body rose from his hands in chimerical ascension . . .

"Yahweh's Hour" concluded, with no heartening closing music, and the highest-rated *human* program in the Patchwork States of America came on: a show about bad cops retraining as horse whisperers. Most attendees stalked back through the ballroom, yielded their lobe-links, and filtered into the winter darkness.

Mercer also stood to go.

No cozy glow suffused him, his flat was blocks away, and tomorrow, if the trackers of the Endless Plague approved the Overman's return-to-work order (as they would), he'd return to work as a foam-extrusion operator for a Dadd-owned insulation firm.

Leaving the ballroom, the ex-con who'd sat next to Mercer bumped him. "Hey, my bad. You forgive me?"

Mercer said nothing.

"Wasn't 'Yahweh's Hour' really great tonight? Real marching music. The best episode in this ever-loving series so far."

"Give me a break."

"Easy. Didn't your own smart-ass dream-shaping work for you?"

Mercer took the man by his shirt front, twisted it, then stopped and re-leased him.

"Yeah, jerk-bro, maybe it did."

Then, in sudden liberating wonder he skipped twice before settling into his usual funk-ridden trudge back to his flat.

ENVOI
A Scaffold

The first thirteen planks of *A Refusal*
    to Mourn the Death, by Fire, of a Child
in London constitute a single down-
    dropping sentence, like a noose leaping up
short of *the majesty and burning* of
    its subject's extinction beneath the gallows
of Dylan's opening two stanzas and the first
    plank of its third. In this fatal suspension
he abjures any recourse to commas or
        hyphens. As if loops and pointed sticks appall

his sense of the aborted innocent's
    existence. As if compound descriptives like
mankind making and *Bird beast and flower*
    Fathering and *all humbling* set before
darkness to radiate it, with no punctuation
    whatsoever, could reunify the ruins
inflicted on a bolt-stricken city's hapless
    casualties, whether man woman or bairn,
even if his titular slain urchin, *London's*
    daughter, was the freest of injury

infliction of her lot during those nightly
    Nazi blitzkriegs. *I shall not murder*, Thomas
tells us in the second load-bearing sentence
    of his scaffold, *The mankind of her going*—
although, had she lived to adulthood, she
    might have preferred *humanity* as a species
specifier amidst her shrouded *long friends*
    and frank blasphemy to her eulogist's
self-flattering discretion in refusing
        to stain with *further Elegy* the dignity

of her annihilation by adopting
    in another plank of his platform the lament-
gainsaying timelessness of *the unmourning*
    water Of the riding Thames. Then nails a
twenty-fourth timber to the full shebang:
    After the first death comma *there is no other.*
Whoa. Is that filigreed blather or an oaken
    spear of warm sagacity?
                  It's just Dylan, friends:
a stick of Easter dynamite to pipe our unspeakable
    grief.

STORY NOTES

Every selection in *A Few Last Words for the Late Immortals* runs no longer than 3,000 words. Together, these pieces span my writing career, beginning in 1969 with a sale to *Galaxy* of "Piñon Fall," for its Oct/Nov 1970 issue. But the earliest story here is "Darktree, Darktide" from *F&SF* (April 1971). A selection from 2018, "The Grape Jelly and Mustard Method," is at once a story, a play, and advice about writing SF, but my newest story, "Yahweh's Hour," reconfigures a briefer tale, "God's Hour," first published in *Omni* (June 1987) and is original to this volume. The final selection, "A Scaffold," a poem in honor of Welsh poet Dylan Thomas, I wrote in April 2021, seven months ahead of this volume's publication.

Ray Bradbury's *A Medicine for Melancholy*, which I read in 1960, Donald A. Wollheim's *Two Dozen Dragon Eggs*, briefly encountered in 1969, and Yasunari Kawabata's *Palm-of-the-Hand Stories*, which first appeared in English translation in 1988, all prompted me to consider compiling a collection of my shorter pieces. The stories and poems in *A Few Last Words for the Late Immortals* are more of a mixed lot than these three writers' anthologies, so here I offer brief observations about each of its selections:

Proem

"Astyages' Dream": Composed while attending the University of Georgia, for the late Marion Montgomery's creative-writing class. My source was Herodotus' *Histories*. Each stanza has fifteen lines, and each line of the second stanza rhymes with its corresponding line in the first. The other king in Asia was Cyrus II (*aka* Cyrus the Great). Astyages reigned for thirty-five years as the final king of the Median Empire before his deposition in 550 BCE.

Part One: Love's Heresy

"Love's Heresy": I took my idea for this one from Jorge Luis Borges, whose work has always awed me. Also, Robert Silverberg noted that his story "To See the Invisible Man" drew on a curious line in Borges' "The Lottery in Babylon," an admission that led me to search Borges' oeuvre for a passage that *I* could riff on. I found it in "The Theologians," and "Love's Heresy," the result of that discovery, remains a favorite of mine.

"HoneyMoonWalk": I placed this love song to my bride Jeri and to our evolving space program with a Bellevue Press postcard series edited by my friend and colleague Jack Dann.

"Darktree, Darktide": My first sale to *The Magazine of Fantasy & Science Fiction*. Its ending is hardly original, and I also use a variation on the same device in another story in this collection. Still, this piece's "atmospherics" marked it as a breakthrough, even if it doesn't raise a candle to Mildred Clingerman's "The Wild Wood" (*F&SF*, January 1957), which sucked my breath away and sparked the writing of this tale.

"I, Cartographer": A prose poem with a narrative element. Robert Frazier, editor of *TASP* (*The Anthology of Speculative Poetry*), was good enough to publish it. At that time, Jeri and I were remodeling her mother's girlhood home in Pine Mountain, Georgia, the house we still live in. I recall our painstaking efforts as feeling, well, endless.

"Tears": This story grew from our observations of the steady mental deterioration of a man who lived in the house on Blanchard Avenue right behind ours on King, and from his wife's efforts to take care of him. It first appeared in *The Chattahoochee Review* under the editorship of Lamar York.

"The Contributors to Plenum Four": This list of mock-bios of writers in a far-future SF venue was based on the contributors' notes in the many recurrent short-fiction anthologies of the 1960s and '70s: Terry Carr's *Universe*, Damon Knight's *Orbit*, Robert Silverberg's *New Dimensions*, Samuel R. Delany and Marilyn Hacker's *Quark*, and Harlan Ellison's two *Dangerous Visions* volumes. Such publications offered a market beyond the monthly magazines of that period, and I exulted when Bob accepted this goofy piece for *New Dimensions* 5, along with my comedic Phil Dickian tale, "Rogue Tomato."

"To a Chimp Held Captive for Purposes of Research": A dramatic monologue addressed to a caged chimpanzee by a young female researcher. Its stanzaic scheme apes that of John Keats' "Ode to a Nightingale," but contains a lot fewer exclamation points!

"A Father's Secret": This story stems from a minor celebrity's matter-of-fact revelation that he was recurrently molested as a boy. His candid acceptance of, or acquiescence in, these violations disturbed me. A literary-journal editor to whom I submitted this story rejected it with the odd and perplexing confession, "I may have made a mistake."

"Wished-for Belongings": This one isn't really a crime or mystery story, but it still wound up in *Alfred Hitchcock's Mystery Magazine.* I'd first tried to sell it to *Esquire*, where celebrity editor Rust Hills shot it down. I now feel that *Hitchcock's* was by far the better fit, and I still like its portrait of the protagonist, its stylistic consistency, and its O. Henry-esque ending.

"Vernalfest Morning": My youthful take on a children's crusade in a future civil war, set in the vicinity of the USAF Academy north of Colorado Springs, Colorado, *not* in an African nation or the Middle East, features children as exploited grunts in a chaotic internecine conflict.

"The Egret": My only sale to *Playboy's* Alice Turner, who, at one point in my career, had likely read more of my short fiction than any other working editor. The ending embodies a plausible natural-history shocker, grounded in the purportedly instinctive behavior of birds like egrets and herons.

"In Rubble, Pleading": My take on a true story told by a man in Mulvane, Kansas, my boyhood home from 1952-57. It concerned the deadliest tornado in state history, which struck Udall (eight miles from Mulvane) on May 25, 1955, killing 77 persons and injuring 200 while destroying the town. After rereading this story recently, I cut it by a thousand words without deleting any scene crucial to it or undercutting, I hope, its palpable bleakness.

"Give a Little Whistle" first appeared in Stuart David Schiff's *Whispers.* It derived from an idea of my wife Jeri's. (If you know Jeri, that may surprise you.) As I once claimed elsewhere, it is "more vicious, and a little less obvious" than "Dear Bill" (which soon follows), but how do we sympathize with the warring adult infants who dominate its plot? (The dog herein, bless him, is another manipulated figure in its heartless machinery.)

"For the Lady of a Physicist": The inspiration for this one? Andrew Marvell's fine "To His Coy Mistress" and the theorizing of the late 20th- and early 21st-centuries' answer to Albert Einstein, Stephen Hawking, who may be as well known for cameo appearances on TV's now syndicated *The Big Bang Theory* as for his mind-boggling black-hole extrapolations.

"Dear Bill": I once characterized this tale and "Give a Little Whistle," in my mini-collection *Emphatically Not SF, Almost* as "set-ups, traps designed to ensnare or impale. Once you've been netted or skewered, neither will again hoodwink you or command your respect." I added, "If you don't quickly figure out what's going on . . . you're probably not a candidate for Harvard Law School." To undercut *that* blow, this: "But we've got too many Ivy League lawyers already."

"Independence Day Forever": Twenty-three lines setting forth the matter-of-fact monolog of a quietly alarmed astronaut bivouacked on the Moon. The piece's title summarizes it.

"A Few Last Words for the Late Immortals": My first sale to a nuts-and-bolts SF market that I feared I'd never crack, *Analog Science Fiction/Science Fact.* We are the "late immortals" of the title, and our protagonist is an avian critter from another planet and another solar system, but *not* Stanley G. Weinbaum's "Tweet" from his story "A Martian Odyssey."

Part Two: In the Memory Room

"In the Memory Room": In 1985, my dad's third wife died in Pueblo, Colorado. This story grew from that event and her funeral. It was the only story in my collection *At the City Limits of Fate* that Gene Wolfe, a long-distance mentor of mine, unreservedly praised. This version streamlines its original deliberately claustrophobic text.

"Extinct": This poem ran in *Isaac Asimov's Science Fiction Magazine*, edited by Gardner R. Dozois, about a year after my father's death. Lee Otis Bishop, then 68, died in Martin Army Community Hospital on the post known as Fort Benning just south of Columbus, Georgia, under circumstances just like those reported in these 48 lines.

"Three Dreams in the Wake of a Death": A real dream inspired this story and constitutes one of its three sections. Often, after reading it aloud, I ask how many of my auditors believe the first, second, or third dream represents my original one. Regardless of crowd size, an equal number of listeners almost always raise their hands for each section, an outcome I find oddly gratifying.

"The Balloon": A science-fantasy-quasi-horror tale with a thin connection to the war-between-neighbors theme of "Vernalfest Morning," with a message-heavy comeuppance for its "patriotic" warrior protagonist.

"Secrets of the Alien Reliquary": Another quasi-military communication, this time from a team of explorers on an alien world. Great fun to read aloud, it also has the distinction, as a poem, of having been chosen by David Hartwell for his *Year's Best SF* 5 (Harper Eos, 2000), as well as by Brian Youmans for his *Best of the Rest 2* (Suddenly Press, 1999).

"Annalise, Annalise": An oddball romantic comedy with suggestions of computer-generated imagery (CGI) and compromised-privacy elements that its male protagonist must examine and resolve, or not, in the real world.

"Epistrophy": In the 1990s, I dived into recorded jazz, including Thelonious Monk's. Asked to submit to an anthology of stories about tombs, I chose an unconventional "tomb" and stole the title of a Monk composition for my story. *Epistrophe*, with a terminal *e*, is a literary device using repetition at the ends of phrases, sentences, or lines for rhetorical/poetic effect, but Monk chose to substitute a *y* for the word's final *e*, so I did too.

"Dead Poet Parable": Here, a woman elevates her own child over the oeuvre of a revered poet. Beyond that, what does this parable mean? I leave that determination to you. Writing this piece, I had in mind a hurtful personal experience and a few of the elegantly enigmatic short poems of Stephen Crane.

"Midwifing the World": I wrote a draft of this story while facilitating a week at the 1998 Clarion West workshop in Seattle, Washington. My students recognized it as a total botch. Home again, I revised it with as many marine references and images as I could cram into it. Ann Kennedy (later VanderMeer) generously featured my rewrite in an issue of *The Silver Web*.

"Menard's Disease": Later, Ann's soon-to-be husband, Jeff VanderMeer, asked me to concoct an ailment for *The Thackery T. Lambshead Pocket Guide to Eccentric & Discredited Diseases* as if I were the specialist most familiar with it. I named my disease after the title character in Borges' "Pierre Menard, Author of *The Quixote*," but also called it, scientifically, Biblioartifexism. *The Lambshead Pocket Guide*, etc., is a one-of-a-kind anthology, and I had one heck of a good time expatiating on my specious disease.

"The Alzheimer Laureate": Another tale about a dreadful ailment, this one evolving from my speculation that a legitimate winner of the Nobel Prize for Literature could publish work in his dotage that aficionados see as brilliantly abstruse and hard-eyed critics as outright nonsense. Forgive me, but at my age I feel pity and affection for the afflicted, ludicrously clad Dominic Celestine McLock.

"Her Chimpanion": This prose-poem story jumped out at me from my interests in anthropology, primatology, and the genetic alteration of surviving animal species for reasons not related to their lives in the wild. Without ever intuiting COVID-19, this piece touches on viruses, quarantining, and even the immemorial human war against loneliness.

"Tired": My second sale to *Analog* under the editorship of Stanley Schmidt, twenty-one years after "A Few Last Words . . ." Surprisingly, then, it owes a debt to Philip K. Dick, who, despite often referencing talking machines and appliances, never placed a story in *Analog*, but in 1953 did sell "The Imposter" to John Campbell's *Astounding*. I owe the last line of dialogue in "Tired" to my astute friend and editor, Michael H. Hutchins.

"An Owl at the Crucifixion": In an unpublished novel of the same title, I attribute this shape poem, which some call "concrete poetry," to a fictive 12-year-old, Susannah Huckaby. Its only other appearance in print had all its lines set flush with its left-hand margin, absolutely nullifying its visual aspect. I groaned upon seeing it, but forgave the book's innocent editor, the late Tom Piccirilli, for what was obviously a horrific typesetting error.

"Sequel on Skorpiós": Written to fulfill an assignment that I once gave my writing students at LaGrange College: *Tell a story that contradicts a belief you hold dear.* I did just that, insofar as I could, but appended a coda that may violate the assignment, albeit ambiguously. Later, some readers' feeling that the story denies the Resurrection almost led a private school in Columbus, Georgia, to revoke my invitation to speak there.

"Outside the Circle": Written, futilely, for a *Writer's Digest* short-fiction contest called "The Eleventh Commandment," which was also to be every submitted story's title. In my piece, I hedged my bets by proposing *many* eleventh commandments and concluding with a *deus ex machina* epiphany. I also changed its title.

Part Three: Last Night Out

"Last Night Out": Written shortly after the September 11, 2001, terrorist attacks in New York City, Washington, DC, and aboard a United Airlines flight over Pennsylvania. As I said in my notes for this story in *Brighten to Incandescence*, learning that "two of the hijackers visited a strip club only days before turning an airliner into a flying bomb" evoked in me "a horror-tinged disgust." And I concluded, "When religion and patriotism couple, their mutant offspring prod us to spiritual wastelands that some . . . seek to reproduce in the world itself."

"The Mockingmouse": The article "Singing Mice" by Rob Dunn in *Smithsonian* (May 2011) induced me to reflect on the auditory researches of the biologist, Martina Kalcounis-Rueppell of the University of North Carolina, Greensboro, and on the possibility of a mammalian equivalent to the mockingbird, as suggested by Dunn in his article. Hence, this poem.

"Purr": This story and "The Library of Babble," as well as a novelette called "The Pile" (see *The Door Gunner and Other Perilous Flights of Fancy*), stemmed from efforts to turn our late son Jamie's computer-listed story ideas, or some of them, into son-and-father collaborations. I recall that Jamie preferred cats to dogs. Ann VanderMeer published the result of our collaboration in *Weird Tales*.

"Miriam": I first wrote this story under the byline "Nōni Tyent" and published it in *A Cross of Centuries: Twenty-five Imaginative Tales about the Christ*, an anthology I edited for John Oakes at Thunder's Mouth Press. I used the female byline because only one other story in my collection was by a woman, Karen Joy Fowler's "Shimabara." Anyway, I regard "Miriam" as an alternative feminist take on the earthly mission of Jesus Christ.

"No Appetite for Communion": One section of a prose-form story devised by Bruce Holland Rogers, the symmetrina. Each symmetrina has an uneven number of sections (5, 7, 11, etc.), a stipulated number of words, stipulated points of view, and the development of a theme common to all its parts. "No Appetite" is the seventh section of a project by six writers bearing the overall title "We Shall Not, We Shall Not Be Moved." In this version, I've cut back my part's stipulated number of words.

"The Library of Babble": Another work inspired by an item on Jamie's computer list of story ideas, this one about a library of sounds rather than of silence. I looked toward Borges again, alluding to his story "The Library of Babel," and made my—*our*—piece about a busy dad and a musically talented son on a field-trip to the titular institution. Editor/publisher Bill Schafer, ever a supporter, featured it in *Subterranean Online*.

"Philip K. Dick is dead, a lass": A eulogy composed using the late Jim Simmerman's recipe for writing a poem if blocked or in need of directions, "Twenty Little Poetry Projects," an aid that I often shared with poetry-writing students. This poem was published in the Quality Paperback Book Club's *QPB 1999 Calendar of Days* and later in Edward L. Ferman's *Fantasy & Science Fiction*.

"Ch-Ch-Ch-Changes": A symmetrina composed for a Festschrift honoring my editor David G. Hartwell on his 70th birthday, eventually posted at *Tor.com* of Tom Doherty Associates, where David worked. Minus title, subhead, and endnote, "Ch-Ch-Ch-Changes" has 2,200 words. Its seven parts have sequential word counts of 100, 200, 400, 800, 400, 200, and 100. The point of view for these parts is 1st person, 2nd person, three successive 3rd persons, 2nd person, and a final 1st person. The overall unifying theme is *changes*. (Given David's profession, what else could it have been?)

"The Making of Kid Dibauda": Using a prompt from *What If? Writing Exercises for Fiction Writers* by Anne Bernays and Pamela Pointer, I wrote this lightweight flash fantasy. Yes, yes, it features a pun. So does Damon Knight's "To Serve Man." I rest my case. Incidentally, *What If?* contains helpful exercises as well as good illustrative story selections.

"Dr. Prida's Dream-Plagued Patient": Written in longhand at our kitchen table on a yellow legal pad soon after teaching an intense elective Jan-term class at LaGrange College in 2006. It first appeared in *Aberrant Dreams*, then in Stephen Jones' *Mammoth Book of Best New Horror*, Vol. 18, in both England and the US in late 2007.

"Did You Want to Talk?": Would you believe another Bruce Holland Rogers-inspired piece in this collection? Would you believe that—like "The Making of Kid Dibauda," "Seevy," and "Yahweh's Hour"—it is original to this volume? Does it surprise you that its two principal characters are an egotistical writing teacher and an irate writing student? Hey, are you a mind reader?

"Seevy": I first called this story "Selfish," which may better suit it. Although it's not SF, horror, or dark fantasy, but an autobiographical piece with fictional components, I offer it in homage to a possibly minor but still nagging boyhood shame.

"The Grape Jelly and Mustard Method": Chip R. Bell, writer, editor, and a board member of the Georgia Writers Museum in Eatonton, Georgia (the hometown of Joel Chandler Harris and Alice Walker), asked me to provide a chapter on writing science fiction for a new edition of a Museum publication called *Book Mark: How to Be an Author*. I did just that, primarily for young aspiring writers, and this is my oddball *RSVP* to Chip's kind invitation.

"One-Rhyme Sonnet on the Mutability of Human Faith": In 2018, I published four novellas in *The Sacerdotal Owl and Three Other Long Tales*, each of which dealt with its own cultural-cum-religious milieu: "Mayan, Buddhist, Christian, and technological," to quote Nancy Kress. I set a passage from Micah and this sonnet at the head of those four stories as an epigram. If you don't care for their translations, blame Ben-Ami and A. H. H. Lipscombe.

"Yahweh's Hour": This story, as noted previously, is a thorough re-envision-ing of a short piece written in 1986. Even as it retains the structural kernel of that original, I think it a better story. I wrote it just before the 2020 presidential election, as I did this note, which I then revised eight days after a heinous attack on the US Capitol incited by our sitting president. "Yahweh's Hour" posits the continuation of a radical regime that American voters rejected on November 3, 2020, so, in this note, I celebrate an outcome that denies, for now, the elevation of a would-be despot over our imperfect but still resilient democracy.

Envoi

"A Scaffold": This past April, writer Rhys Hughes told me that his friend Vatsala Radhakeesoon, a Mauritian poet and visual artist, was asking for poems for International Dylan Thomas Day, some of which she would post on her blog site around May 14, the anniversary of the day on which Thomas' *Under Milk Wood* was first read on stage at 92Y The Poetry Center, New York City, in 1953, the year of his death. I leapt to contribute because Thomas' lyrical, often obscure poetry haunted me; indeed, I wrote my master's thesis at the University of Georgia, "Dylan Thomas' Obscurity: The Legitimacy of Explication" on it. Chapter One of that thesis contains a defense of the famous last line of his poem "A Refusal to Mourn the Death, by Fire, of a Child in London." You could, possibly, look it up.

January 19 and April 16, 2021
Pine Mountain, Georgia

ACKNOWLEDGMENTS

First, I heartily thank the editors who encouraged and accepted the short work of mine constituting this volume, or, in one case, an earlier version of a story that I totally rewrote for its first appearance here:

Pat Cadigan, Jack Dann, Edward L. Ferman, Ellen Datlow, Robert Frazier, Lamar York, Robert Silverberg, Shawna McCarthy, Harry Smith, Cathleen Jordan, Roy Torgeson, Alice K. Turner, Stuart David Schiff, Jerry Pournelle, David D. Deyo, Jr., Stanley Schmidt, Kathryn Cramer and Peter D. Pautz, Gardner R. Dozois, Kristine Kathryn Rusch, Steve Pasechnick, Peter Crowther and Edward E. Kramer, Ann Kennedy (later VanderMeer), Scott Edelman, Gordon Van Gelder, Tom Piccirilli, David Pringle, Marty Halpern, Bruce Gillespie, William Schafer, Kathy Kiernan, Jeff VanderMeer and Mark Roberts, Patrick Nielsen Hayden, Joseph W. Dickerson and J. Lonny Harper, Chip R. Bell, and Vatsala Radhakeesoon.

I also acknowledge all who have supported me from the beginning of my association with Fairwood Press/Kudzu Planet, starting with the one abiding, overseeing presence from book to book, Patrick Swenson: writer, editor, publisher, art designer, PR man, teacher, workshop guru, public-school teacher, father of Artemis, long a social-distancing friend (even before COVID-19), and a great deal more.

Then there's Michael Hutchins, who likewise wears several sombreros: website designer, editor, proofreader, map contributor, logo designer, co-creator, and friend. Michael has been an additional set of eyes for every title I've done at Fairwood Press, often going over the text of a book multiple times before publication. He introduced *Ancient of Days*, my second title here, and acted indispensably as editor-in-chief for *A Few Last Words for the Late Immortals*.

Others who provided introductions: Elizabeth Hand *(Brittle Innings)*, Jack Slay, Jr. *(Who Made Stevie Crye?)*, Paul Di Filippo *(A Funeral for the Eyes of Fire)*, Daryl Gregory *(Philip K. Dick Is Dead, Alas)*, John Kessel *(Count Geiger's Blues)*, Hugh Ruppersburg *(Other Arms Reach Out to Me: Georgia Stories)*, Joe Sanders *(Transfigurations)*, Kelly Robson *(The City and the Cygnets*), Gregory Feeley (*Unicorn Mountain*), and Sarah Pinsker (*A Few Last Words.*). On one or more of these titles, I received extensive editorial help from, respectively, Brad Strickland and Greg Feeley, who also helpfully critiqued this book's *Envoi*, "A Scaffold."

Those in addition to Patrick who created covers or other art for these editions include Paul Swenson, Patrick's brother, who did eye-catching covers for my first four novels here (*Brittle Innings, Ancient of Days, Who Made Stevie Crye?,* and *Count Geiger's Blues*); Orion Zangara, who did the cover and the striking black-and-white interior illos for *Joel-Brock the Brave and the Valorous Smalls*; and, finally, Amit Dutta of New Zealand, who obligingly modified his painting of a domed city for the cover of my Urban Nucleus fix-up, *The City and the Cygnets*.

The following persons submitted publicity comments for one or more of the titles already cited: Gregory Frost, Jack McDevitt, Jeffrey Ford, Robert Sawyer, Gregory Benford, Nancy Kress, Andy Duncan, George Zebrowski, Pamela Sargent, James Morrow, Mary A. Turzillo, Steven Utley, Samuel R. Delany, Lisa Tuttle, John Clute, Eileen Gunn, Suzy McKee Charnas, David Gerrold, Jack Skillingstead, Ian Watson, David Zindell, Kim Stanley Robinson, Bradley Denton, Nancy Jane Moore, Jane Lindskold, James Patrick Kelly, Rick Wilber, Lisa Goldstein, Paul Williams, David G. Hartwell, Rhys Hughes, Faren Miller, Jane Yolen, Marly Youmans, Brad Strickland, Nathan Ballingrud, James Van Pelt, A.M. Dellamonica, Dale Bailey, Karen Joy Fowler, Kelly Link, Terry Kay, Bruce Holland Rogers, Dan Chaon, and Lewis Shiner.

Some of my editors also provided publicity comments: Pat Cadigan, Jack Dann, Robert Silverberg, Gardner Dozois, Ann VanderMeer, and Gordon Van Gelder. Others of my revised FP/KPP titles reuse comments that appeared *on their original editions* by Greg Bear, George R.R. Martin, Vonda N. McIntyre, Paul Preuss, Norman Spinrad, Theodore Sturgeon, Michael Swanwick, and Paul Williams. I must also thank my lifelong friend Ray Cavender for his useful comments on the newest story here, "Yahweh's Hour." I now confess that I would never have written any of these pieces, or revised them, without the unshakable love and support of my wife Jeri.

January 2021
Pine Mountain, Georgia

SOURCES

Note: All selections have been revised to
varying degrees from their original publication.

"Astyages' Dream, Which He Relates to the Magi" first appeared in *Windows & Mirrors*, Tuscaloosa AL: The Moravian Press, 1977.

"Love's Heresy" first appeared in *Shayol* #3 (Pat Cadigan, ed.), Kansas City KS: Flight Unlimited, 1979.

"HoneyMoonWalk" first appeared (as "White Power Poem") in a postcard series edited by Jack Dann and published by Bellevue Press, 1976.

"Darktree, Darktide" first appeared in *The Magazine of Fantasy and Science Fiction* (Edward L. Ferman, ed.), Cornwall CT: Mercury Press, April 1971.

"I, Cartographer" first appeared in *The Anthology of Speculative Fiction* #3 (Robert Frazier, ed.), Sand Ridge WV: TASP Press, 1978.

"Tears" first appeared in *The Chattahoochee Review* (Lamar York, ed.), Dunwoody GA: Dekalb College, Fall 1987.

"The Contributors to Plenum Four" first appeared in *New Dimensions 5* (Robert Silverberg, ed.), New York NY: Harper & Row, 1975.

"To a Chimp Held Captive for Purposes of Research" first appeared in *Isaac Asimov's Science Fiction Magazine* (Shawna McCarthy, ed.), New York NY: Davis Publications, January 1985.

"A Father's Secret" first appeared in *Pulpsmith* (Harry Smith, ed.), New York NY: The Smith, Autumn 1984.

"Wished-for Belongings" first appeared in *Alfred Hitchcock's Mystery Magazine* (Cathleen Jordan, ed.), New York NY: Davis Publications, December 1982.

"Vernalfest Morning" first appeared in *Chrysalis 3* (Roy Torgeson, ed.), New York NY: Kensington Publishing / Zebra Books, 1978.

"The Egret" first appeared in *Playboy* (Alice K. Turner, ed.), Chicago IL: Playboy Publishing, June 1987.

"In Rubble, Pleading" first appeared in *The Magazine of Fantasy and Science Fiction* (Edward L. Ferman, ed.), Cornwall CT: Mercury Press, February 1974.

"Give a Little Whistle" first appeared in *Whispers* ##19-20 (Stuart David Schiff, ed.), Binghamton NY: Stuart David Schiff, 1983.

"For the Lady of a Physicist" first appeared in *Black Holes* (Jerry Pournelle, ed.), London UK: Orbit Publishing, 1978.

"Dear Bill" first appeared in *All the Devils Are Here* (David D. Deyo, Jr., ed.), Atlanta GA: Unnamable Press, 1986.

"Independence Day Forever" first appeared in *The Magazine of Fantasy and Science Fiction* (Edward L. Ferman, ed.), Cornwall CT: Mercury Press, July 1984.

"A Few Last Words for the Late Immortals" first appeared in *Analog Science Fiction/Science Fact* (Stanley Schmidt, ed.), New York NY: Condé Nast Publications, July 1979.

"In the Memory Room" first appeared in *The Architecture of Fear* (Kathryn Cramer and Peter D. Pautz, eds.), New York NY: Arbor House, 1987.

"Extinct" first appeared (as "Extinction") in *Isaac Asimov's Science Fiction Magazine* (Gardner Dozois, ed.), New York NY: Davis Publications, December 1991.

"Three Dreams in the Wake of a Death" first appeared in *The Magazine of Fantasy and Science Fiction* (Kristine Kathryn Rusch, ed.), Cornwall CT: Mercury Press, July 1996.

"The Balloon" first appeared in *Isaac Asimov's Science Fiction Magazine* (Gardner Dozois, ed.), New York NY: Davis Publications, January 1992.

"Secrets of the Alien Reliquary" first appeared in *Time Pieces* (Steve Pasechnick, ed.), Cambridge MA: Edgewood Press, 1998; later in *Asimov's Science Fiction* (Gardner Dozois, ed.), July 1999.

"Annalise, Annalise" first appeared in *The Magazine of Fantasy and Science Fiction* (Kristine Kathryn Rusch, ed.), West Cornwall CT: Mercury Press, October/November 1996.

"Epistrophy" first appeared in *Tombs* (Peter Crowther and Edward E. Kramer, eds.), Stone Mountain GA: White Wolf, 1995.

"Dead Poet Parable" first appeared in *Time Pieces* (Steve Pasechnick, ed.), Cambridge MA: Edgewood Press, 1998.

"Midwifing the World" first appeared in *The Silver Web* (Ann Kennedy, ed.), Tallahassee FL: Buzzcity Press, 2002

"Menard's Disease" first appeared in *QPB Calendar of Days 2002* (Kathy Kiernan, ed.), Mechanicsburg PA: Quality Paperback Book Club, 2001; then in *The Thackery T. Lambshead Pocket Guide to Eccentric & Discredited Diseases* (Jeff VanderMeer & Mark Roberts, eds.), San Francisco and Portland: Night Shade Books, 2003, whose editors had commissioned it.

"The Alzheimer Laureate" first appeared in *Science Fiction Age* (Scott Edelman, ed.), Herndon VA: Sovereign Media Co., March 1996.

"Her Chimpanion" first appeared in *The Magazine of Fantasy and Science Fiction* (Gordon Van Gelder, ed.), Hoboken NJ: Spilogale, Inc., March 2001.

"Tired" first appeared in *Analog Science Fiction and Fact* (Stanley Schmidt, ed.), New York NY: Dell Magazines, November 2000.

"An Owl at the Crucifixion" first appeared in *The Devil's Wine* (Tom Piccirilli, ed.) Baltimore MD: Cemetery Dance Publications, 2004.

"Sequel on Skorpiós" first appeared in *Interzone* #134 (David Pringle, ed.), Brighton UK: Interzone, August 1998.

"Outside the Circle" first appeared in *The Thirteenth Moon* #17 (Jacob Weisman, ed.), San Francisco CA: Tachyon Publications, 1996.

"Last Night Out" first appeared in *Brighten to Incandescence* (Marty Halpern, ed.), Urbana IL: Golden Gryphon Press, 2003.

"The Mockingmouse" first appeared in *SF Commentary* #87 (Bruce Gillespie, ed.), Greensborough, Australia: Bruce Gillespie, April 2014.

"Purr" first appeared in *Weird Tales* #352 (Ann VanderMeer, ed.), Rockville MD: Wildside Press, December 2008.

"Miriam" first appeared as by "Nōni Tyent" in *A Cross of Centuries* (Michael Bishop, ed.), New York: Thunder's Mouth Press, 2007.

"No Appetite for Communion" first appeared in *Indiana Review*, Vol. 27, No. 1 (Grady Jaynes, ed.), Bloomington IN: Indiana University, 2005.

"The Library of Babble" first appeared in *Subterranean Online* (William Schafer, ed.), Burton MI: Subterranean Press, 2010.

"Philip K. Dick is dead, a lass" first appeared in *QPB Calendar of Days 1999* (Kathy Kiernan, ed.), Mechanicsburg PA: Quality Paperback Book Club, 1998.

"Ch-Ch-Ch-Changes" first appeared on Tor.com (Patrick Nielsen Hayden, ed.), July 11, 2011.

"The Making of Kid Dibauda" appears for the first time in this publication.

"Dr. Prida's Dream-Plagued Patient" first appeared in *Aberrant Dreams* #7 (Joseph W. Dickerson and J. Lonny Harper, eds.), Peachtree City GA: HD-Image, 2006.

"Did You Want to Talk?" appears for the first time in this publication.

"Seevy" appears for the first time in this publication.

"The Grape Jelly and Mustard Method; or, How to Write Science Fiction, Maybe: A Short Play," first appeared in *Book Mark* (Chip R. Bell, ed.), Eatonton GA: Georgia Writers Museum, 2018.

"One-Rhyme Sonnet on the Mutability of Human Faith" first appeared as by "Muni Ben-Ami" in *The Sacerdotal Owl and Three Other Long Tales*, Bonney Lake WA: Kudzu Planet Productions / Fairwood Press, 2018.

"Yahweh's Hour" appears for the first time in this publication.

"A Scaffold" first appeared online (Vatsala Radhakeesoon, ed.), in commemoration of International Dylan Thomas Day, in May 2021.

ABOUT THE AUTHOR

In 1988, Michael Bishop won the Mythopoeic Fantasy Award for an earlier version of *Unicorn Mountain*. His other prize-winning novels are *No Enemy but Time* (1982), winner of a Nebula Award, and *Brittle Innings* (1994), winner of a Locus Award for Best Fantasy Novel. He has also published poetry, reviews, and essays as well as story collections, notably *Other Arms Reach Out to Me: Georgia Stories* (2017), winner of a Georgia Author of the Year Award in 2018. He continues to live in Pine Mountain, Georgia, with his wife Jeri of fifty-one years, a retired elementary-school counselor, a yoga devotee, and an avid gardener. On November 5, 2018, Bishop was inducted into the Georgia Writers Hall of Fame.

www.ingramcontent.com/pod-product-compliance
Lightning Source LLC
Chambersburg PA
CBHW020104030726
47498CB00006B/1935